Jaguar Child

Catherine Mintz

www.copper-publishing.com

Cover art and design by Catherine Mintz
Art and text copyright 2020 by Catherine Mintz

ISBN 978-0-9839589-5-6

To the crew of the *Rosario Bay*.

A vortex of flecks of fire, a fuego fantasma, forms in the street beyond me and drifts toward the noise of the plaza, trailing glittering debris. Through the cloth of my dress, I touch the copper sun hanging at my breast and stand, shivering, shoulders against the quinta wall, one cheek pressed against the fine shuck-work of the basket on my shoulder. The sweet scent of death—fragrant oils, wine, spices, and precious woods—eddies up our street.

I shiver, and draw my veil over my face with my free hand.

Tonight a fortune will be burned so it may go to the dead lands with the alcalde, Leon Ildefonso, the ruler of our town. In the distance, I can hear the funeral crowd roar, then roar again. They have lighted the pyre, its smoke and sparks turn the sky into glowing lizard skin. Drifting against the wind, a cloud of fantasmas, brighter than the dull red moons, speckles everything below them with lurid light.

On every major occasion, the fiery vortices come, leave drifts of the glass lentils we call witches' eyes throughout our town. In Misericordia del Mar, the eyes are everywhere, decorating the gateposts of houses, heaped into play quintas by children, used as gamblers' tokens, so common they sparkle in the dirt of our streets. Some say they bring good luck, others, bad.

No one is interested in me: time to go.

I am on my way back from taking almond liquor and braised jack to the feast in the plaza. Like all slave women who brought food to the funeral feast, I was expected to serve, but by my owner's order I have slipped away. After midnight, the town will celebrate the festival of reversals, when men dress as women, and women as men. From the clamor in the poorer quarter the party has already started. Glassy bits crunching underfoot, I shift my basket to my other shoulder.

I should be on my way.

Lady Mercedes told all her servants she wanted her people home behind her barred gates before the festival began. "When conventions are suspended, law often fails too," she said, earbobs of jade swinging at either side of her turtle throat.

"Yes, my lady," we chorused.

No matter that she seldom goes out anymore, my lady rises and dresses every morning as if she will have guests. She is seldom disappointed. When the day grows cooler, and the back of the house smells of good things cooking, people come, to ask advice, to pass the time, and to gossip. Everyone says she keeps a fine table, a happy house, even for her slaves.

I know I should be grateful.

The plaza crowd roars, drowning out the chanting of the priests. A trio of fantasmas drifting by me pauses; a handful of witches' eyes rattles on our doorstep. I close my eyes, hoping to seem lazy or drunk. A slave never wants to attract attention. We are property, invisible, to step out of that protection, to be seen, brings punishment, swift and sure, from owners and slaves alike. You must know your place.

Or act as if you do.

The three fantasmas drift on, more glassy spore clattering onto cobbles.

I am afraid.

If I go in, gather my nerve again in the sanctuary of my owner's house, I can say I was asked to bring more valentina sauce for the jackrabbit. Our household makes the best, which is the only reason we can hold our heads high and send so poor a meat as jack to any funeral feast. The distant crowd roars again. The sky over the plaza glows red. There must be hundreds of fuego fantasmas gathered about the plaza.

The alcalde has gone to his gods accompanied by his most favored servants as, when her time came, I will be sent to sent to serve my mistress, who is older by far than Leon Ildefonso. Rosa, our ancient housekeeper, says my lady can remember the last silver ship landing. I wonder what a ship of metal looked like, sailing toward our shore and whether the sea was green, gray, or blue as turquoise. The ama de llaves tells tales her grandmother told her, of the days before the ancient things failed. In those days, Rosa says, there were no slaves, but how can there be no slaves? Who would do the work?

There will never be a better moment than this.

I swing my basket from my shoulder to my head. It is harder to balance empty than full, and I think of leaving it behind, but it is my excuse to move freely anywhere. I am coming from delivering something or going to get something. I wove it myself in the black, red, and blue patterns I was taught as a small girl. Child-like, I touch my it with one hand to keep it steady, listening to raucous laughter beyond our wall.

Even our slaves are tipsy tonight, although my lady's servants are always frightened they might fail her. Those who go to the dead lands as slaves are forever enslaved. I— I was born free. I have a birthright and must claim it.

Do it. Do it now.

The scent of ripe apricots comes and goes on the breeze. I touch my basket again, then drop it into the garden. Slipping over the banister, I make my way down the tree espaliered against the wall. It has been a long time since I sneaked into my lady's quinta this way. Basket in my arms, I go into our orchard. I move from tree to tree, trained fingers seeking out the fleshy softness of the ripest fruit in the dark. A gift of apricots will let me pass unquestioned. I can feel the gaze of the house's duende on me as I move but the old thing in its niche is decades past the time when it could speak. Its best use is to roll its eyes and make the children laugh.

Loaded basket on my head, I let myself out the side gate, shake the bars to make sure the latch drops into place. Back to the street, I put my gift down and drape my head cloth to conceal my face. I am fifteen and well grown for my age. I do not glance back, although I feel shame at what I am doing. Lady Mercedes is kind, treating her few servants almost as if they were her young family, killed by fever a quarter century ago. She will be hurt by my running away, but she will not keep her grip on her affairs forever, and I want to live, to be free.

Go. Now.

My feet know the way, if my heart does not, for all I was five when she bought me in the market. The slavers had taken a poor haul. A rich one, with many strong adults, and such good businessmen would never have bothered with a girl too young to be useful. I'd have been abandoned to starve or given the mercy-stroke. Worse, perhaps, had there been evil men among them.

The captured women were kind to a silent, unresponsive child. It might have been that they missed their own, who had not been as lucky as I. I was too stunned to care, for I had seen my mother die and stripped her of the one thing of value she might have taken to the dead lands, the bright copper sun that she wore as a pendant.

Now it is dark with my sweat.

The day I was sold was a fine, bright morning, and though it was going to be hot, it was still cool when my lady came with her cook and her assistants to shop. They were looking over the hanging carcasses of deer and antelope for those young and fat enough for her table. She was enjoying the bustle of the early morning import market: the heaps of spices, the lengths of red and blue cotton cloth, the shrieking monkeys and parrots in their locally-made cages of colored wire.

Child that I was, even with one ankle chained to a block I was all eyes for the toys. There were stick whistles, bright wooden parrots that really flew, bottles filled with gray ant colonies that you could see right into. There was a yellow kite with flapped eyes that fluttered open and shut in the wind—but more wonderful still was the proud lady, ears and hands heavy with rings, followed by her servants. Although gorgeous jewels and glass beads were all one to me, I had never seen anything like her and I stared as she and her servants passed the slave market without a glance.

However, seeing she was rich and well dressed, well able to afford a whim, the slaver sang out after her, offering me. "A little flower from the south for the beautiful lady of the north." She looked at me and laughed at him, her face all twisted with age-wrinkles, then drew her veil across her face, said something to one of her maids, and walked on. I was much older before I understood how kind she was, for there was no other servant in the house that had not been born into slavery and raised to serve. First generation slaves did heavy labor so their uncouth manners could not offend their owners. Their children might hope for a house position, if they were comely and quick-witted.

The maid—it was Consuelo, the cook's helper, charged with dressing the dinner table for the evening—put her trug of gladiola sheaves on the ground and counted out my price, a scanty half-handful of small change, leftovers from the marketing. All the while the dealer was unlocking my chain her appraising eyes ran over me. She grinned when I lifted my chin and glared at her. "You do as you're told, soon enough." Offering me a bit of caramel from her apron pocket, she ate one herself. Tongue coated with sweetness, I limped after her.

Strong for my size, I was able to haul the water for the fruit trees, and sprinkle and sweep the summer patio set among them. That was where my lady always received guests when the weather was fine. I stood and pulled the fan-cord, learning the ways of a fine house. Lady Mercedes' father had left her a nice patrimony, and despite her years she did not lack for suitors willing to add it to their own bit.

However, she relished what her great age had brought her: freedom from the eternal woman's round of pregnancy, birth, child-care, and man-care. She wanted a few years before she, too, bowed her neck to the yoke and joined her father's and her husband's spirits in breathing the fragrances of the sacrifices at the family shrine. That time would be too soon for me as well as her.

Where am I?

Lost in my thoughts, I have come by my usual way, skirting the center of the town. Below me, where the street runs down to the beach in wide steps, I can see the white tumble and break of the rising tide lapping the lowest tier. The sea is restless under the pressure of the wind still coming off the water. It is a sultry night, and it will be hours before the land cools and the temperature drops.

When I look far out, I can see the waves breaking over the carcass of the great ship that brought our ancestors here. The ship's great curving beams of metal have resisted decade after decade of storms. It still is uncorrupted, only now it has sunk too deeply into sand to allow any further salvage, other than the colored wires and glass that divers harvest for cages and fancy-work.

Wiping sweat from my cheeks with the tail of my head cloth, I set off at a brisk pace. I will, as I planned, stop at Lord Xavier's quinta. Set against the town wall, it offers a good escape route and it will hurt my lady less if she thinks I've been swept away by the rabble at the far edge of town. I owe her that trifle of kindness, surely. I look back at the fantasmas' glow at the funeral and sigh silently. I owe my owner too much and nothing at all. I must get away now: it is not likely there will be another opportunity. If my cage is not of bright-colored wires, it is nonetheless tightly woven.

I will leave by the water gate at the rear of the quinta and make my way up into the sage-scented hills that I missed so desperately when I was a child. I am not loath to have my trail end within Lord Xavier's precincts. The son is not so kind a master as the mother, being handy with both tongue and whip, ensuring his slaves will not have noticed anything when questioned. He will want to recover me, if not as part of his mother's grave goods, then as part of his inheritance, although failing to send me to her pyre would be slightly scandalous.

A quick clop of hooves is overtaking me. I slow slightly, force my mind to go over what I will do next. On the side away from whoever is passing me, I lift a hand to my basket and grip a handle, hard. My lady, if she has noticed I am still out, may be thinking of scolding me, but no one will be looking for me yet.

It's nothing. Nobody.

Slave searches follow the main highway down the coast, to the cities where well-trained house servants bring higher prices and could, the marketplace gossips said with a wink of complicity, even be indentured. To be a bondsman is a step up from slavery for any born into that state, but I cringe at the thought.

I am old enough to be attractive to men. My lady would have been speaking of a husband and children for me if she had not had been planning that I go with her. She is thrifty enough not to waste a young man from her son's inheritance for my comfort in the dead lands and, given her age, my children are not likely to be old enough to be counted assets.

If my people thought I had left on my own, they would suppose I would go to Los Tegues. If they think me stolen they would think farther, maybe even the vast city of Orocan, with its Well of the Maidens.

Now.

A white-haired old man on a sway-backed mule passes me without a glance. Hoof-beats fading away ahead of me, I let my legs reach out in stride after stride as I follow the familiar way for what I intend to be the last time. I have a good plan.

May the eyes of whatever gods there are be averted, I think, as a glowing trail zigzags across the dark and seemingly starless sky. The lights of the town make the glories of the heavens invisible, for here every great house keeps lanterns burning all night high up on their walls and there are always the fires of the fantasmas, drifting, as though impersonally curious.

In this affluent residential section, the streets are quiet. I can hear a soft echo from my own bare feet as I walk and now and again a guitarra being tuned. Even here you can smell cedar smoke and burned flesh from the alcalde's pyre. Hot wind licks my ankles when I stop at the great gate in the adobe wall. It may be days before the rain that will release Leon Ildefonso's soul.

Lord Xavier's gate is only one on this elegant street made of thick planks, deeply carved in leaves and vines in the style of the first settlers. The rest are the now fashionable curlicues and twists of hand-hammered iron, offering glimpses of courtyards and fountains, but my lady's son does not want people looking in. He says it encourages the maids to gossip and the menservants to flirt. He certainly gives them plenty to gossip about, if little hope of flirting.

I tug at the flat strip of stamped leather hanging in the flickering shadows of the portal torches and hear the high chime of the bell, then somebody on the other side grumbles to his feet and fumbles back the wrist-thick daytime bar. The night bar takes two men to lift into place, and so is seldom used on festival occasions. Basket of apricots heavy in my arms, I wait, careful not to look around me, as if intent on my errand.

The gate swings open a hand's breadth and old Rico's lined and seamed face appears in the gap. He looks at me and grunts, pulling the gate open enough so I could get in, but not so open that I don't have to brush close to him to do so. I go by him with averted face and downcast eyes as always, think, It's the last time, as his hand brushes one of my breasts.

"Apricots," I say, offering the basket to him. Sometimes his ancient lechery cloaks itself in enough gallantry to carry the girls' burdens. This time he shakes his wine-fuddled head and resettles himself in the watchman's alcove in the adobe wall. I can smell piss from when he has relieved himself against the portal. There will be trouble about that tomorrow.

"Take them to the kitchen," he says.

I swing the basket to my head again and pad off down the dust-soft path under the arcade, bare feet feeling the coolness of the always-shadowed earth. It has been weeks since the last rain. All the unpaved paths and byways of Misericordia del Mar are ankle-deep in dust finer than the cornstarch I separate for my lady's most elegant desserts.

When one of the household cats slips across the path, its patchwork fur blending into the dappled shadows cast by a pair of aimlessly drifting fantasmas, I have to pause until my heartbeat slows. I mustn't look nervous, it will raise questions, even if only out of kindly concern that I was accosted on my way here.

15

Take cornmeal, thrice ground, and sieve it well. Mix it with cold water. Place it in a settling bowl, and leave it undisturbed.

The fantasmas drift up and away, surrounded by a haze of befuddled insects. The glowing lights seek the company of their kind in the Plaza, perhaps, but a savory gust tells me why they were here. The buffet in the great hall must be grand indeed.

A blind man could find his way to Lord Xavier's kitchen by smell alone. There is roast pork and the sharp spices of the obligatory five sauces. Something with steamed mangos. Toasted rice with shreds of dried coconut. I swallow saliva. At my lady's quinta, we went hungry today, to honor the dead.

Everyone is making a grand occasion of the alcalde's funeral. There are few excuses for revelry in the dry season, even though the ancient aqueduct brings enough water to the town that the patient labor of several hundred slaves can irrigate the fields that support us all.

The waterworks make Misericordia a rich town by the standards of the coast, and many captives from the interior are glad to be taken here. The lowest pump-slave has enough to eat and drink, and the adobe walls and ditch protect those inside from the roving parties of raiders that plague the small farming settlements.

The splash of water in Lord Xavier's fountain reminds me it is a long, hot walk out from the interior and not everybody makes it. When, wooden neck-yokes balanced on our shoulders, my group topped the last rocky hill before the town, the green fields and the ocean were like a mirage to most of us. Many didn't know the seawater was undrinkable and forced their way forward through the weaker captives, near mad with thirst.

It was fortunate that we came to the stock market beside the town gate first. I remember one slaver throwing his head back to roar with amusement as we all rushed forward to plunge our faces into the horse-troughs and drank our fill beside the animals. It was the first time in our lives some of us had drunk all the sweet water we wanted.

I pause to dip my hands into the fountain's cool water. It may be the last time I see such wasteful abundance. When I came here, two or three of my fellow captives, groaning as they vomited the excess, swore the water was poisoned. The rest, from further inland, laughed at their self-inflicted misery. As if, bound for the slave market, we all had not had enough to be miserable about.

Those of us from the interior knew the true balance went awry when the blazing white curves and zigzags appeared in the sky. Not many of us had seen the fuego fantasmas then, and as a child, I wondered about them as they drifted about the slave market. I would have been frightened but no one else was. So much that was familiar now was strange then.

The reverse is true, too. Padding through the dark, leaf-rustling garden, I remind myself of that. It will be dry up in the hills, and, although it has been years since I was a lean and leathery child, my luck will turn as I leave the rich coast. I must be sure to take water, even if I can't get food.

It is the one part of my plan I cannot compromise, and the one part I am not sure how to carry out, for the great pottery ollas that I use to water my lady's fruit trees are nothing to carry into the wildness. The kitchen door stands wide open because of the heat, but I tap on it to announce myself.

"Delores!" said Elena. "I smell apricots!"

We laugh.

Lord Xavier's kitchen is filled with the half-full pots and disarrayed platters of a big party. They have not waited for midnight here. On such nights, by long-established custom, the house servants eat as well as the masters, and the gentry in the main dining room are sending back plenty of every-thing. On other days the servants' appetites have to be a little less choice, unless they are friends with the cooks.

A frequent and welcome visitor, I soon have my own full plate and quiet corner, watching Elena skin, stone and mash the full-ripe apricots from my baskets. "Smell them," she says. "None to be had in the market like Lady Mer-cedes', and Lord Rafael here again tonight, looking at Lord Xavier's eldest daughter."

Looking up from her work, her night-black eyes flash as she grins. I grins back, teeth clenched on a mouthful of roast suckling. Lupe, the eldest daughter, is not pretty, but she is well bred, accomplished, and good-tempered. Her father will sweeten the marriage compact with a few of his well-trained household servants, and Elena, a junior cook, is a likely choice. She will enjoy having authority over her own kitchen.

"Good luck," I say sincerely, chin greasy from rich meats.

Elena, who knows her own worth, nods, complacent, hands busy with the fruit. She washes her hands with care, dries them, and begins to stroke flour and ground almonds into butter. All the gentry know her pastry. Plump Lord Rafael likes the table and may think twice about turning down a suitable offer sweetened with such cooking.

She will be prized until she is too old or too ill to stand the long hours and the heat of the kitchen. If fortunate, she will end up with an owner kind enough to let her live out her days in comfort, shelling beans, shucking corn, or keep-ing an eye on whatever is on the spit as the fire flares blue with salted wood.

Now, she is skilled, pretty, and expensive.

Soon, I am too full to be comfortable but know I must eat more. It is a long way into the sagebrush hills where I can find water and food. I go get a second plateful, careful, this time, not to select anything fatty. It will not do to be ill on the way; water is always far more important than food.

I eat, slowly, chewing carefully, although I cannot taste what I am eating, and watch Elena as I have often watched her before, although for different reasons. Her cool fingers flutter skillfully.

Of all house-slaves, a fine cook is one of the luckiest, for the kitchen is her kingdom. If she marries the steward, a clever woman can set the tone for the whole inner household. When I was twelve or thirteen I haunted our cook, Ines, hoping to make myself handy enough that she would ask for me as an apprentice.

My effort was doomed, for my lady was too fond of me to countenance it. I was trained to be her body servant. I cried in my bed for weeks, although I held my head high in the daytime. That was when I admitted to myself that I would come to this night if I wanted to live beyond the few more years of Lady Mercedes' life.

Remembering what I am doing, my hands shake and the food goes sour in my mouth. I swallow with an effort and look at Elena to see if she has noticed, but she hums contentedly, absorbed in her work. The kitchen is quiet as before, pots bubbling on the stove and whispering flames licking the meat on the spits as the rattling clockwork turns and turns it.

Seeing the witches' eyes above the fireplace brighten and then dim, I stop thinking, and chew and swallow with determination. Soon I am going to be far away from all this. Free.

When my stomach is as full as I can reasonably make it, I ask, "Something to drink?"

Elena nods at her busy hands. "You know the way. Take what you like, no one is checking tonight. They're glad enough to be rid of the Old One, but if you ask me, they'll be singing a different tune when they sit down to fill his place."

Her voice fades behind me as I make my way down the stone steps into the cool depths of the larder. There I have some of the luck I have wished Elena. The field workers' water skins have been left in an uncounted heap by the cistern. I take two from the untidy pile and plunge them deep until they are full. Then I fill a pottery cup from one of the jars of buttermilk on the stone shelves. I leave what are now my water skins in the shadows under the rosemary hedge outside the larder door and go in. I settle back into my corner with a fresh plate.

"Tell me one of your stories," says Elena. "Tell 'The Coyote Who Stole the Moon.'"

I laugh. "That's for children."

She smiles, eyes cast down, and I guess children are on her mind. Joaquin and she have hopes they can stay together. They have planned to wait but maybe they haven't or maybe she is dreaming of what might be if this batch of apricot tarts is perfect. "Tell me," she says.

"When I finish this."

She nods, in no hurry, for the oven needs to cool a bit more.

I eat a last scrap and begin. "In the beginning, when all things spoke the same tongue, and greeted the dawn and greeted the dark together, there was a coyote who loved the sun. Day after day he spent, leaping higher and higher, trying to catch the object of his desire."

As I talk, I roam about the kitchen, tugging on the cords of the fans, sweeping up a fine dusting of flour, setting a lid straight on a crock. I pass and repass the great dinner platters with my back to Elena. One by one I slide pastry—skulls crusty with bubbled sugar and thighbones stuffed with almond paste—into the pocket that runs across the hem of my apron.

I am crouched, rewinding the clockwork for the spitted chickens as I come to the end of the tale. I pause to add a bit of salted wood to the fire. It flares, blue and lavender. "He was alone, in the darkness, with nothing but wet paws to show for his pounce," I conclude.

Done, I stand up, take my apron off and bundle it into a corner next to the door, smoothing my hair and shaking my dark leather housekeeping skirt. After that story my mother had told me while she combed my hair on our doorstep, I want to be in the hills. There is flour caught on the dark suede and I rub to get it off. I can still see a white smudge when I am done.

No matter, I think, and touch the copper token at my neck.

"You'll have to dress finer to catch the men," says Elena, eyes still on her work. Her blue-black hair is strained to the nape of her neck with a knot of red ribbon to match the border on the full sleeves rolled nearly to her shoulders.

I say nothing. Wishing won't change my high-cheeked face for Elena's smooth oval. I have the narrow eyes and droop-cornered mouth of my people. "Everything smells so good," I say.

The cook glances at me, mind on the butter and bolted wheat flour she is working with feather-light strokes. The apricot filling stands cooling n its yellow bowl.

I check for her, but the oven is still too hot for pastry, so I leave the door ajar. In the day, the staff can bake with the ancient solar oven and keep the kitchen cool, but now, in the dark, they use wood fires like the poorest of the poor.

Elena's voice runs on and on, comforting and familiar. It would be so easy to stay. "You should get some ribbons from the marketplace," she muses, "although who has some to match the gray-green of your eyes I'm sure I don't know."

21

"Blue would do as well," I say absently. As if I ever wear ribbons. I dress plainly, in dark colors, as is proper for a body servant. I sit down with my apron-wrapped bundle of food against my leg, and mime finishing another helping.

Then I take the plate to the tub in the corner, already filled with scraps for the pigs, scrape it, rinse it in the barrel in the corner and put it in a basket, ready for the dishwashers in the morning. They will have a mighty task and probably mighty headaches, too.

"Not at all. You pay too little attention to things. Your lady may still think you are a child, but the time will soon come when she'll ask you who you like." Elena's pastry is excellent but she does not pay much attention to the ebb and flow of life around her if it does not directly concern her. My lady will not be asking me whom I fancy as a husband. On this night of all nights, Elena might at least realize they will burn me, too, alive, as they did the alcalde's body servants.

But she isn't, in some things, clever. I doubt Elena ever gives a thought to something so simple as why they will take the baskets of crockery to the head of the irrigation ditch at the foot of the garden to be washed. The used water irrigates the herb patch and the kitchen garden. The kitchen rinse barrel's water will go directly to the poultry yard. Food scraps must not be wasted. Water is always precious.

I slide the cheap pottery cup that had held the milk into my bundle. I will take it with me. There are springs in the hills where you wait, drip by drip, for one swallow. On a full belly, with water waiting, I want to be on my way. I make my farewells to Elena, who doesn't give me a second glance, her hands being busy patting pastry into a form, tasting the filing, stirring it briskly to make sure it is cool enough.

Outside, I hang the heavy water skins from my shoulders, knowing they will seem too light far too soon. The moment of truth comes when I turn down the paved path to the back of the quinta. Here and there it is softened with dust but the rising wind will brush the traces of my footsteps from it. My shadow dances around me as another batch of fantasmas drift overhead. I hurry, wanting to be well away as soon as possible.

My lady will send men to look for me soon enough. Rico is so often drunk and unreliable that they won't be sure I haven't slipped out the main gate while he slept unless there is some other evidence. When he falls into a tipsy doze the servants often raise the bar and leave without disturbing him. The old man always replaces it without asking questions. He'll swear he's seen me pass, and lead them all astray.

I smell the fragrances of the different plants my skirt brushes as I pass. I want that, too, well away on the wind, before they come looking for me. I hurry, skirt gathered tight, inhaling sage and rosemary as if they were incense.

The gate in the thick rear wall was originally put there to allow the water bearers of the household to go down to the aqueduct before there was a wooden pipe with its slave-driven pump to bring water to the gardens. These days it is mostly used to toss out trash, to bring in adobe materials when the household turns out for the yearly replastering. Adobe houses melt a little in the winter rains and the witches' eyes must be renewed: bad luck always comes if they are not.

One can get out readily enough but the bar trips and drops back into its socket in the wall once the panel is closed. When it is in heavy use it is propped open and a watchman sits in the niche beside it, but tonight there is no one there.

The heavy beam swings up until I can duck under it. I push it shut again slowly. The thud of the bar going into place sounds very final. Now, if I want to get back in, I will have to circle the town wall in the dark and explain myself to the watch at one of the main gateways. They will hold me for my owner. Tonight would be a bad night to be in their hands, for most of them are likely to be drunk. The ones that are not would be wild with the festival for the dead. I cannot run back; I must go forward.

Nose crinkled at the stench of garbage from other, less well-run households, I set out. Nervous though I am, I still take time to push my face into the aqueduct's flow. I drink until my food-swollen belly almost rebels, then hitch my two heavy water skins to comfortable positions and trudge up the well-worn path into the brush.

I take my time. It is unlikely anyone is looking and if one of the watchmen on the wall towers spots me he will assume I am going to the piles of unsalted firewood gathered high on the slope. Despite the heat, there are cook fires and bonfires all over the town, and someone has to get the wood to feed them. They are using plain wood tonight, not the salt water soaked wood that keeps best through winter. Only an unwilling kitchen drudge would be sent to haul in weevil-infested wood that had not yet been treated.

When the wind shifts a little, I smell smoke and spices, strong enough to mask the odor of garbage in the ditch at the base of the wall. A day or two, and all this will start on its way down into the saltpans to be cured. Then they will burn the garbage and brush in the ditch and toss the alkaline ashes upslope to keep the approaches clear of cover and vermin.

Right now, though, if anyone wishes to attack, the means to enter the town lie, the result of hundreds of hours of slave labor, on these slopes, convenient to the wooden doors that lead into the back gardens of the great houses and the main courts of the poorer ones.

They will all be bricked in for winter after the ditch burning. Some households wait until the day before the alcalde's inspection to properly barricade, for it is easier for slatterns and the mistakenly-thrifty to toss the household trash out for the wild dogs than to cart it away.

I pass the woodpiles silently, hearing the rustle and crackle of dry grass and half-stifled moans from behind one: lovers. As long as I am quiet, no one here will think anything of another servant girl hurrying through the night. Where the path passes the partial concealment of some bushes, a man steps out for a moment.

Seeing the shine of long, dark hair and the flutter of some decoration at the tops of his light-colored boots, I draw my head cloth across my face, hoping it is too dark under the thorn trees to reveal the lumpy outline of the water skins at my back. Holding my breath, I keep on my way as if I have an appointment.

Not everyone who comes here has a particular lover in mind, and some of the women will accept a little money from the menservants for the pleasure of their company. Some few of the older ones don't ask anything, but go with whoever asks them. At the edge of my vision, I see whoever it is step back into the shadows.

When I've gone beyond the usual bounds of the town's foot traffic, the trail is rough beneath my bare feet. There are stones sharp enough to pain me despite my calluses. Never sent beyond the gates, I don't have a proper pair of sandals, shoes, or boots to my name, and I was afraid to take any of the mistress's or my fellows.

What I do have is a pair of well-worn fancy slippers that went with my lady's favorite dress until they became too shabby to be worn, even under the concealment of a long skirt. I stop and pull them on awkwardly, balancing on one foot and then the other.

I was given them when I cut my foot nearly a year ago and saved them for this, wrapping my foot in rags whenever I knew my lady wouldn't be about, telling the other servants air was good for the wound.

I've cobbled a leather layer, but even so the thin soles won't protect me from bruises and stubbings. They are better than nothing, and, should they send the dogs after me, second-hand shows may confuse the scent. Thinking of that, I pluck a few half-withered leaves from a wild sage bush and tuck them under my feet.

Dry brush all around me, I am following only the faintest trace of a trail when I hear the sound of one stone turning over on another behind me. I stop and crouch beneath a jaboncillo sapling, smelling the tang of sun-cooked resin in the dark.

In the true dessert, stones crack in the temperature change from day to night but they don't often bounce and roll, and it is flat here. I remember less than I want to from my country childhood, but I do remember that. Something is on the trail behind me. I stay very still.

Time passes. Presently I hear the soft hiss of breath. He may have been careless once but now he is so close to me I can hear him exhale. I hold my own breath. If I can hear him, he can hear me. There is just time to slowly fill my lungs before his hand closes over my mouth. I try to bite, but he has a good grip, strong fingers locking my jaw shut.

He pulls me back against him and feels the water skins. "Good," says the soft, accented voice. "You'll need some smarts out there." He dumps me in a careless heap, pulls a nightglow from somewhere about him, squats and blows on the tiny light. It flames.

I can see his face as he studies mine. It is narrow and foxy, surrounded by a waterfall of coarse black hair. His forehead has no slave mark, and if he were a Lord I would know him. An outlander, then, in town to trade. Curious about the local girls, he's come to the hill to try his luck, seen me and followed.

Or maybe he's seen my forehead. There'll be a good reward for a runaway house slave. One way or another, he knows enough to persuade a lot of girls to please him.

When he's looked me over, he puts the light on the ground and closes the two clamshells in their metal frame.

Now, night vision gone, I can only see him as a darker outline against the night sky.

"Running away?" he asks.

I nod, half-hoping he is still night-blind. There is not much point in saying no. No use trying to escape, either. He has a bow case at his back. An arrow in the leg and I won't get far. Wounded, I'll be a burden, not an asset. The bright starlight will make me any easy target in a moment, when his eyes readapt.

Still, he sees the motion and laughs softly. "Know anything about living in the hills?"

"No," I say. If I say I know a little, he'll question me to find out how much.

He touches something hidden at his throat under his shirt, sits back on his haunches and says, "I'll make you a bargain. I came into town to buy a likely girl for my bed and to work about the camp. You come with me for a year and you'll know enough to get by on your own. If we both like, we could make it permanent. If not, we part, no hard feelings."

"If I get pregnant?"

He shrugs, then says, reluctantly, "Maybe you can please me without that."

Maybe I can.

The town bravos think nothing of stopping a slave woman for their pleasure but it is considered poor form to force one into full sex. Her owner might make difficulties. Most plan which woman they wish to breed with which man, for sound slave children increase the value of an estate like any other fine livestock.

Almost all men will settle for your mouth and hands without a fuss. When I was nearly of age, I learned a good deal from my fellow slave women. It is wise to be friendly.

He's offered a good deal. If he keeps it. "All right," I say, rising out of my crouch and brushing dirt from my suede housekeeping skirt. "Where do we go?"

He stands in one smooth motion and says, "Off this trail for one thing. By those clothes, you're a woman's body servant. Does your lady have a husband? A son?"

"She might have to ask her sister's son. Her son is entertaining a suitor for a daughter tonight. It should be a while before I'm missed."

He sniffs the eddying air and hesitates. Soon, now, the land wind will start, carrying our scent back toward the town. The gentry hunt with dogs. I've taken precautions but I don't think he has. "We'll have to move fast for a while. You can rest in the daytime. For a little."

I tug at the straps for my water skins and he lifts one away. I can hear it slosh as he re-slings it on himself. It is not courtesy that he take half of my burden. With half my water plus whatever he already has, he can outlast me in the hills if I should change my mind about our bargain or if I've lied even as I agreed.

"Follow me closely."

I do. He starts off fast and finds I can't keep up on the rougher ground. Then he changes to fifty strides fast, followed by a hundred at a slower pace. Fifty strides fast, a hundred slow. The change gives the body some ease and the counting soon makes the mind numb.

I follow blindly. Lady Mercedes keeps no horses or mules, it being convenient to borrow from her son and

nephews in exchange for her raising fruit for all the households. As a result, I am far more accustomed to walking
than the average body servant, but I am glad when we stop
for a rest and a mouthful of water.

The lesser moon, a knife-like crescent of cinnabar, has
risen, and I can watch our trail being blown into the sandy
ripples and waves of the higher desert. We are a long way
off any path. I wonder if my captor knows some hidden
source of water, that he is so confident.

Anyway, I judge I should act as though I believe him, so
I waste a little of my water wetting my palms and the tight-
drawn hair at my temples. It may go better if I look as if I
wanted to be attractive for him.

"What's your name," he asks suddenly.

"They call me Dolores," I say.

"But that's not your name."

"No," I say, frowning at my slipper-shod feet. Already,
there is a small split over one great toe. I lie. "I don't remember that." My mother always called me my daughter. I
have not had a dream-quest. Because of that, to my own
folk, and despite my age, I am still a nameless child.

"You weren't born a slave."

"They took me in a raid south and inland of here, eleven
years ago."

"Not a very profitable raid, if they were collecting," he
looked me up and down, "four- or five-year-olds."

"Six," I say. I'd just turned six, for we count the year
you spend in the womb. My mother made sweet cakes for
the two of us with the last of the dried cherries. We sat on
the stone slab before the door and each eaten one hot.

The hills before us had been pale green with fleeting
spring of the dry lands. We were hoping my father would
be back soon from a successful hunt: one of the knee-high
spotted antelopes or a bush deer.

I was so happy.

Then we had heard the distant thunder of many hooves. My whole clan did not own so many horses. My mother stood up, fluid and graceful, ready to flee, and sat down again heavily. "They've seen us," she said. You can see a long way across the grasslands and it takes skill to move without leaving a plain trail. Neither of us knew how.

So we sat, licking crumbs from our fingers, and waited. My mother must have known but I didn't understand. When the men rode up they didn't bother to pretend they were anything other than they were. "Yoke her up," said one man, and two others pinned my mother.

"The girl?"

"If the woman wants her."

My mother, not knowing if my father were alive or dead, took my hand in hers. We walked away without looking back, smelling our burning home.

My mother touched her throat and I saw she had concealed her copper pendant within her dress. She let herself be lead where they willed. Older now, I think would not have been so tame as she. Better to die trying than to be so meek.

Remember that, I tell myself, as my most recent captor stands up and looks around from horizon to horizon.

"I'm Guapo," he says. "Of the coyote clan, if that means anything to you."

Coyote is the clever one, sometimes the trickster, occasionally the fool. I shake my head, no. A townswoman would know nothing about clan matters and calling a townsman a coyote is an insult. Coyotes are scavengers at the tip heaps below the walls. If he belongs to an upland clan, whatever this man's name is, it isn't Guapo. That is town slang for a coxcomb, a dandy.

"I'll call you Luz, and give you the coyote's protection—unless you know your spirit?"

Again I shake my head. I have no guardian spirit, no name, and my eyes are the gray-green of the sea the townsmen's ancestors had come from. In my clan they had thought that unlucky.

No proper person goes upon the sea, only witches, ghosts, and the fuego fantasmas, which are not often seen so far inland. I had never seen one until they brought me to the town. One drifted about after me all one long summer evening, and my fellow slaves laughed at my badly concealed terror until I, finding the thing did nothing, laughed, too.

I am much more frightened than that now and hope it does not show. Perhaps it does, for Guapo selects something from around his neck—there is more than one cord there—and hangs the little leather bag on mine, still warm and greasy from his body.

The unclean touch is unpleasantly personal. I don't shudder. I have already agreed to be far more intimate than that with him. He is offering me status of a sort I'd never had. Among the uphill peoples, prisoners are stripped of their totems. Slaves, what few the clansmen keep, have none. He's given me one and I am, therefore, a person to him.

I wet my palm with another few precious drops of water and rub at my slave-mark—my lady had been so kind I was never branded but wore, instead the monthly-renewed slave stamp on my forehead—and become something like a free woman. "Thank you," I say, trying not to sound grudging. "I will be Luz," I add, remembering the light in my childhood visions. I offer him my water skin and we seal the matter with a swallow apiece.

He gets up and we began walking again. Maybe my feet move a little faster in their new freedom. Maybe not. I fall into the steady rhythm that can carry you for miles without thinking. Pale pink dawn finds us far out on the barren desert. The mud plates we are crossing are baked so hard they won't shatter underfoot even if you stop and stamp.

The bowman's stride didn't vary and I wonder if we'd keep moving through the midday heat. It is easy to die of thirst in such places. The rising sun casts long, fantastic shadows from everything. Presently Guapo says, "There."

I look and see a dark smear at the horizon line. "What is it?"

"A bunch of bushes where the water comes close to the surface. It's out of the sun. We can rest." He breaks off and I know he means to see if I'll keep my bargain. It takes almost two more hours of walking before we reach the thicket and work our way into its hollow heart. It is, really, all one plant: the oldest shoots dead, and the newest battling on the exposed rim.

It is cooler here and he doesn't rush me. I do the things I know mostly from telling, not practice, even though I dislike the unfamiliar male odor.

Afterwards, satisfied, he rebraids his hair, whipping the loose ends tightly with red cord. Then, piece by piece, he removes all his finery, a shell neck plate, two fine bracelets of silver so smooth and regular they must be very old, and the fringes wrapping the tops of his boots. He takes off his sash, puts everything in its folds, and reties it tightly at his waist, but not before I see the lump of gold, big as the tip of my thumb.

He came to Misericordia del Mar dressed in his best, prepared to pay well for a slave-girl and been disappointed since the Old One's funeral had closed all the markets. He is short for a warrior, shorter than I, with thin lips that look bitter in repose.

Even stripped of his finery, he is fussy about his dress. The skins of his leggings are stoned near white and stenciled with blue-black geometry, and the string-shield for his forearm matches his bow-case. Guapo, I think, carefully not smiling. Maybe he really is named something like that.

He looks me over a bit, too, with cautious sidelong glances, apparently satisfied with what he sees. Eventually he draws his knife and gestured me closer. I hesitate an instant and then go. He has no reason to harm me.

Guapo grabs a fold and began cutting my skirt shorter until it falls only to my calf. Then he cuts some of what he's taken into two temporary shoes for my feet, pleated bags laced across my instep, and bound around my ankles: awkward but effective. Most of the rest gets turned into leggings for my legs, for only leather will save you from the desert thorns.

He tucks every scrap of the well-tanned material into his own bundle. We each take a scant mouthful of water and set off again, the hot glare of the descending sun in the west on our backs. That is the first night and day we spend together.

Our first camp is a cold one, our dinner the squashed pastries and cakes I took from Lord Xavier's kitchen. Guapo gobbles down his share and more and I make no protest. Soon I'll be dependent on his hunting skills. But I savor every titbit, wetting my fingers to save the crumbs that fall on my skirt. It will be a long time, if ever, before I eat flaky pastry and fruit from sheltered gardens again.

Stomach appeased for the moment, licking the last smear of almond paste from my thumb, I look around. We are in a hollow, invisible from any distance in the flat desert. The constant wind sends gauzy streamers of dust weaving over our heads, blotting out the stars as they began to come out. I can smell the dry, powdery scent of the land itself, taste its grit on my tongue.

The long muscles in my legs quiver so hard that tremors shake my feet. I begin kneading my calves in the twilight, watching Guapo, still sunlit up on the hollow's rim. He looks tired, too, but his hands are busy cutting and splicing leather. Frowning at his task in the fading light, he holds a loop up, slides it closed, then open.

He's making a snare, I think, wondering what there was in this barren land, where all the water is bitter and un-drinkable, to snare. Jackrabbits, perhaps. The town disdains the tough and stringy flesh unless the animals had been caged and fattened. Serving them at a feast was always a boast among the oldest families, showing someone had in-herited a recipe that made them palatable. Wild jacks are at their poor best stewed, but we have no pot and no water to stew them in, for we can't afford to lose what would cook off.

I lie down, sending my tongue in search of fugitive tastes in my mouth. If we are going to be eating roasted jackrabbit, there is hard living to come. I had expected to go to the gentler hills, where there was sweet water, herbs, and roots: where I knew what to do. Here, in the true des-sert, I am ignorant and in danger.

This land is not mine.

Stretching out flat, I try to relax. There are no blankets, no bedding. The sand is as hard as stone under my weary body. I scrabble a witches' eye or two out of the way—they are rare so far from a settled area—then restlessly twist from one position to another, watch Guapo's busy hands until he either finishes or decides he's done enough in the failing light.

Once he has packaged everything ready for the morning, he slides down into the shadows, scoops two hollows in the sand, one for his hips, one for his shoulders and head, lies down and goes to sleep, comfortable as a dog drowsing on a street corner. He has said nothing about maintaining a guard, so I dig out two hollows, dust off my sandy hands, and lie still. I can rest my body even if I cannot sleep.

I stare into the vault of the sky, at the river of stars. How long since I have been able to see so many of them? Even here the dust haze reflects the lights of some distant hamlet and hides a few of the faintest back the way we had come. There are so many I find it hard to find the partial patterns I have grown used to in the darkest part of the night in town.

Four parallel white-hot lines burn down toward the horizon and are gone. Another flashes up from the horizon in a long, smooth curve that crosses over its own path. I blink.

Jaguar claw marks on the sky are a bad omen. Counting the true stars will avert bad luck. I stare up, willing myself back into memories I will need, if I am lucky. I am far too old for a quest, but I hope that in the lands where I was born my spirit and my name will reveal themselves to me. My spirit had begun to come to me when I was child: a light, coming closer, filled with a something that I always woke before I could see. Without my spirit and my true name, I am forever incomplete.

Count, I tell myself. Count.

One is the baleful red eye of the wolf, plus seven, the blue-white stars that collar the bull. Three plus two are the fox-child's ears. Thirteen in a patch smaller then I can cover with my hand at the end of my extended arm, and there must be room for hundreds of hand-sized patches in the sky, a number beyond imagining with your eyes closed.

I stop my counting without knowing why and crawl to the edge of the hollow. Down slope, Guapo lies, turned on his side, asleep in the pale light of the rising crescent of the greater moon. What I had taken for a hamlet is still alight, and its lights have moved. Is there a sound? I wait, intent, and hear it again. A hound bays. I am sure it is a dog, and not a coyote.

"Guapo," I say softly.

"Hmp!" he says and his eyes open. "What?" he breathes.

"I heard a dog."

He rolls to his knees, and waits, listening.

I point: behind us, the way we came yesterday. The dog howls again. The sound stops abruptly, as if a huntsman has closed its jaws with his leather-gloved hand.

Guapo is on his feet, hanging his few possessions about himself.

I follow suit.

"If you've changed your mind and want to go back," he says as he pokes his head through the looped carrying strap of a water skin and settles it at his back. "You can wait here." He sniffs the wind, which is from us to them. Hand on my water, ready to take it from me, he adds, "If you're with me, we run until I say stop."

I nod, pull away to check the ties on my improvised shoes. The hunters may take me safely back to my lady, particularly if I say Guapo forced me to come. If they take the dandy they'll hang him. Eventually. After he's screamed and bled enough. I know he knows that when he puts his hand on my arm, a hard, unfriendly grip.

"You're sure?"

Once more I nod.

The bowman releases me and jogs off, deceptively slow for a man running for his life, but we'll have a long way to go.

I follow.

The greater moon has risen a hands-breadth higher up the sky when we come to the first arroyo. It is too deep to scramble into conveniently. Guapo turns right and begins running alongside it at a much faster pace.

I catch his fear and keep up, feeling the soft soil dint beneath my feet. My thighs ache with the effort. I can walk for miles, but running in soft soil is harder than anything I have done since I was a child. I can hear Guapo breathing heavily, and my own heart pounds loudly. Straining to go faster, I can no longer listen for any sound from behind us.

It seems a long time before we come to a place where the arroyo's bank has collapsed into a natural ramp and we can slide and stagger our way into it. My mouth is dry with haste and fear. We are trapped unless there is some way up the far side.

There isn't. The soft crumbling walls pass us as we flee, always nearly vertical on the side we want, sometimes even overhung. Guapo runs with determination and I run with fear. I don't want to go back. Even if all they do was kill this casual acquaintance, there'll be a sharper watch on me from now on. I'll not get an easy second chance. My lady is so old. I think of the curved knife, and the blood, and the prayers. They give the most favored to the pyre's flames alive that their spirits may serve those they had served faithfully in life.

My father told my mother, when he thought I was not listening, they gave them, not to the true spirits of the land, but to the evil that flies among the stars. It has been a long time but I remember his face as he said that, bitter and hard. He lost a brother to slavers. He had probably chosen to die rather than be taken if they came upon him.

I run harder, passing Guapo.

He makes a greater effort and draws even with me again.

The footing changes abruptly and we both stumble and fall.

The dandy curses, feels his legs and feet, then stands, cradling his left arm in his right.

I am shaken but unharmed, except for scraped palms and a skinned cheek.

We've come to the roots of the hills. All around us the walls are split and layered like the pages of a book. Guapo seizes me by the elbow and swings me next to the side of the arroyo, his hands looped into the stirrup menservants offer their mistress to mount. I put my foot in and scramble up.

I haul myself inelegantly over the edge to lie, panting, with a few moments to think about what his knowing how to do that meant before he makes his way up. Not quite such an outlander as I'd thought. Leon Ildefonso kept a guard of native bowmen.

"You," I say, as he gets to his feet and pulls at me to rise.

"Not now," he says, jogging off again.

He sets a slow pace. We both need to get our wind. A dog howls somewhere behind us, and he curses. "Fond of you, is she, your Lady?"

"Yes," I say.

"You might have warned me."

"I," I say, then save my breath for the running. He could have told me about himself, and as for me, I am so used to Lady Mercedes' kindness it hasn't occurred to me that a stranger's assumption would be that a personal servant would run away because she was unsatisfactory. Such a one, unfaithful and too soft for fieldwork, might not be pursued with vigor by a wealthy household.

A chime of hounds sounds behind us. The hunters have let the whole pack run free, hoping they'll corner us. That means it is Lord Xavier's hunting hounds. They know me and I am safe. I can take the chance of the dogs distracting Guapo to escape from him. Hung-over and angry, the men won't be too sorry if the dogs simply pull the bowman down and worry him to death.

A few simple lies, and I'll be on my way back to my owner, the grateful trophy of the hunt. At that thought, I run harder, the wind whipping my sweaty hair into cold flames that lick my cheeks and neck.

Overhead the star river flows across unmarred heavens. If they catch me I must say I was afraid of the man, the hounds, of being mistaken in the dark. It is rough running. The ground is uneven, almost always climbing. Every tiny relief of a down slope is paid for twice when you start to climb again.

My throat is sore from the strange, electric air, and I can see the play of heat lightning in the hills we run towards. A cool gust paws my face: it is raining there. It is a long way away.

Guapo turns sharply and I follow, down the bank of a small arroyo, up the other, down the one beyond, up the other side, climbing hard, almost on our hands and knees. I wonder what he was about, if he thinks we'll find a place the dogs can't leap to—then I hear what he's already heard.

The distant roar of water in a waterless land: a flash flood. It will grind sand, stone, and boulders together until nothing will stand in its path. The only safety is high ground, if we can find it.

I run as I have never run before, indifferent to pain.

We climb out of one last arroyo and scramble up a low hill, turning constantly to find the steepest upslope. The men and the hounds behind us seldom come so far into the high desert, for there is little to hunt. They may not know their danger. They may continue to follow the easy path of the dry streambed.

When we cannot hear one another when we try to speak, we both sit on the sand-scoured rock and wait, shoulders heaving. All the directions from here are down. We have done what we can.

The roaring water comes. The spray wets us where we sit, watching the moonlit froth and fume torn by the gusting wind. In minutes it is over.

When everything is silent again, Guapo unslings his bow case, takes out the bow and begins rubbing it with a soft rag, looking up from time to time to judge how long until sunrise.

We can't continue without light. There are pools of mud and traps of quicksand in the high desert after a rain. I sit, rubbing my skinned knees and hands, pulling thorns from my forearm by touch. I tripped and fell twice when Guapo hadn't.

That done, I watch the smoky light make everything around me paler and paler until, between one moment and another, I can see color, the soft pastels of dawn and the harsher earth tones of the desert.

All around us the land is littered with stones bigger than my head and the bedraggled remnants of jutillo bushes. A deceptive desolation, for those broken branches will be sending roots into the ground, stretching toward the sunlight, maybe even flowering, before the end of the day.

In the morning light this is a beautiful land, simple rather than harsh, all soft colors and rounded forms. The way the world must have looked in the beginning, before man, before animals, almost before plants, a creation fresh and unmarred.

In silent agreement, we stand and begin walking. Someone will come looking for the men, dogs, and eventually us. The two of us walk fast and hard and I hardly notice it, my eyes are so busy with what we pass, and my mind so occupied with remembering. It is not my homeland, I know that, but for all that it makes me homesick.

I find myself looking for some familiar landmark, some foot-worn trail. Guapo, glancing over his shoulder at the vast and shelterless expanse, does not seem to share my curiosity. Maybe Lord Xavier's men and dogs have been scattered or killed by the flood, but if they are still following us, they will be savage. He glances at me from time to time, eager to find fault and finding none.

My legs are sore, but I match him pace for pace. I have never been so sure that I want to be free. Even when the stupefying heat of midday comes on, and the dry steady wind leaches the moisture from eyes and mouth until my eyeballs feel sandy and I can hear grit squeak between my teeth, Guapo keeps us moving, not fast, not slow.

There is no place to shelter. I say nothing, for there is nothing to say. By now it is plain we have come too far or by the wrong way. We are in the high dessert. The horizon is a level line and the sky is a blue bowl specked with black. To the high, circling vultures we are as ants crawling across a plate.

Guapo curses monotonously.

Myself, I imagine I am sitting in the shady patio, doing that dullest of tasks, the one assigned maids as punishment, hemming sheets with small, careful stitches so the crafts-women can do the fine embroidery.

I flex my fingers, thinking of how careful I would be if I were there, the sounds of the fountain soothing my ears, the hot wind languorous with the fragrance of roses. Every so often, leaning against the soft cushions at my back, taking a slow drink of water from my olla, then making more small, small stitches.

Presently my shadow begins to lengthen, a little puddle of darkness that my feet reach and reach for and never fully achieve. I walk and watch the darkness grow toward distant evening and relief from the heat, stupid and mechanical, the sun broiling my aching head.

The water on my back is too heavy and not heavy enough. It takes energy to move and it is not going to be sufficient to get me to the purple horizon. Now, in late af-ternoon, clouds sail the ocean of air above us, majestic as great ships, offering us only their insubstantial and racing shadows. Heat-dazed, I wish I could walk, mouth open, feeling the rain on my face.

I nearly step on it.

We have been following the dusty trace of a game trail. Someone has placed the trap right at the point where the path dips and turns toward a little hollow that suggests there may be water a foot or two under the sandy surface, just at the place where one's attention is distracted by the need to keep one's balance in suddenly soft footing.

It is a metal trap, cruel and toothed, with a dried smear of something on its trigger pan, although most of the bait has been stolen. By gray ants, I think, for the thing is so sensitive it leaps shut at the wind of my passing.

Guapo, eyes as glazed with heat and fatigue as mine must be, turns back at the clang of metal on metal. "You all right?" he says flatly, knowing I am. No one with their foot trapped in one of those things could stand calmly.

I nod, trying to make some sense of what I am looking at. Outlanders don't use metal traps. They are expensive, and unreliable. Small game is often taken from the trap by something larger, and large game fights itself free.

Here there was not even a way to anchor the device firmly in the sand. It is just lying there, intended, I realized, the hair rising on my neck, to cripple, not capture.

The bowman comes back to look at it, but I have no confidence in his judgment. I remember his boosting me with a stirrup lift. He is one of the Old One's, tracking skills gone stale with years of soft town living.

Maybe he had not been so very good in the wilderness anyway, if he found town living so much to his taste. A man soft enough to think of finding a woman before he ran for his life is no one to depend on. I stay silent, while he sniffs and pokes at the trap with a show of professionalism, and look suitably impressed.

We need to get away from here. Now.

The bowman stands looking around us, frowning. "There's nothing here?" he asks in the half-interrogative of a man seeking confirmation of an obvious fact. "Is there?" he says more sharply, his accent made noticeable by his alarm.

Nettled, despite my fear, I poke at the sprung trap with a booted toe. "Why is this here, then?" I whisper.

"Good question," he says, and squats, making himself small.

I follow his example. It is more than time we act like the prey we plainly are.

He pushes his face close to mine, and says in a low voice, "I think there's a well near here."

I look around, puzzled, for there are none of the usual signs of water to be seen, just the slow sweep of the flat, barren land.

Guapo adds, more softly still, "In a dugout, under-ground." The soil is soft, certainly, perhaps pounded to powder by the passage of many hooves and paws.

I listen for the sound of water, sniff for the smell of it. Nothing. If the well is in a dugout and covered, it can be anywhere, invisible unless you are right on top of the en-trance. Any bush will be enough to hide the opening. It will provide luxurious living in so dry a country. A bowl of wa-ter set out every day will draw game.

However this trap has to be for people and whoever has set the trap will not be friendly to two thirsty runaways who lead a search party through his territory. I think of my hap-less flesh used as bait, maybe even for the pot. When I think of what might happen to a woman, my interior twitches with fear. My bargain with Guapo is only demean-ing, has been forced on me by circumstance, and may do me no long-term harm. "What shall we do?"

He shakes his head, mouths, Be quiet.

I say very softly but also very firmly, "What shall we do?"

His eyes on the trap, Guapo considers the lay of the land. Then he sniffs the wind, appraises me, and says, "Can you run?"

I nod.

"Steadily?"

I nod again. The heat has baked the stiffness from my body. I am ferociously thirsty but capable of a fast steady pace.

Without a warning word, he touches the thing hidden within his shirt, stands, turns, and runs in one fluid motion.

I follow as quickly as I can. Death stands very near to me. Perhaps worse than death, unending pain. There is a reek in a flaw of the wind. Someone nearby, sweating because his body has water and to spare in this dry land. Someone who likes to cripple what he catches. Someone, like Lord Xavier, who takes pleasure in others' agony.

We go separately, in swooping curves and sudden zigzags. I could fool myself that it is all imagination, if it were not for the arrow. It passes so close to my cheek I feel the breath of its passing, see the odd, triple-feathered fletching.

I give myself to entirely to the effort to escape. Turn this way, that. Duck! Fall and roll. The bowman goes right. I, left. Up again, then one last hard run toward the horizon.

Guapo doesn't stop abruptly. He slows down gradually, until we are finally both going at a walk. "Close," he says, coming back to my side.

I nod, knowing he isn't the preferred prey. There must have been sign, rocks overturned, exposing their whiter undersides, for example, if someone is living in the area. I didn't notice anything and I wonder if the bowman should have.

Guapo doesn't seem much worried by our close call, but he too may figure most of the shots will be at me. To bring me down. A man alone on the desert for any length of time might begin to think about women. The thought had occurred to the bowman.

Ah.

I have value. Before, my bargain was forced, made out of instinct and habit. Not that I can do much to realize my value, but there is no reason I should be any more loyal to the bowman than he to me.

I keep my thoughts from my face. Slaves learn that it does no harm to always be pleasant and to seem a little simple. I'd learned that long ago, although my lady had sometimes seen through me.

We pass stunted bushes and follow the dusty trace of a game trail. It winds on and on, around huge boulders split by the sun, and across flat, flaking shelves of rock where scree slithers underfoot and the wind sings and moans through twisted trees.

Finally it peters out. Climbing slowly, we keep walking, hoping to strike a track that leads to a pool or spring. When it is near dark we just stop, in no particular place, with leagues behind us, and leagues more before us.

I let my bundles slide to the ground and sit down. I can smell the dust, the dust that may have us yet. We haven't found any water. The search that caused Guapo to almost lead us into the hidden camp, also lead him to follow one game trail, and look for another, but either we turned in the wrong direction, or the traces were too old, or the paths served some other purpose altogether.

Thirsty.

A vision like those of my childhood blurs my sight for an instant and is gone, but I do not need its warning. We are in trouble. One water skin is empty, except for a foul and leathery lees. The other is flaccid, half-full.

Guapo's own water bottle must be hidden somewhere about his person. I haven't seen it. It would be rash to assume that he will offer that to me, and in any case there will not be much. Indeed, since it is an ordinary part of his equipage, it may be empty or filled with wine or beer.

Thirsty.

He does not seem prepared for the trek, hasn't brought any food or much water, hasn't found any water or stopped to hunt, and we've drunk and eaten almost everything I had. I find a small round pebble to suck and walk on, tasting dust.

Thirsty.

It is a dry and hungry camp that night. I am dubious about Guapo's trailcraft, too. I can't do better, but that doesn't mean he is any good. As the bowman lies down to sleep, I ask, "Shouldn't we post a guard?"

Guapo props himself up on an elbow. "They're only two of us, and we're tired. I opt for taking my chances. Do what you like." He settles back, rolls over on his side, his breathing settling into the slow rhythm of sleep almost immediately.

I sit on a large and comfortless rock, listening to the click and shift of stone, the whisper of the wind, and feel very alone, nameless and without a spirit to call on for strength. Living in the town among those who do not have totem animals, I did not feel my need as acutely, but in the wilderness and no longer a child, I yearn for one.

All I have is that childhood glimpse of light in darkness, black and gold: the warning that comes to me if nothing else does. It is not something to appeal to or depend on, just a sign to heed when it comes. Nameless, I am no adult and I have not an adult's protection. Guapo's coyote, trapped in the bag around my neck, is not my totem. I feel its indifference. Surely the powers can understand my need and can open the way to me if they will.

Sitting on the stone, tired muscles twitching in my legs, I close my eyes, and lift my face to the wind. I can smell the sharp scent of pine trees and ocean salt, the distant hint of some fire's wood smoke.

Thirsty.

Stretching my front legs down, then my hind legs out, I pad off. It has been a hungry time for a while, and it doesn't look like things will be better the way I am going.

Too close to men. Too little water. I lash my tail, once, and go into the long, slow stride that covers distance.

I wake with a jerk from the odd dream, having accomplished nothing more than make myself uncomfortable sleeping upright when I might have lain down and eased my back and legs. There is a feral smell in the breeze that I can't identify, but I doubt Guapo will appreciate being waked to take a sniff.

Sliding down to sit leaning against the rock, I wait. A minute or two and the scent is gone. It might have been blown for leagues, like the smell of the sea. I ease my head cloth down around my shoulders and settle myself, eyes closed, but ears still awake. I wish the bowman had been interested in setting a watch.

The two slivers of moon, one bright, one smoky, rise slowly, casting long double shadows through the ragged trees and across the tumbled rocks of our sleeping place. It is getting cold enough to make standing and walking around for a bit a good idea. I rise stiffly and pace around the edge of our dusty bit of nowhere.

The trails of the wildlife are dark as ink on the moonlit soil. There the scribblings of a tumble bug, rolling its burden toward some safe crevice; here the delicate footprints of a long-eared mouse with the furrow of its tail running between; and this is a pugmark as broad my outspread hand when I place it next to it.

I stare at my fingers in the dust and felt a warm breath of terror at my neck. When I wheel around, there is nothing. But it had been there, two or three body lengths from where sleeping Guapo lies, less from where I was sitting, keeping watch in the wrong direction. Jaguar. It had come silently down the hill against the wind.

I shake the bowman awake.

"What," he says, hand fumbling on knife.

"Come see," I say.

He blinks at me, starts to say something short and reroll himself in his improvised bedding, then changes his mind. Breath hissing as the cold air hits his chest and arms, he drapes his tunic around himself and comes.

He squats, looking at my handmark and the footprint in the dust. "Jaguar," he says. "Big one." He takes a deep breath. "Did you see it?"

"No," I say, "and I was awake."

"You wouldn't of, either." The bowman stands up, looks around. "Hungry, I'd bet." He wipes his hands down his thighs. "They don't usually go for people, but there're no deer in the great dry, and I haven't seen any hares."

The prints of the beetle and the mouse were the first signs of wildlife I'd seen since we'd started walking. "What's it doing here?" I say. If it shouldn't be here, perhaps I'd found my totem, although the jaguar is very powerful, and the powers punish those who overreach themselves. More likely my spirit is the hard-working beetle or the shy, quick mouse, or something else altogether.

Guapo tightens the tunic around his shoulders, said, "Out of the cold fires, maybe."

"Where's that?"

"North of here," he says, crouching down and squinting as he looks for our visitor. "A big half-moon of a valley, with a hot spring. Trappers come east to show their pelts and traders north and west to sell supplies, trade news, and haul the furs to the towns. Tell me if you see anything silvery."

I start looking.

"One day some traders found the whole center of the valley all smoke and steam. They thought," Guapo freezes and considers something, then dismisses it, "that maybe the hot spring was heating up. So two stayed behind to make camp. The rest dumped their stuff, put a claim sign on it, and climbed down." The bowman pulls his nightglow from his belt. "Twigs," he says. "Light stuff."

I start gathering.

Guapo breaks a branch, pulls a few rocks together. "Come on," he says. "Quick."

I come, skirt full of tinder from beneath the nearest bushes. He tucks a handful or two into a cone of sticks, lights one, and tucks it underneath. Then he puts the ends of some of the longer branches into the struggling fire. I squat, pretending I want to warm my fingers, not just cower.

"If something comes," the crouching bowman says, blowing at the base of the flames and feeding the fire with light worm-ridden stuff, "then take a brand in each hand. If it's just hungry, it may do some good."

I look around. "What else could it be?"

He shakes his head, intent. I spring to my feet and turn around and around, leather skirt slapping at my calves. Guapo grabs a fold, pulls me to a halt, and growls, "Don't go funny on me."

I stop, more frightened by his tone than by the jaguar. He is here right now and the jaguar isn't. The man stands up, a little shorter than I, pushes his face up into mine and says, "The traders didn't come back. A big white bear did. Came sniffing and pawing like it was counting the goods. The two who'd stayed behind broke and ran. Nearly starved to death before another party came along. They went back."

Guapo squats again and so do I. He piles green twigs together, handy to feed into the flames for smoke. "The bear hadn't opened or eaten a thing. The whole load was there. Worth a season's trapping for four or five men. Nobody would touch it. The grass grew over what the mice and the bugs didn't get."

He looks into the fire, and I shake my head, marveling at the stupidity. Good food left to rot. Properly honored, the bear spirit is kind to men. Although of course I don't know, I guess that my father was a bear man, for our household made do with deer hides and the rugs my mother wove during the winter months where other families had good, thick bearskins for their beds and floors.

The bowman takes my expression for wonder and goes on. "That valley was full of white animals. Deer. Bear. Everything. Spirit animals." He looks around at the clearing, enclosed in the light from our fire. "The traders left the food as an offering, hoping to escape with their lives." Sensing disbelief, Guapo looks at me, and adds. "Not all of them did."

"What do you mean?" I warm my shaking hands at the fire.

"They lost three or four men. Found them just torn open, not eaten." He starts as something pops in the flames. "One guy's head was set in the crouch of a tree." Flaming twig in hand, the bowman sits back on his heels and delivers his punch line. "No natural bear did that."

Shadows leap back and forth in the trees as the fire grows. Resting one hand on the butt of a stick in the unnatural red and yellow flames from unsalted wood, I look around me with more care than the bowman, trying to catch the gleam of an eye, the outline of a feral face. The firelight doesn't make me feel safer, just conspicuous.

I glance up. Although the glare means I cannot see all the stars, I can see enough to be sure there are no jaguar scratches. Guapo's fire is probably wise. I would have started it earlier and hidden it better, myself.

If we come to water, I might do worse than leave him behind. In such rough country I can travel without leaving much of a trail. After that, there are the stars to lead me back toward the fertile lands along the coast. I guess that to my lady and all I knew in Misericordia, I am dead. One of the smaller cities may have a place for me. I can make baskets and sell them. Weave rugs. Plait cages.

Relaxing in the warmth, Guapo crosses his legs, relishing his story now. "They weren't really white," he continues. "Some of the later guys shot at a few. Their hair was ashes at the tips." He stares at the darkness without seeing anything.

Then the bowman prods at a stick already covered with fine white flakes. "It fell off easy, so whatever happened hadn't happened long before the first traders showed up." He looks at me. "They went through the cold fires, and it changed them."

I glance away, face as expressionless as I can make it. True spirits don't run around in the bodies of scorched, bewildered animals. They come and go like the wind, everywhere and nowhere.

"That's where I'm going." He gives the fire a decisive poke and makes it sputter and smoke.

"Why?" I say carefully, instead of, What?

He slides a hand in the collar of his shirt and scratches his chest, then shakes his head. "Curiosity, I guess."

"Guapo," I say.

The bowman's eyebrows knit in quick anger. "That's where we're going."

It takes an attentive ear to catch the stress on we but I hear it. I don't say anything more. As far as Guapo knows he doesn't have to do anything to force me to follow him because I don't know enough to survive on my own. I have let him believe that and that was wise.

I sit, looking into the fire, apparently submissive. In truth, I am nearly ready to leave him. Things from my childhood are coming back at odd moments. The pattern of clouds, suggesting an area with more water in that direction. The faint smell of dampness in this tumble of rocks that hints at an underground pool that small things might be able to reach. The warning cries of birds.

It is near dawn, but still too early for the sand doves to fly. Their shadows flash across the blushing sky. Something is prowling along the face of the rock where the roosts are. Guapo gets up, and listens, slowly turns around until he faces a dark patch of brush. Terror claws its way into my belly. Last night I'd gathered tinder at the edge of that patch.

As I watch, Guapo slides his bow from its case and strings it, finds and nocks an arrow.

Fingering the finger-long utility knife at my own waist, I get my legs under myself, ready to spring.

Without looking at me, the bowman says, "No. Take a long branch from the fire."

I pull one stick out, slide another in. I doubt I'll have time or need for another if an attack comes, but why not be optimistic?

We wait, listening to burning wood crack and shift, smoke sharp in our nostrils. Nothing. The sky turns from rose to gold and it is dawn.

I relax my cramped hand, knead it with the other, settle back on my heels, and feed the flames. I listen to my heartbeats as the sky grows lighter and lighter as the dawn flowers, gold and orange. Whatever had been in the scanty cover of the brush was gone.

The bowman goes and scouts the bushes without result. He comes back shaking his head, looks at me, and says shortly, "Big one. Probably just hungry."

I heat a little water and steep sage leaves as we wait until full daylight. It takes the sour taste of hunger from the mouth and settles the empty stomach for a little.

When we resume our journey, Guapo is careful to keep to open trails, detours around what little vegetation there is. His bow never leaves his hand all day. We see no game, not surprising since we avoid any place that might provide cover or water. The jaguar, if it is tracking us, will be traveling shadowy, cooler terrain.

At my suggestion, our next camp is in the middle of a rocky sheet that has a fault line running across its face that provides some shelter from the rising wind. Although it is early, it is cold, and I say I am tired and smell unseasonable snow.

Guapo denies it but, being tired himself, yields ungraciously to my feminine weakness. All you have to do is look out and up to see that on the heights winter has begun. A night with no fire, no water, and no food will be hard. The bowman has become cautious later than is good. The preceding night, one of us could have been killed as we slept. I remember our positions by the fire and shiver. I had been the nearer.

We settle into the crack and Guapo presses himself against me. Although it is close to freezing, I don't want his hands groping me over, but I'm not any less alert for it. Neither is he, much. He stinks, but it is from fear, not lust.

I hear the crunch of stone on stone. Something heavy is moving very carefully toward us, maybe. Guapo hearing it, scrabbles around, finds a loose stone, and throws it. The loose scree begins cascading down and down, the slide growing as it goes. The echoes go on and on, and a convoy, complete with shouting horsemen and lowing oxen, could pass us without our knowing.

Hissing something, Guapo eels off down the crack, knife in teeth. There were a few cold, lonely minutes before the bowman comes back, crawling backwards, and bumps into me with a start. "Nothing," he gasps.

He gets his icy hands inside my clothes and I his and we wait out the frosty hours until the dawn listening to sounds of rock shifting and breaking, frightened by the growls of our empty bellies. At false dawn Guapo rises and starts down slope, a complete change of direction.

White spots in my vision and light-headed, I know why. Food we can go without for a while longer, if we must, but water is a necessity if the two of us are to keep moving with any real purpose.

We go from patch to patch of dusty greenery, but all the plants are rooted in cracks in the rock, their water sources unreachable. Noon comes, and we squat in the shadow at the foot of a cliff, watching the band of darkness slowly grow wider, neither of us saying we should get up and go on.

Finally, numb with hunger and thirst, I prowl the base of the cliff. Although it is in shadow, the rock is near hot enough to bake corn cakes. Wishing I had had its heat the night before, or could have it in the night to come, I walk along, one hand trailing, then stop and press my cheek against the stone, thinking my fingertips are deceived.

It is damp.

I look up, head back, eyes searching the shadow of the cliff-fold. Somewhere above me a few drops of water are leaking through the face. There is extra vegetation at the foot of the rock, a few sparse stiff-stemmed plants nibbled by the wind. Stepping back to look further up, I am instantly blinded by the glare.

"Luz?" Guapo can see me from where he sits.

Tongue thick in my mouth, I point up.

He gets to his feet as I move back into the shade. Guapo touches the cliff.

I scuttle out of the way of the shower of rock chips that he knocks down as he scrambles up.

High above me, Guapo grunts. Then he drops to the ground and touches wet fingers to my lips.

I taste grit and sweat.

"A seep," he says hoarsely. "We could soak a cloth in it, maybe."

I kneel and fumble in my pack.

The pottery cup I once drank buttermilk from is chipped, but Guapo tucks it into the folds of his belt and climbs again. After a while the bowman leans out and says, "Come."

Hitching my skirt around my waist, I get a purchase on the stone, work my feet into the cracks. Guapo pulls me up the last bit. I lean against the rock, panting, false snow making it hard to see. My cup lies, spilling over, in a crack in the stone.

The bowman offers it to me as if he were giving me first taste.

He isn't. Despite the shade, I can see moisture on his lips, but I nod appreciation and sip the spoonful of water.

Turn and turn about, we sit in our perch and drink. The wind-worked rock is crimson and ocher; the sky so pale it looks silvery. Corn colors, I think: yellow, red, white. No birds soar in the warm updrafts, no green softens, no clouds obscure that pitiless glare.

It takes a long time to fill the piece of pottery, and we are too thirsty to turn away from water, even if it is gritty with fine sand and tastes of iron. The shadows turn purple, the night comes and we stay, trying to fill a water skin by touch.

Night-flying insects come, pale flutterings in the moonlight. Guapo grabs, de-wings, and eats one, then is noisily sick. A little later he tries another kind, and is even sicker. He almost tries a third. He is that hungry.

Fool, I think. Insects need to be ground fine in a mortar or they irritate the stomach, and vomiting wastes energy and water I understand why he tries, though. We have had enough water to feel hungry again. I press my legs against my belly to soothe the aching inside.

The melon-yellow moon sets slowly, and then the smoky one, and the bowman falls into a doze. Alone in the starlight, I watch, while sand hisses and scratched stones whisper. So far away Guapo doesn't stir, there is a scream as a predator takes its prey.

The sound pierces my ears, opens my eyes. The door to the spirit world swings wide. I fling myself through it and into the light without hesitation. It is my fourth birthday, and I am to plant three grains of corn—red, yellow, white—and one chosen with my eyes closed and tucked into the earth by feel, for the lost blue corn. My tongue trips and falters in the growing-chant. I stay past dawn, hoping that the spirits will answer me anyway, but my mother brings home nothing but me and my tears.

Sitting on the door stone of our house, I sigh, smelling the desert, dreaming I am at home, but awake enough to know I dream.

Now.

With vast hands, the powers of the place where I truly am seize me. I hold my breath, hoping to hear the squeak of the mouse, the rustle of flame, some sign of whose I was. To find your totem alone, without help, even so late in my life, was a token of great favor. I feel it coming, closer, close, then nothing.

Nothing. Nothing. O, nothing!

I press my hand against my breast, shuddering, as I crouch, back in the mundane world, hearing the drip and trickle of water, and the faint snore of Guapo, slumped in sleep. I drink what is in the shard, then put it away, careful not to further offend the powers of the place. There are plants that depend on this moisture. They belong here and I do not.

I press my shaking hand to my chest, feel the lump of the leather sack under my shirt against my palm, and know what I have done wrong. At the crucial moment, I touched the alien totem at my throat, as if asking its aid. It is coyote and I am not.

Please, I think. I know it's not mine. Whoever you are, I need you now and forever. Something stirs in me. I hold my breath, lift the pouch-strap over my head, slowly, slowly. I plead without speaking, Tell me who you are, who I am.

Then the jaguar comes.

A town-bred woman might say it is drawn by the double scent of the water and our flesh. I know better. Long before my ears know, I hear it, silent as shadows fleeing moon-light, padding along the path of water-smoothed stone that would be a stream once or twice in as many years. It comes up the slope of rock and turns toward me.

Seeing the lean form below us, I hear Guapo stir and take a deep breath, and think, No. He must not interrupt. I have to know the message. I am not important enough to be the jaguar's, so this was not a totem vision, but a warning. Beneath us the jaguar's hard-muscled haunches bunch and gather. Its tail twitches as it judges the distance to us. I can see its eyes shine in the starlight. It means to leap—at Guapo.

No, I breathe. This is my fault. A wise woman would have seen to it that I was stripped and clean, ready for the totem vision. If I had thought, I would have known that was necessary myself. The powers are always dangerous, as fire always burns. I have offended the greatest power of all.

Far away, a coyote yaps.

The cat turns away, leaving only its feral scent. Guapo sleeps on. The bowman's totem has saved him. That it also saved me was no more than happenstance, but I will not be ungrateful. I resettle the leather straps, totem and pendant, around my neck.

I am, it seems, to have no name, to have no clan forever. A single claw mark scribbles across the sky and blooms in gold. I shut my eyes and sleep.

The next morning Guapo walks along, silent, head down, eyes on the ground, the knotted leather of a bird snare slapping at his empty belly. There are no animal signs, not even jaguar tracks or scat. We and the drifting dust may be the only moving things on the entire face of a dead earth.

There were many living things in the desert I remember, not the least of them my parents. Mother, whose hands could wring water and food from the harsh soil. Father, who saw to it we had a roof over us and seldom lacked meat for the pot. It was a hard life, but as a child I did not know that.

I also did not understand why we had so little and the kinfolk that occasionally passed by had so much. My parents, a love match, had fled the wrath of my mother's kin, angry that my father had not paid the full bride price before my conception. If my mother had borne a boy, she could have named him for one of her uncles or her grandfather, and that man would have paid the debt in return.

However, since I am a girl, there was nothing for the couple to do but flee into the desert and hope my mother's womb would soon quicken with a male child. Years passed and it didn't happen. Perhaps their diet was too spare or their souls too bitter toward their kin.

In any case, isolated, we were easy prey for the slavers. I was not old enough to understand the horror when my mother and I were captured. I never knew what became of my father, if he fled the slavers, or died at their hands, or if he came home from hunting to find us gone and then went on with his life.

Two days after we began the walk, my mother died. She had not spoken a word since she was yoked and joined to the chain that swung between all the adults. Mother was a strong woman but something within her broke. I, secured to a light wooden yoke that rubbed my shoulders, had been left to run beside my dam, like a foal beside a mare.

When Mother slumped and fell, pulling those on either side of her to their knees, a guard unfastened the chain and dumped her still-living body by the side of the road. Near blind with tears, I watched them go, looked at my mother's dark staring eyes, pulled her sun pendant, its copper darkened from her sweat, from her, and then I followed the coffle.

All my mother could see was death and child that I was, I knew there was nothing else to do but go with my captors, even though the road they followed lead to the coast. I knew the hard tribal law that I must carry my lineage forward if I could.

If I had seen my future, perhaps, I would have curled up beside my mother and waited for death and the coyotes. But as it was then, here there is nothing to do but follow Guapo. I am stubborn by any standard.

Bit by bit the land we cross shows signs of life. In the shadowed folds of the ground, there is green stuff, even the occasional flicker of motion.

Food.

I look for fist-sized rocks, hoping for a horned toad, perhaps, or a snake.

Now, arrow nocked to string, Guapo's bow never leaves his hand and his eyes search the ground and the sky above us, alert for any prey.

Silent, unwilling to break his concentration, I think him over-nice. Most reptiles are edible. Finally, I gather some round stones but still I don't throw, afraid I might scare off the hare Guapo hopes for. My mouth fills with liquid, thinking of it mud-baked under a fire, steamed in its own juices. I'll pick every shred from every bone, crack them open, suck out the marrowfat. My mouth waters at the thought. The seep saved me. I have plenty of life in me yet.

Sniffing the wind, I smell damp earth. There may be permanent water nearby. Scanty and curled though the leaves of the plants are, it had rained here not long ago, for there is pollen streaming from the dry grass heads.

I look among the scrub and grasses for the blue sky reflected in some puddle caught in a hollow. It is better not to drink from the evanescent pools. They will already swarm with spadefoot tadpoles, almost invisible monkey shrimp, and waterbears, rushing to complete their lifecycle before the next dry year or three.

Besides, many of the pools will be salty, and we cannot tolerate much salt. There may even be arsenic and I see no nopal cactus to clear and settle the water. But game will come to the water and flesh is water-rich.

If I have to, I will drink what there is.

Guapo fires, and misses. We search for the arrow. I find it, its blunt wooden tip shattered by a rock. The bowman looks at it and puts it away. He'll have to carve and mount a new point, but the fletching can be saved.

It is time for my methods. Stone still, we sit on a patch of short fine grass. Out of the corner of my eye I begin to see the flick, flick of the ears of feeding hares moving in our direction. They crouch in the succulent grass as they scent us.

Guapo gets one with his first shot, to the head. I carry the gutted kill while he goes ahead to look for a second. We'll need two for a decent meal, there is little enough flesh on the first, and the smell of blood will warn our prey.

I could gnaw it raw, just for the moisture of its flesh, if it was not for shame. I am strong; I can wait. Nonetheless, my trance of hunger broken, I see there are other things to eat here, some so common that I know them from the marketplace, like the thick pads of horse cactus that only need their spines charred away and the thumb-sized, fleshy fruit of the jutillo.

Gathering, I wonder how much food I passed before I saw it for what it was. It is abundant. I hear the thrum of the bowstring and hurry to Guapo, my awkward, prickly burden bouncing in the swag of my skirt.

He guts the second hare without bothering to salvage any of the innards and dumps the guts of the first.

We can afford to carry only the choicest meat, abandoning the offal, with their dubious contents, to whatever scavengers there might be.

Walking on, mouth full of jutillo fruit, I am lighthearted. It is rich country, compared to what we had come through. There are flocks of birds running in the striped shadows of grass as high as our boot tops.

Guapo stoops to examine the dry, gray dung where some herd of carus or deer passed a day or two before. Like the hares, they are after the wild grain, cropping it close to the soil. There is no need to spend time tracking such big game. The meat would only go to waste and offend the spirits. Everywhere around us hares' ears show above the grass as they pop up, curious, to look at us.

By the time the sun is westering, Guapo has shot a third, and the rustle and flutter of life is still all around, oblivious of our presence. Men do not come here. I am a free woman and I will live.

Joy, ah, joy!

We find a camping place near a thicket, build a substantial fire in a stone-lined hollow, wrap the hares in leaves, coat that with mud—mud!—and set our hares to bake.

I scorch, peel, and dice my wild harvest in the waning daylight, enjoying the homely chores, the familiar pull of muscles in my legs and back as I squat at my work as I had when I was a child.

Guapo tries to re-head his arrow without success. His knife is too dull. Putting the damaged one back in his case he counts nineteen, most of them headed with the long iron spikes that can punch a hole through a man: war arrows.

Leon Ildefonso's bowmen did not do much hunting. Not of animals. The Alcalde's men patrol the borders and the croplands, and whomever they kill is left for scavengers. I look at those arrows, good only for man killing, and at the bowman, and think it is time for us to get who we are straight. "You ran away from the Old One," I say calmly. I want the truth out of him for once.

Stroking a whetstone down his knife's edge, Guapo shrugs.

I peel a jutillo fruit in a long, spiraling ribbon, and feed the scrap to the flames.

When he'd joined the Alcalde's bowmen Guapo would have sworn to follow him into death. Most recruits assume this means death in battle, something one would expect of a warrior, and this one found the funeral obligation an unpleasant surprise. Few were in a position to rectify their error. He had.

I look at Guapo, and shrug, too. The Old One lived his life as he pleased, what right had he to take another's for his comfort? My obligation to my lady is greater than that and I am here. "I didn't say I blamed you."

"No," Guapo says. The corners of his mouth jerk with annoyance.

It could be that where he came from women are supposed to be silent, submissive. Where I come from, they are not. It could be he feels guilty, I think. I do. Someone else may have died in my place. Someone I know, most likely. It is not a pleasant thought.

Anyway, I have questions to ask and need to establish my right to ask them. "Why are you going to the cold fires?"

Surprise and puzzlement twist his forehead, then he says, "It came to me in a dream. I hadn't dreamed for a long time." He frowns down at his hands, unwilling to meet my eyes after the admission.

People whose lives are in balance dream, so I know he meant the messages that come from the spirits, not the casual fantasies that come to everyone between waking and sleeping. Sitting at polite attention, I wait to hear what he will say, and regret it almost immediately.

He spins a tale, bits and pieces of every dream telling he had ever heard. Because their wishes must be honored, saying the spirits spoke to you is one way to have your way. It is a cheat to say you dreamed when you did not. When the liar stops with the traditional, "So I dreamed," I do not answer, "So you dreamed."

Instead, I rise and walk away. When I am well away from our fire, my temper cooling, I turn around.

There is nothing in his face.

I hope there was nothing in mine.

The spirits will deal with him. There is no need for me to do anything. It is his right not to tell me but I would prefer he simply say he could not rather than lie to me.

There is something dark and sour at the heart of this man and I wish I had better choices to make. I can, if I have to, make my way here in these soft lands.

Squatting in the dark, I strip a tuft of dry grass, crunch hard kernels filled with raw starch, chew slowly to get the good of it. You must listen to your dreams; you must honor the spirits. Those with skills may use other means, but neither of us is shaman or brujo. Guapo is playing a dangerous game and I want no part of it.

I go back to the fire and sit in silence.

Presently, the bowman sucks in a breath, holds it, and looks around. "That cat's back," he says to the ground, avoiding naming the thing correctly, which would give a spirit animal more power. I didn't think he was awake.

"Where," I say, without looking.

He jerks his chin, politely.

"Welcome to all gathered here," I say, as my father had said at every meal, welcoming unseen presences. Something rustles and is gone. I shrug. I know it cannot be my totem animal.

I shudder and gasp as the spirits seize me, shake me, fill me with conviction like a woman fills a water skin. My wishes have been answered many times and I have failed to understand. "I have dreamed," I say, and the bowman's back straightens to attention, "the jaguar spirit."

The words are no sooner out of my mouth than his hand extends, asking for the bag at my neck.

I bow my head, lift the sack off, and give it back to him. "Thank you," I say to the sack. If it has done me no good, it has not harmed me, either. Living as I had as a child, apart from people, and then growing up in the safe walls of the town, I can only guess that jaguar and coyote are not friends. The clever wild dog may pick up scraps from the great cat's kills, but they can never be harmonious, like crow and hare.

"Perhaps it's guarding you," he says, bowing his own head to his totem and hiding it in his shirt with the other bag that bulges beneath his shirt, the one that he touches at moments of stress. "Following us like this."

"I don't know," I say. I do not want the jaguar for my totem, it is powerful and dangerous, but there is the dream I do not dare deny, when I was in a jaguar body, mind clouded by instinct. No matter whether I like it or not, I am one of the sky lord's.

Staring into the coals, I frown, then look up to see what is on the bowman's face.

Nothing.

For Guapo the moment has passed. He is poking at the fire pit, intent on the baking hares.

Whatever has been there, now I can only smell well-cooked flesh. "That's done," I say.

Guapo glances at me, nods, and uncovers the meat.

Each with a carcass of our own, we eat, throwing the sucked bones into the fire, where they sputter and flame in a funeral for our prey.

The third carcass, which we meant to split between us, we save for the morning, unwise though it is to keep meat through the hunter-filled night. Our stomachs have shrunk too much to hold more and we cannot bring ourselves to burn it.

Almost too full, I settle back to watch the flames. For all the heat of the day, now it is cool enough to make the fire's warmth welcome.

Guapo yawns widely and stretches out on the grass, wriggles his shoulders to get comfortable, and yawns again.

"One of us has to keep watch," I say firmly. Even if the jaguar is my guardian that does not leave me free to be foolish.

"Luz," he says, annoyed, then grimaces and breaks two twigs. Recent history is on my side. Juggling them in his hand he offers the ends to me. "Short stick, first watch."

When I draw the long one, the bowman makes a sour face and obviously repents his fairness.

I am not pleased either. Guapo looks sleepy. Still, we have to start depending on one another, and here, with a good fire, and plenty of game for the predators, is as good a place as there is likely to be, cooked hare or no.

I draw my head cloth over my face, settle myself to feign sleep. I sleep, deep and well, until my companion rouses me with a hand on the ankle and lies down himself.

It is moonless, clear and dark, with the river of stars flowing from horizon to horizon. I sit and watch the wandering lights drift across the sky, bobbing and twisting in the invisible current. Two or three parallel scratches flare and fade, leaving afterimages everywhere

I look for several heartbeats.

They may have been natural, born of the sky stones. They may have been jaguar marks. I wonder what the birds know that I don't. The shape of the land, certainly, but do they fly high enough to see the wandering lights that were not moons or stars but seem to move with purpose? Some bird or insect so high it catches the light and never needs to land?

Our legends say the jaguar marks were not always there, but legends are only history that has turned to poetry, and not necessarily true. Still. I wonder.

I feed the coals slivers and scraps of wood, reluctant to rouse any flame to spoil my night vision. Something small and quick passes by, pausing to stare at me with reflective eyes. A capped fox, perhaps, by the sharp-pricked ears that twitched as it watches me, watching it, watching me. It leaps and is gone, silent as a fuego fantasma.

When the stars begin fading, the wind comes up to walk through the grass, whish, whish, like a reaper, harvesting time. Back to the moving air, I begin to feed the fire more generously against the pre-dawn cold. Above me the moving lights in the sky flock together and are gone.

I don't see it come. It is just there, sitting across the fire from me: the jaguar, lean and ribbed with muscle. I see myself through its eyes, thin and dirty, one hand on a stick not quite in the fire, the other, lax and loose in my lap, frozen by—not quite fear but more than respect.

We sit and look until, like the fox, the jaguar gathers itself together, and springs off with a bound. It, too, is noiseless in the sounds of the wind brushing leaves and stems. The sky begins to pale before I rise and walk back and forth, around and around, until my feet have obliterated the paw marks.

I do not want to talk about what just happened with Guapo. I must think. I have a totem animal, but no wise woman to give me my true name. I must guard my thoughts and wait.

We fall into a routine. Guapo takes the first watch, I the second. We hunt early in the day and late in the afternoon and walk endlessly north at all times when we aren't sleeping or resting. The moons appear and wax and wane and still we walk.

Every morning at first light the jaguar comes to look and be looked at for a few cold moments before fading into the grass for another day.

After one dawn encounter Guapo turns over slowly and asks in a sleep-fogged voice. "How much longer?"

I stop moving and the dew-wet rag I was washing my face with dribbles down my arm. I shiver as one cold drop breaks from the point of my elbow.

"Until what?" I say, briskly wiping the back of my neck.

"Until you'll wear its totem."

"It hasn't left anything."

He sighs and rolls onto his back, looking up at the sky. "Luz."

I know I am being difficult. His own bag probably holds a tuft of hair or a fragment of gnawed bone. Still, my own spirit animal, if that was what it was, left only paw prints. I squat and take a pinch of earth from the middle of a broad pugmark.

Guapo offers a scrap of leather from my skirt.

I place the dirt in the center, twist it, and whip the top around with red hair cord. Ducking my head into the loop, I drop the bag down the front of my shirt. There is nothing more to do. I am the jaguar's.

Whether it is coincidence, or just that we are so far out on the grassy plain that there was no longer game it can hunt, the great cat does not come again. I still have no name, unless Nameless is a name. I should not summon my spirit animal unless I am protected by a proper name. It is hard to wait, be patient.

The days pass, and except for the aching of our legs and feet each evening, we might not have moved at all. Guapo and I walk through unending monotony: grass, sky, and wind.

Robbed of the more familiar objects of a landscape, the eye becomes accustomed to watching the gigantic towers of the clouds, or the tiny serrated barbs at the tips of the grasses. They brush against you, covering you with tiny cuts from their endless touch. Bugs swarm to feast so the sores never close.

Dream-walking, we call it, and in the company of this man I cannot trust, I am in danger. I need the knowledge hidden in my memories. It is hard.

I recover that childhood morning when the slavers came down into our sheltered valley, watered their mules and horses, took the feed we had for our two skinny cows, and then killed my father. His blood turned earth to mud, his eyes stared, as if watching for crows to come.

All these years, I've told myself that he didn't come back. My mother wailed, roasting the antelope my father had brought for our family. The dogs snarled and tugged at his body, until at last their masters, eating, flung bones and gristle to them.

There. Then. Here. Now.

I regain my sense of time and place with tears streaming down my face. I scrub them away with my fists.

Guapo is a few paces apart from me, eyes moving everywhere, probably thinking of nothing more complex than the weather or the birds that fly up out of the grass.

I am glad he has not seen. He is not a man to sympathize.

My mother I mourned properly. I wear her token, the one I took from her when she was dead only in spirit and not yet in body, that sun of darkened copper that I touch whenever I need to be brave or to think through some problem.

Now, with nothing to remember him by, I mourn my father. I cry when it comforts me, silent tears that streak my cheeks and ease my heart. I miss being a child, and protected.

We go hungry, and sometimes thirsty. Hunting is trickier here. We walk on the endlessly springy mat of years of dead blades packed down over the roots. An arrow that misses will most likely be lost for good; there is no wood to make more.

I know how to make a sling, but there are no stones. A net might have done if we had the time and skill to twist one. Guapo still has his leather snares but there is no place to set them in the endless sameness, and in any case, for all the illusion we never move, we do not retrace our steps.

Chewing grass as we walk, we bite the sweet pith of the stems, and feel our guts rumble with roughage. At a patch of low-growing plants that shelters seedy orange berries, we crouch and pluck them by the handful, scaring birds up out of the leaves.

I search, but can find no eggs or nestlings. The birds, too, may have come a long way for the fruit.

We both lust for their fat, their flesh. Incautiously, Guapo risks an arrow that I find only by touch, half-slid beneath the matted leaves. He takes it from me and returns it to his quiver without a word, defeated.

I am the one who swats a feeding hen with the edge of my head cloth and strangle it like any chicken. I take two, then stop. I do not want to eat them raw. Limp bodies swinging in my hand, I wonder if I should have killed them, for the spirits avenge useless deaths.

Guapo nursed the spark of his nightglow well out onto the plains, but it failed when no slow-burning fuel could be found. Now, all the bowman has is the rough pebble of glass from his fire starter. Lighting a wisp of hay, he watches it burn in the palm of his hand, and blows the ash away.

He looks at me, but says nothing, not pleased that my spirit guide seems to be the jaguar. It is suitable for a man; his own guardian is weak by comparison.

Seeing the initiative must be mine, I prepare the birds and hack a pit in the soil with the haft of my knife. We cover the plucked and gutted carcasses with knots of dry grass, twisting it as hard as we can to give the fuel some substance, then Guapo focuses the brilliant sunlight on a strand.

The fire flares up, near invisible in the sunshine. We crouch upwind, feeding the flames and knotting more fuel. The first smell of hot fat makes me swallow until I am near sick from my own saliva.

At the earliest moment they can possibly be considered roasted, I pull the carcasses out, throw handfuls of dirt on the pitiful fire. We tear the birds apart, chew cartilage, and gnaw bones. Then we graze like beasts, filling our mouths with the sweetness of the orange berries.

When we are sated, our faces war-painted with grease and dirt, Guapo looks at me and looks away. I wipe my hands together. Without a word we set off again. I am eager to leave the scene. It is different eating something that you have killed with your own fingers.

We have gone a good distance when a pale shadow slides across the turf in front of me. I turn. There is a thin column of smoke rising out of the grass. Even as I look it grows thicker, and I can see flames flickering at its base. My mouth goes dry.

Guapo turns to see what I am looking at, and curses. He starts back, then stops. There is nothing to put out a fire with. We have been saving a few good swallows of water in the last skin for some emergency, living by licking the dewy grass at dawn as the wildlife does.

It takes minutes of picking with a knife to free the earth from the tangle of roots. I dug deep, but not, it is clear, deep enough, and the earth is rich with humus. The flames flicker, grow brighter.

The bowman wets his thumb and checks the wind. From the north, pushing the flames away from us. "Let's run," he says. We start off, slowly, for we are logy with food and may have a long way to go. I don't waste effort by looking back, but Guapo does.

The breeze grows stronger as the fire draws the air to it, and the daylight becomes a ghostly gloom, the sun's face obscured by rising smoke. We are safe as long as the wind holds. Nonetheless, we jog until we have to stop, bent forward, gasping.

I am surprised to notice that I have more endurance than Guapo. I can outrun him. The rustle and flutter of fleeing life is all around us. The still-sweet air rasps in my lungs. Behind us dark smoke veils the sun and a deep threatening roar is growing louder.

When we look back to see a sheet of fire licking the sky, we turn and run again. My luck is bad, has been bad for a long time, only now I know it. I touch the token at my breast and run on, as if tireless.

Whatever good we got of the meat is long used up when we cross the last stretch of short grass and stand at the edge of a head-high tangle again, watching the sullen glow of the fire burning its way south.

Neither of us needs to remind the other that the wind still may shift. Nonetheless, we batter out beds amid the tall stems and the exhausted bowman settles to sleep and I to watch.

Toward morning there is a little rain and there is no light to be seen against the clouds. I wake Guapo and settle into a dream-filled and restless doze at false dawn.

When full morning comes we push our way into the tangle of grass. There will be no more fires. Days pass when we hardly speak a word. The slightest change in the landscape, an insect flying up, leaves scissoring in a rift of wind, a trail where something had passed, is like lightning from a clear sky.

Finally we come to a ridge and can see that beyond this point the endless grass is no more than knee-high. There are tossing tawny waves for leagues. A white-topped darkness on the farthest horizon draws our eyes.

At first I do not know what it is. Like a storm rising over of the sea of grass, the mountains top even the clouds. Lean and hungry, we have come to the wall of the world I know anything about. Knees weak, I stare at the things I know only from stories, the vast bones of the earth.

We walk until our legs fail beneath us. I sit down, fall back, look up at the river of stars. I have, in all my process of self-discovery, virtually forgotten why I am walking.

Morning comes and we don't bother to forage. There will be game and water, firewood and a place to build a fire at the roots of the mountains. We walk until noon and after, and although the range is higher against the sky, still the grass flows away to its unseen feet. By mid-afternoon it is apparent even to people as hopeful as we are that it will be another day, perhaps several, before we actually come to even the foothills of the range.

Guapo and I do what we can to fill our bellies with raw
seeds and shoots, then lie down on the turf. We are ill tem-
pered from fatigue and disappointment.

In the middle of the night, Guapo strips and comes to
me. Slipping my skirt and shirt off, I place my hands in the
deep hollows of his hips as he thrusts and plunges. I am too
thin to conceive, and doubt he will leave me if I do. The
jaguar gave me power. Guapo will want me for that.

We spend the rest of the night wrapped around one another, clothes piled above us both. Dressing is a hasty,
chilly business in the blue dawn, and I fumble in my haste.

Never handsome, hunger has erased most of the evidence of my sex. I think that from the rear I could pass for
an emaciated boy. Certainly from the front, only the promi-
nent nipples and unadorned patch of hair at the groin give
evidence I am a woman.

Guapo draws his leggings up over the long, lean muscles
of his legs. A dandy once again, he sits to comb and rebraid
his hair.

I do the same. Hands busy with my braids, I wonder if
any of the bowman's stories are true, if there are cold fires
in the foothills, and animals touched by something unnatural.

Why am I doing this?

Part of my mind that had been slumbering as I walked is
awake again. Guapo's quest is not mine. I should leave this
man, for plainly he is obsessed, but the trip back, alone,
seems impossible.

As things are, it is two more days before an occasional
outcropping of rock breaks the smooth flow of the grass.
When we pass the first stunted, wind-twisted bush, the
bowman scavenges dead twigs, and spends an anxious half-
hour re-igniting his fire glow.

I watch the two metal-bound shells go into his pouch
with hungry hope. Without speaking, we agree that we will

keep walking until full dark. If we are lucky, that will bring us to someplace where there is water, wood, and perhaps some game. My concave belly growls at the thought, even as I hunch my shoulders at remembered cold.

Guapo glances at me and pulls his bow from its case. He knows the things I am thinking. We seldom talk these days. There is little to remark that cannot be indicated with a gesture and the vast whisper of plains dwarfs mere human voices.

More important, I am now very afraid of his fixation on the white fires and do not want him to guess that. I want to make things right with the spirits. There lies my safety and my hope of happiness. I intend to leave him when I reach some place I can care for myself, regain my strength before deciding what to do. I would not be welcome in my clan but where else can I go? South? To the cities?

As I mull my choices, the bowman walks alert as a house cat stalking. When some fat, ground-burrowing thing with a dappled hide and black ear-tufts climbs to a rocky lookout and is so entranced by our unaccustomed presence that it makes no effort to run away, he gets it with one snapped-off shot. We eat its liver raw, sliced thin, but takes its meat with us.

Later that day we come over a slow swell of the land and see our first water, a stream, so narrow you can bridge it with two hands, chuckling in its deep-cut bed in the low, tufted grass. I do not run to it. I walk, as if I knew all along that it was there waiting for me. I crouch down, and drink and drink, for the feel of water on my lips, in my mouth, in my throat.

Drawing back from the bank, I am unable to do more than lie in the grass, smelling damp earth, crushed leaves beneath me, and my own unwashed body. There is grit packed beneath my nails and my toes are dark, knobby roots.

I don't have to guess with what horror sleek Elena would greet me if I were suddenly to appear at her kitchen door. I am too skinny and dirty to even be a fitting object of charity. The scene clear in my mind's eye, I laugh.

Guapo, wiping water from his still-filthy face, laughs with me, for whatever reasons of his own. We both sit, staring at the rising hills, until the delightful pain of overfull bladders overrides the ache in our legs and we stand and turn away to relieve ourselves, suddenly modest as we had not been in the grass.

Suddenly immodest in fit of desire, I run my fingers over every blue-hollowed rib and knob of his spine as he leans into me. Settled on the grass, I buck and dance beneath him. The overwhelming urge past, we roll apart and reorder ourselves, aware of the emptiness of our bellies that we have denied while we walked north.

The one carcass looks very small and its liver has left a vile taste on my teeth. I want cooked flesh, eaten with clean hands. I gather twigs, most not as thick as my little finger, but still huge and substantial compared to the forest of stems we have pushed through. The bowman makes a fire pit of rock, coaxes a fluttering flame from the coals of his nightglow, and sits back on his heels.

I feed the fire, muscles falling into the long-accustomed motions of the hours spent maintaining a steady blaze for the cook when I hoped to build a safe place for myself in some kitchen.

When the meat is done, we eat flesh, marrow, and cartilage. I cut the hide in strips and turn the inner surfaces to the fire. Then Guapo and I scrape the crisped fat with our teeth. There is little left for scavengers when we finish.

However, as we lean against one another, glutted, I see the tawny flicker of a coyote tail. The bowman throws a ragged handful of scraps and a sharp-toothed head rises out of the grass and seizes it with a snap. "Feed well, brother," says Guapo, then pulls me against him with renewed purpose.

I worry. Not today or tomorrow, but soon this better living will make me capable of bearing. I am very certain I do not want the burden of a child, especially not this man's child. I will have to find new and more inventive ways to please him. It is only because I am in no condition to make the long journey back that I do not leave him now.

The two of us make no haste into the mountains, walking from stream to stream, stopping to eat, not only in the morning and at evening, but often killing and cooking at mid-day too. Even as we walk, we pluck berries and leaves and stuff them into our mouths

Day by day, the land grows rougher and more hospitable, rich with game and greenery, cut by small streams, and pocked with hollows suitable for hiding from the searching winds. The nights are cold, and Guapo and I are driven to sleep close together.

Unable to see around us while we were in the grass, we have fallen out of the habit of keeping watch. I awake one night to something was walking around our camp. I know the scent.

Guapo, coming awake, does too. Slowly, cautiously, he pushes a branch into the glowing bed of coals. The dry leaves catch, and light washes over the huddle of boulders at the far side of the fire. One opens and blinks sleepy eyes.

A jaguar. My jaguar. It is the same. I know markings of the face. She is a gaunt rack of ribs, leaner than even Guapo and I had been. I touch my fingers to my totem bag, part my lips. The fire flares higher and the jaguar flows into the black velvet darkness and is gone.

It snows toward dawn.

Guapo, whose whole will has been directed toward moving north, sits on a boulder by our fire, large and well-built-up but not really warm, and says, "We'll have to find a winter shelter."

The knot in my throat loosens. He has some common-sense, still. I have been fearing the cold climb into the mountains, into the teeth of winter.

If I ever go back to Misericordia del Mar, no one will doubt I have been stolen, my body is so rough with criss-crossed scars. I would go cheap in the marketplace there, for I look as if I had been whipped, often.

Lifting an icy-cold water bag, I drink, remembering licking the dewy grass and tasting blood from cuts on my tongue, and considering my words. Finally, I ask, "What kind of shelter?"

"A cave, if we can find one. We don't have the tools to cut wood."

"We'll need it anyway." Even in Misericordia, close to the tempering sea, you need wood for the winter. Here we will need more, although we will not have the broad roaring hearths and fragrant ovens that take so much of every winter's cutting. We will be hard pressed to gather enough to keep us alive, here. Solid shelter will make all the difference.

Water carves stone, and we do not want to go far for water in the heavy snows of winter, so we look along a fast flowing stream that waterfalls plunge into in clouds of mist. On the third day, the bowman finds a cavern, with a low entrance that opens out into a high room with hard, smooth floor. Guapo rejects it, "Too big."

Thinking of the fire needed to heat such an enormous space, I nod reluctantly. Ideally, we need a shelter that will stay above freezing with the heat of our own bodies. There will be days in winter when there will be nothing to do but wait for a storm to pass. "Let's look around anyway," I say.

I have never been in so large an enclosed space. Seeing the folds and drapes of stone, I can believe that if I propitiate the earth spirit it may give me protection. For an instant, I see the light I had seen in my child's vision, as it had never been before, like a door opening with a brilliant light beyond.

Stunned, I stand, blinking, blinded by a light that is not there. It is dark so far from the entrance to the cave. Un-tranced, I can see frozen water glittering on the wall as a sign. We must be near, but this is not the place the spirits had in mind. The vast bones of the earth will shelter me. It is up to me to find the place.

Ignoring the dim light from the distant entrance, I close my eyes and listen. The surrounding earth seems to enfold me securely.

Stop. Think. Wait.

I go back into the large room at the entrance, to find Guapo, who, seeing me come out of the darkness, shrugs and says: "We'll make this do for the night, anyway. There's snow coming."

I glance at him but he does not meet my eyes. Perhaps he feels the strength of the earth, although he does not un-derstand the spirit world. Guapo did not grow up among the clans. I am sure of that now. Perhaps one of his parents was from the town. He is a good bowman, but he does not feel the powers.

We make and light two torches. Guapo forges ahead, his light bobbing and weaving away. Lifting my own, I follow. It would be convenient to be close to the main entrance and that is where Guapo is searching.

Once his attention is not on me, I step back. That sliver of darkness on my left is not a shadow. I eel my way in, raise my torch, and stare, mouth open.

It is a temple, its walls white with stone that drips and flows as if it were water in slow motion. Invoked with crude, quick strokes, a woman stands, breasts full and proud, belly round and fertile, genitals ripe.

She is very old. The water-stone, thin as it is, has draped her more modestly than would please her and narrowed the entrance so only a determined person can enter. There is nothing feminine about her. Earth is female. A mere man would have to turn away as his manhood shriveled in awe.

I touch myself in reverence. "Mother," I barely breathe. I touch my forehead in respect, not knowing the proper words or gestures. Thank you for the food, I think. Shelter us if you will. I am grateful that she shows herself so plain to her ignorant, erring child.

It is a trick of my wavering torch that the carved woman seems, for an instant, to lean over me. The spirits use such unspectacular means to communicate with us when they can. I have been blessed. My heart, which I did not know was heavy, lifts.

This is the one spirit that will always protect me. I kneel and kiss the stone at her feet, then press my cheek against the slick rock, thinking of the broken woman dying by the side of the road. Surely my mother was safe with her spirits.

"Luz?" calls a distant voice.

I blow out the last flickers of my torch. "My light's out," I call back.

The crevice is invisible. I feel about with my hands and force my way back through in the dark. I leave a good deal of skin behind in the process. Guapo must not find me here, or find this place, although I think, empty, it can protect itself from any man.

"Stay there," calls Guapo in so confident a tone I wonder what he has found. There will be male symbols, too, beneath the earth. The Mother must be satisfied. Perhaps he has come on such a one. Perhaps we are twice lucky.

I will not ask nor will he tell. Men believe other things than women, and women keep their mysteries secret. In any case, Guapo, ignorant, is dangerous company. I am well away from the entrance to the Mother's Room when Guapo relights my torch and looks me over, appraising: it is a cold gaze.

Knowing I am going to be leaving him, I also know that if he does not leave me first, it will be because I am convenient. He will be unkind if it suits his interests.

On the way out our torches show what has been concealed from us before. There is a smaller cave opening off the main cavern, no more than the size of the smallest bedroom in Lady Mercedes' house, the one that had been mine.

"Here?" I ask, knowing the answer before the bowman speaks. It is a good place. We are not the first to discover it, for the floor is littered with grass, leaves, and bones. Fire-blackened stones form a rude fireplace.

Guapo pokes about enough to know nothing is fresh. He says judicially, "We're not likely to find better quickly." As if obeying him without an actual command, I take off my skirt, load it with debris, and dump that in a corner of the main cavern.

Then I scrape the earth fresh and clean, and dig a hearth-pit. Later will do to conceal the spoor of our presence more thoroughly. I wash in the icy stream, scrubbing myself with sand, and get warm hauling back cobbles for the hearth.

We need wood, but I am too tired to do more heavy work, so I am lining the pit with stones when Guapo returns. He has a yearling carcass and its fresh hide filled with clay. I mortar the stones temporarily, wrap the carcass in frost-withered grape leaves and bury it. I go and bring in extra vines for the cooking, leaving the easier pickings nearer the cave for emergency.

As I come and go in the failing light, I can hear Guapo tumbling the piled trash into some deep hole in the rocks. I go to see that he does the job well. It is late in the season, and snowing a little, so anyone who comes will be desperate.

I have my small knife. Guapo has a larger one and his bow. Tomorrow I should make a greenwood spear and harden the point in the fire. With my help, Guapo finishes the debris cleanup with scree topped by a few large stones, sealing the debris in so it will not attract animals.

Then, when I go back to tend our supper, he drags a branch about the main cave floor. Its smoothing will not confuse a careful eye, but it is the best we can do for the moment. Tomorrow there will be more to do.

Already the wind is rising outside, and the icy snow ticks and rattles in the oak leaves. We may have a deep fall before morning. We, warm and well fed, are optimistic and full of plans about what we will do when this first storm of the season blows itself out.

There will still be plants to be harvested, meat to be dried, and perhaps even fish. We are both happy to be indoors, out of the wind and the increasing cold. Warmth and food are luxuries to such as we are. Hard as the cave floor is, I sleep as I have not slept in months.

Next morning we find the wind has blown away most of the snow, and we can move freely, and without leaving obvious tracks. Neither of us comment on how very good the place we have found is. Though the bowman thinks the main trail is some distance to the east of us, this could be a crossing point to the trapper's hole.

We came up through the empty plains, rather than skirting the more hospitable edge as the traders do, but it is possible that we have found a less traveled, easy way into the range. It is the sort of thing men would keep secret.

Throughout the short daylight, Guapo cuts branches for bedding while I gather firewood. That night we burn fat-rich bones for their bright yellow light and dream of the comforts we may put by and make.

Dried fruit, surely, for, although I haven't seen many yet, there still are frost-shriveled grapes and they will be none the worse for a freeze. A better bed, when we have time to build a frame and lace it and a mattress sack. A hide curtain for the door will stop drafts and hide the light of our fire.

Guapo is careful to hunt far from home. At first it is that he wanted to save the nearer game for harsher days. Later it is that we know many of them. The old, stiff buck who comes to drink only in the half dark before full night, ears twitching and turning to every sound of the wind. The pair of big-eared pocket mice that we rob twice before we let them keep their hoarded seeds. The hunting owl that tells us nothing else is near.

The deep snows come as the days began to lengthen. The female animals grow thin along the backbone and full in the belly and I discover that, I, too, have quickened. I told myself my failure to bleed meant I was not in condition to bear, but one morning the bowman puts a hand on my rounded belly and smiles, and I know he knows. I cry when I am sure he is off hunting. I am sixteen and the second half of my life—if I am lucky—has been determined for me.

My pains come on me one day in the mountain spring, a few weeks early by my calculations, when it is cold but the days are already longer. Guapo leaves to go hunting and something makes me say nothing. Birth is woman's magic and I did not want his presence to spoil it. The earth will help me.

After the first pains abate, I go back to the opening of the shrine—I am far too big with child to enter—and invoke the mother's aid. I am caught by another wave of pain. Concentrating on my body's signals, I crouch, then lift my head as the contractions ease. I must go further back in the cave, beyond where Guapo explored. The blessings must be renewed if his male presence has spoiled them.

I wonder that I had not thought of this before, but then so much of winter he was by our hearth, only venturing out briefly. This is, by my count, going to be an early birth, unless I conceived when I was gaunt and weary, there on the plains. In any case, it will be hours before I bear.

Making my way back to the fire, I build it up to last, and put more wood ready to hand. I have water, even food, should I want it. Then the pain comes again. I crouch patiently, waiting, until I have another respite. I make torches, twice what I think I will need, and take my digging stick.

Guapo has not been gone very long, but I may need to be. I want the security of the earth's power with me, and it is mine to take merely for bearing pain. I laugh to myself. Men can lift and haul and push, but it is women who can go the longest and bear the most hardship. The earth made us so. I embrace what I am, a strong female, ready to bear her first child.

I light a torch and raise it high, exulting in my good fortune. However irregular my life until now, I will make one passage in the proper way, protected within the earth itself. I touch the proper places to invoke the mother and set out.

The man's footprints run out at a large slab of stone not three hundred paces beyond the first twist in passageway. He sat there a long time. I look at his sign, amused. How like Guapo not to venture too far but to save his pride by sitting long enough that it would seem he had gone further.

However, since I have been able to track him, he will be able to track me. I trust in the shrine to hide itself as it had before. What lay deeper in may be so powerful that it cannot be concealed. Once again the pains take me, and I crouch, letting my torch burn low. I know the way back, should the light go out.

There, huddled on myself in the flickering light, I see it. I should have known, I think. I am sure Guapo had not known it, but he stopped here for a reason. It is nothing but a crack in the rock floor that might have escaped notice except that the dim light of my failing torch its blackness shows clearly.

Pain easing, I light another torch, which flares brightly. It is as if there is nothing there. "Mother," I breath to the air. I strip off my makeshift shoes, then go through the curtain of air that rises from deeper in the ground. I am awkward with my great belly, yet the stone beneath my feet is smooth, as are the walls that enfold me. Many have passed here before me and none has left a trace.

A womb of stone opens before me and, putting my bundle down, I light a second torch. I know the place, although I have never seen it or anything like it. Maybe, long ago, my people came from here, for where I lived there were no caves and still we believed that the best births were those sheltered beneath soil, and built platforms of sticks and mud as roofs over birthing places.

Towering phalluses of stone rise from the floor, hang from the ceiling, wet and dripping. As with the figure in the shrine, they have been shaped with a minimum of cuts to make it plain what they are. Looking, I imagine that there was a chant for the task, a word for each stroke.

Pain comes again, although not so intense. I go forward, and find what I expected. The enormous double oval of the female sign, carved into the stone, frames a dark passage. Before it are many flat stones. This is the place to bury the afterbirth, the material evidence of the spirit-child always born with the human.

I do what is necessary now, while there is time. Unable to chip a hole in the rock, I find a hollow. I seek out one flat stone and then another, and set them ready. I will be tired when I come this way again. I set my torch upright, so it will burn slowly, and leave the others I have made next to it, ready to hand.

Then I go through the great vulva into enfolding darkness. Pain comes and goes, good strong pain that tells me all is well, the child within ready to come out.

My body knows what to do, although I am not as certain. My mother, my clanswomen, should have been around me to help. It does not matter. Here I am safe, safer than they could make me. Silently, I invoke the mothers who have been here before me, then the greatest of them all.

Too soon for me, liquid splashes down my legs and it begins in earnest. Leather birthing strap looped over a knob of rock found by touch, I squat, teeth bared in pain, intent. Time goes slow. I work and rest and work again, all without a sound, until the baby emerges. My questing fingers tell me it is a fortunate birth: a male. Guapo may want a son as he would not want a daughter.

I chose a secret name that honors the earth.

Lying my son on my warm bare chest, I wait for the second birth, the spirit child I must hide. The boy is small but strong, restless and active in my hands. I lift him to my breast and sink back exhausted to feel the contractions as my womb tightens and the bleeding stops.

The second birth is easier than the first, as it should be. I lift the cord and felt the life ebb from it until the spirit child has gone free. Then I cut and tie it, bundle my baby, and the shapeless mass, and go, slowly now, for I am sore, into the outer room in the deeps of the earth.

My torch has only a faint red glow, but I hold a fresh one close, and breath upon it. A flame leaps to life. I do what is necessary. With a spent torch, I close the way in with the double oval bisected by a line, the one sign men may see, a warning that they not trespass.

The place of strength has given all I need to me. Legs shaking, back straight, I bear my son away from the place he must never enter again, no matter how dire his need. The shadows leap and flicker as I make my way back to my own fireside.

I burn my extra torches, as if cleaning the mess of a birth, and make my son and myself comfortable by the fire. Holding him against me, so small, so strong, I hum softly without saying the words of the song. Sleep takes us both. The fire burns low, but the bed of coals is warm and I welcome the darkness.

Waking, I help him to my breast and sleep again, feeling my womb tighten. I will be well; he will be well. Sleep, sleep, sleep without dreams, sleep.

Mouth dribbling milk from my teat, my son is annoyed by the blast of cold air that accompanies his father and greets him with a sturdy yell.

"It's done," says Guapo.

I lift my son and show him.

"A boy," he says, indifferently. "Good."

I am glad he was not here. He does not know the proper things for a man to do for his son. Guapo doesn't name him, as he should.

Still, he makes up the fire and treads down the ash-strewn earth where he thinks I've burned the debris of birthing his child. Women's work that only he is here to do. Then he goes off, about his own business, outdoors.

I lie, warm and tired and sore, and dream of finding clay and making pottery, of knowing every patch of berry bushes, and of the tender green leaves of spring. I think I have time. I cannot cross the great grass plains thirsty and hungry with a baby. My son would die. I need to plan and instead I sleep, do the little necessary things, cook what Guapo brings—

Mostly I sleep.

I wake one morning to gusts of warm wet air tossing our hide drape back, a rainstorm in progress outside the main entrance to the cavern beyond. I stretch and ease the sleepy child to my oozing breast, yawning comfortably.

My companion is a softly snoring lump under the patchwork fur blankets. Something shifts in the outer chamber and I clutch my son to me. Then a hand pushes the flapping skins out of the way and a hairy face looks around the edge.

I must make a sound, for the bearded man grins and says something. His accent is so peculiar that it is a moment before I understand he is apologizing. He calls to someone out of sight.

Guapo rolls over and leaps up. Below his tattered shirt his scarred and wiry legs look vulnerable. He says something in a language I don't understand, the man nods, the curtain drops, and we are alone again, although not really.

I can hear the domestic sounds of men settling themselves in the cave outside. The bowman is fastening on his leggings. "Traders are here. Pack everything up, we'll leave as soon as the rain's over." Fingers flying on the laces of his leggings, he doesn't even look at me, he is so eager to join the other men in the outer cavern.

The baby, Guapo's unnamed son, shifts and gives a thin wail. Hastily, I hush him with a breast and begin bundling together what food we have left after the winter. I don't want to go. I don't have a choice. Guapo has lied by omission. He has been waiting for the traders, here, where he knew they would come.

Seething with anger, I choke it down. I can't care for the baby and myself alone. It is still too early in the season for most plants and I have not enough skill or weapons to live by hunting. Nothing in our little home has been touched, yet everything has been destroyed.

Cautious, I don't go out until my ordinary routine demands I get water, then I cross the outer cavern, eyes down, modest and retiring as any Lord's daughter. I still hear comments and coarse laughter tells me what they are think-ing even if I can't understand the words.

It is a hard trip with the baby and two full water skins, and my leather clothes are soaked and clammy before I make the trip back. My long hair fallen around my face like a head cloth, I count the invaders from its shelter as I come back in.

For all the noise, there are, after all, only four of them, one scarcely more than a boy, for all his straddle-legged bravado. It is still four more than I want to see. The baby wriggles and cries, and I hurry past, water skins thumping at my back.

Guapo's face when he looks at me from his squat by their hearth is as distant and male-alien as the rest of them. Features shadow-streaked with firelight, they all watch me with bright, unblinking eyes, like hungry foxes prowling at the edge of a campsite.

I cannot hide in the shrine or, safer, the birthing-place: I may draw them after me. If these unbelievers see the im-ages, worse, destroy those focuses of power, I will not be forgiven. I will become as a man, separated from the sister-hood of women.

Someone whispers something that would be too loud if I could understand, and they all laugh, Guapo the loudest of all. I look at my hair, swinging in front of my face, dark and stringy with a winter's lack of grooming. Good, I think. Good.

I don't let myself feel anger until the door-hide falls be-hind me, but I can see how it is going to be. Mostly the group will stay together. Sometimes two of the men will scout and hunt. I will walk with those who are carrying doubled trading packs. At night and in the morning I'll cook for all of them.

Hands busy packing dried berries, I wonder if they have cornmeal or flour with them. Most likely they do. My angry mouth sweetens a little at the thought of corn cakes. I have been eating meat and fruit for months, and before that, grass. I long for grain and beans and yams. Apricots, I think, and my mouth floods with saliva.

The food I ate as a slave.

My mouth goes sour. I shiver. It would be so easy to give up, do as I am told, to accept what fate brings. Now that I am a mother, a representative of the earth, I must be strong. I press my hands against the rocky floor and beg that all go well with my son, always, that he do a vision quest, have true name, find an honored place among both men and women.

The traders spend a rowdy day and a rowdier night in the outer cavern. Listening, I worry about what to do. Most of what we have isn't portable. The snug stone room, the handy stream, the comfort of knowing the animals and their habits.

I don't look too closely at the skinned and gutted carcasses they bring to their hearth. I doubt they've gone far to hunt and the animals around the cave are trusting. The spirits of the place will be angry. Away from their eyes, I burn an offering in my fire, murmuring apologies. Even so, I know the place will not shelter me anymore.

It is no excuse that I was fooled. I fooled myself. I knew what Guapo was from the first, he hardly needed to lie. I am wrong about one thing, my value to the men. The boy is a deft cook, and, from the jokes and gestures, serves other feminine functions as well.

I am beginning to understand their dialect, but I make myself as if deaf with an effort of will. Knowing what they are saying when they don't know I know is an advantage I may need. I am glad I did not show Guapo how much I remembered of life in the wilderness.

From the way the bowman is eyeing the flirtatious boy, he is not averse to trying something new, and once he's tried theirs, the question of their trying his will be as natural as sunrise.

I bend my head to my work, hide my face with the dark fall of my hair because I cannot trust my composure. It is not likely that they would be as easily satisfied as the town bravos. They already have all of that they want.

These men may use me worse than any whore, for I have no pimp to take an interest in me. I don't want to be pregnant again, and regret the baby's weight in my arms. Without him I might have tried to slip away.

Frightened, listening to Guapo in the outer room talk and talk, I watch my firelight's shadows dance on the rock for the last time. The best I can do, if he won't protect me and I can't reach a compromise with the traders, is hide.

I may have to follow them a day or two behind, hoping to find someone willing to claim and defend me when they join the larger body of men at the trading ground. There is no course of action that will not be very dangerous for me, and even more so for my child.

The following morning dawns gray and cool, but with the promise the sun will burn off the early morning mist. I shoulder one pack of our household belongings and look regretfully one last time at the heap of things to be abandoned.

The hides I'd tried so hard to cure were heavy, and we've been given blankets from the trading stock. The hollowed-out stone I'd cooked in, dropping fire-heated rocks into the simmering broth. The plaited framework of our bed had already been broken up for kindling, not even left to comfort someone else who passed this way.

Despite all I am leaving, my shoulders sag under the weight at my back and the baby at my front, where I can modestly slide his head beneath the loose folds of my new shirt to reach my breasts.

Wondering who had given the shirt, I take my first good look at the four as we start up the trail. Enrique, thin and stooped, who probably looks older than he is, is the trail master. His brother, Sancho, is bigger, blonder, with an evasive eye I don't like. The boy, Rafael, is smooth-cheeked and as pretty as a girl. And the forth is gentle Jaime, whose hairy face startled me so.

Except for Rafael, they are a ragged-looking bunch. Guapo and I look no better. They might let us camp outside the town walls, but they'd never let us in to the market at Misericordia. Even the pump-slaves avoided travelers like us, fearing lice.

At the very thought, I begin to itch. The pair of us do not have lice, but the traders must. They will be hiding in the seams of the shirt I am wearing. It will have to be smoked at the very least. A thorough washing is impossible and even arranging to do without the shirt for long enough to smoke it will be hard.

I find no difficulty with the pace they set. I have time to care for my son and myself. Enrique's group camps every night at what, judging by the remains of last year's black-ened fires, are well-known stops.

Game is plentiful, and the foursome brought plenty of flour and meal and even a sheet of iron to cook on. Sancho roasts the game. Jaime is an expert at the thin corn cakes that are swept onto the griddle with a bare hand, so my un-distinguished talents in that department are not called on. Had he been a woman, I would have made friends with him, for a gentle spirit guides him.

My only cooking duties consisted of filling their one small kettle with greens if I can find them, or with stewed dried berries if I cannot. They have a jar of honey that I could eat with a spoon, I am so hungry for sweets. We eat well and I find the sound of human voices and jokes pleas-ant, as long as they do not look at me.

When they do, I want my head cloth. Guapo doesn't make any effort to shield me from the rough horseplay of the men, and it is obvious that Sancho, in particular, only refrained from pressing his interests because he thinks I've given birth only days ago. My son is a small child. I think Sancho's restraint won't last once he knows the truth.

The bowman makes no secret that he has not paid a bride-price, so the men think they have as much right as he to court me. I get a shy offer from Jaime, but despite my liking his manners I cannot keep my distaste for his hairy, smelly person from my face, and he backs away, stammering in confusion.

Coward, I hope he puts my reaction down to my poor understanding of their speech. I know he doesn't, but he still is kind. Under other circumstances, he might have won my true friendship, and perhaps even more. I wonder what flaw let him fall among this company.

Handsome Sancho has nothing so permanent or personal in mind as Jaime. Once he learns I have been a slave, he reminds me often that I am traveling with them, not necessary and hardly even useful, and it is fair I pay my way in some fashion. That I don't want to be one of their party makes no difference: I owe them.

For four or five days Sancho does nothing but talk and touch, furtively. Then on the fifth day he surprises me as I fill the water skins, trips me with the casual ease of long practice, and pins me down. Shoved aside on the muddy ground, my son's high thin wail must carry to the camp, but no one comes.

I can tell by their curious expressions as I warm the baby at the fire afterwards that every one of them knew what was happening. Even Guapo. Especially Guapo. Only Jaime has the grace to look embarrassed.

I have been free and I have become a thing, a possession again. Although I am both angry and frightened, I cook my share of the evening meal as if nothing important has happened, pack everything ready for the next morning and lie down to sleep.

Guapo comes to me in the night. Painful though it is I don't refuse him, afraid that if I make a fuss the others will wake and join him. Sancho will be eager to be the first.

Nonetheless, when the first hint of dawn causes the stars to fade, I stuff a cold corn cake into myself and take the water skins to the stream as I always do, but this time I cross it and keep going, my son's mouth stifled by my breast.

If I want to be a whore, I can do that in far more comfort in the grubbiest town on the coast. I expect them to track me, and aim to travel fast enough in a wrong direction for them to discourage their following me, for they need to reach the trader's meet as swiftly as they can.

I spend most of the day wading upstream, climbing, and wading again. Not knowing the country, the only certain direction I can move in is up. By the time I come to the bare stone of the mountain I know I have to find shelter for the night or my son and I will die.

Wrapping myself and the child in my two blankets, I roll into a crack in the stone. I regret the stinking hides left behind. The blankets are warm, but they do not stop the wind. Still, safe in the crevice, with my milk flowing freely, I manage to spend a tolerable night until the earth shakes.

The rest of the night is spent listening to the groan of settling rock punctuated by the rumble of sliding stone. Something has offended the earth. Perhaps some later trader has found the shrine in the cave or something even more sacred further in.

It may be that the powers are offended for me, but I did not dare hope. I have not, after all, seen a jaguar for many months. I have no name, no spirit. Only determination. On that thought, I doze and wait for dawn and what fate would bring.

They come hunting up the side of the mountain shortly after true dawn. Like the rock around me, the coarse blankets of undyed wool are gray and brown. I am completely covered, having hooded my head in a fold. I stay still and listen to the men call to one another.

I chew a cud of hastily plucked herbs to stay my hunger and drug the baby. I intend to save what I have, dried, as long as possible. I finger my bundle ever so often, reassured that I have them.

Just before noon, Guapo comes out onto the stone shoulder that my crevice crosses and stares so hard that I, peering through the loose weave, think he sees me until he turns away. I long to relieve myself and don't dare move enough to even lift my skirt. The baby had no such inhibitions and soon our inner blanket is wet and filthy.

Sometimes near, sometimes far, their voices echo and re-echo most of the day. When the sun cuts through the black outlines of the trees to the west, the mountain has been silent for a while. Now I can hear the whistles and chirps of wildlife about its business.

I roll out.

"Are you all right?" says Guapo.

I almost let go of the child but he is securely tucked into my shirt. "No," I say.

The bowman has been sitting, crossed arms on his knees, on the shelf of stone that formed the upper half of my crevice. He gets stiffly to his feet and comes down. When he gets within reach, I hit him as hard as I can and feel pain jolt up my arm to the shoulder.

Wiping his mouth, he looks at the smear of blood in his palm while his tongue tests his teeth and explores the inside of his cheek. He spits, scarlet, on the gray stone. "They would have killed me, you know, and probably the pair of you, too." He spits scarlet again. "I never called you a wife or that whore's child," his chin jerks at the baby, "my son."

I stifle my anger. No matter what I think of him, I will need him a while longer.

Hungry?" he says, lifting a hare's carcass from the rock. "We'll have to go down to get wood for a fire."

I back away, looking around.

"They've gone on," he says. "I told them we'd catch them up once I found you."

I swing again and he ducks.

"We don't have to do it," he says.

"Why don't you just go along with the rest of them." I have enough self-control left not to yell. Sound carries a long way in the mountains. I snarl like an angry cat and tell him what I think, finally concluding, "—take better care of myself without you!"

The Old One's traitorous bowman looks away, then up at me. I had never been more conscious that Guapo was shorter then I.

"No, you can't," he says, flatly. As I double my fists he adds, "Don't hit me again." He touches his cheek tenderly.

If I've knocked a tooth loose, he is not going to enjoy eating for a while.

I look down at him, a small man, tongue busy with the dribble of blood at one corner of his mouth.

"Why not," I say. I want to pound on him until my fists are sore and then pick up a rock and grind him into a smear that flies will swarm on and their maggots eat.

He rubs his mouth with the back of his hand. "There were four of them," Guapo says, "and my honor was not involved."

"So?"

"I couldn't do anything."

I open my mouth to list some of the things he could have done. It would have helped if he'd even objected. One word. If just he'd kept his mouth shut. But his honor wasn't involved.

Oh, I have fooled myself, fooled myself very badly. I must get away from him. He has not the honor of his people nor the honor of a townsman. He is filth.

The bowman looks at his feet, takes a deep breath, and says, "May the great ones turn away your rightful wrath. I lost my way."

My mouth falls open. In one instant he has changed from a Lord's bowman dealing with household slave to a native man addressing a native woman, a pair of the true people. Cruel. Clever.

Liar.

Too angry to answer, I lower my head, veiling my face with my dirty mane, and wait. We are two strangers joined by a child that I have not chosen to bear and that he denies is his.

Guapo jerks the hare's carcass by its crossed legs—he has as is his duty, provided meat—and looks at our son. "The kid all right?"

"He's filthy."

Reluctantly, the bowman takes the baby from me, face twisting at the stink. Some of the shallowest pools of the stream have been sun-warmed above absolutely icy, but my son screams mightily at the cold. Guapo muffles the boy's yells with one hand and slaps water over him with the other. I say nothing. The child has to be cleaned, and fast is better than slow.

My own skin rough with goose bumps, I scrub baby shit from my belly and breasts as fast as I can, then start a handful of fire in a hollow among trees. Tucking the child against me, I sit, barelegged, draped in my one clean blanket, feeding the flames with bits of dry wood.

The bowman scrapes the worst of the filth from the soiled blanket with a flat, stream-smoothed stone. Then he rolls that and my dirty shirt into a bundle. I hope that we can wash them soon: they stink. We can't afford to throw them away.

Guapo cuts and laces one of his blankets into a crude tunic. It bristles with coarse fibers at the neck-hole and leaks cold air at the sides where it is laced together, but I wear it as is, too exhausted to do anything more for myself.

I watch the sun rise and set, stirring only to keep the smokeless fire going and the baby fed. All through the short sunlit hours the bowman sleeps. When I dig the hare from the roasting pit, he wakes. We eat every scrap of it.

Full night come, I rebury its bones where it was cooked and lie as close to the fire as I dare while Guapo sits sentinel. Cuddling the baby to silence, I watch the bowman keep watch until I doze.

In the morning Guapo conceals the remaining traces of our pitiful camp. Without a word between us, we hike uphill. The drowsy, milk-filled baby at my breast, is still half-drugged by the herbs I chewed yesterday. I don't need to finger a pinch from my bundle and tuck it into my cheek. I climb and climb, my legs aching with the constant ascent.

Finally we cross a sloping shoulder of rock and start down. The mountainside we descend opens to the north like a hand, the palm the broad stone of the heights, and the gaps between the stone fingers warm valleys. Guapo picks the gentlest slope. We reach a slanting meadow sprigged with scarlet flowers and their bobbing seedcases.

Sleep poppies. I need more for my medicine pouch. I slit a dozen seed cases to gather what gum I can. The long wet grass pulls at our leggings, and we take them off, spread them to dry on a ledge.

Easing my sore back against warm stone, I sit, legs swinging. The air is rich with the fragrances of plants, the season weeks in advance of the one we just left. I find ripe strawberries tucked beneath their sheltering leaves. While nursing my son, I share a sweet half-handful with I'm-not-his-father as I look around.

A herd of deer trots out into the meadow to graze, a bowshot or less below us. Guapo considers, but leaves his bow case in its position at his back.

I am relieved. The extra meat and the hide would be wasted, the spirits offended. Also, and I guess that this is what he thinks of, scavenging vultures may draw unwelcome attention. However, he does bring down two pairs of birds without losing an arrow. He is a good shot in the right circumstances.

When he goes to fetch his kills, I stand and cradle the baby inside my improvised tunic, knowing that, tired though I am, we must move on. I cull the gum quickly, roll it in a leaf, lick a bitter bit for myself.

But, dinner swinging at Guapo's belt, we find a shelter—not quite a cave—of stone hidden behind a screen of bushes. In the warm spring night it is enough to protect us from the weather, even though it storms toward morning.

Wishing I had pegged the filthy blanket and shirt out to be rinsed by the drumming downpour, I lie listening to the rush of wind, the crash of thunder. The air is sharp with the odor of lightning, thrashing foliage leaps into view and disappears.

Our trail is gone.

I spend several peaceful days gathering herbs and harvesting opium gum before we confront the inevitable question, What are we going to do? I am not so sure that it will be we that do anything, if I can pick my moment. I want to go south, where I know the land and the people and I can build a place for myself and my son.

Guapo intends to go to the cold fires, although whatever compels him, it is no dream from the spirits. He shakes his head and frowns at the fire. The baby moves and gurgles and we both look at it. He frowns. It is a boy. He is the kind of man who wants to boast how many sons he has and he has denied this one.

Finally he says, "We can go around, to the west. It'll be safe."

I say nothing. Caution may be the best I can win. "All right," I say and touch the bag of dust-turned-to-hardened-mud at my throat.

It is a great relief to me next day when the pains in my lower belly turn to streaks of blood down my thighs and my womb begins to empty itself. At least, when I leave the bowman I will have only one child to worry about.

Saying no more than I am trail-weary, I stop at noon to brew and drink willow tea while Guapo goes to look over the possible routes and check for game. He comes back at mid-afternoon to propose we stay in this spot for another day, there being nothing better a convenient walk ahead.

Nearly immobile with pain and the baby, I assent silently, then sit and sip, coddling myself a bit in the familiar misery of womanhood.

Guapo works at his arrows and bow, cleaning, polishing, and sharpening. His three dozen arrows have dwindled to seven. He has points from some of the others, but he was unable to do anything over the winter, for there was no suitable wood, dry, cured, and straight, to be found.

Now he sits with a bundle of sticks, sighting down their lengths, setting aside the hopefuls, and sliding the others, one by one, into our small fire. Though he can carve the blunt tips used for small game, when it comes to fletching, he spoils many more feathers than he splits successfully.

I eye him unobtrusively. As one of the Old One's he had no need to make his own equipment. He is out of practice at anything but whittling. He knows what to do, but his hands do not. His face is dark as storm clouds.

My father had been expert at producing arrows, might have gotten away with trading game for equipment, had he wished. He hadn't. He'd done his own hunting, unwilling to be dependent on anyone.

Ignoring the bowman's fumbles—I must not laugh, I must not—I watch the sides of the small kettle that Enrique's traders gave us blacken with soot. Savoring the bitterness of the willow bark and the painful heat of the new metal cup on my fingers, I mull over how to get away from Guapo.

Toward evening, the pressure in my bladder wins out over the pain in my groin. I unwrap myself from my blankets and go apart to relieve and wash myself. Uncomfortable though I am, I am some time about it, wanting to keep myself as clean as possible through the night.

It is the smell of blood that draws it, I am sure, but when I look up from wiping myself on the last of the frayed rags I have for myself and the baby, I look squarely into the cold and golden eyes of a jaguar, crouched, nostrils fluttering.

I scream.

Leaving my son behind, unprotected, hands fumbling with his bow and an arrow, Guapo comes running. From a range so close he could hardly miss, he shoots and hits.

Scratched across the ribs, the jaguar charges him. The bowman rolls over and over, body doubled forward to protect his guts.

Furious, I grab a stick thick as my arm, and swing, feeling it break, although I am not sure on what.

The jaguar snarls and leaps at me.

I can feel its hot breath on my face as I fall backwards. I expect it to rip my throat out.

Instead, it bounds over me and into the woods. Gasping for breath, I stagger to my feet, and go to Guapo.

He is on his knees, arms wrapped around himself. At first I think the blood is the jaguar's, then I see the deep claw marks in Guapo's shoulder. The bowman looks at me, then at the flood of crimson, near-black in the dim light, and faints onto his side.

I go and get my son. Then, child safe in my shirt, I haul the groaning man back to the fire. It is our best protection and I promptly build it high.

Then, flaming brand in hand, I drag wood on-handed and stack it near for the long dark hours. Only then do I turn to the bowman's deep and ragged wounds.

After forcing as much of my tea as possible down him, I wash his shoulder with the rest, then sit through a night where every shadow is the jaguar come back to claim its prey and every spark a beacon to draw outlaws.

I fear the mountain cat will think I am wounded and an easy kill. Now that there are two of us who smell of blood, other things may come to feed. Not all of them will wait until we are dead.

Guapo looks better in the dawn, although I can see vultures high overhead, watching, waiting. I give the baby to him and venture to the stream to fill the water skins. It is a fast trip, for the broad pug marks of the jaguar dapple the smooth sand at the inner edge of the stream's curve.

Back in camp I mingle precious cornmeal with cold water and a pinch of salt and bring it to a near-boil. We need food. I try not to think what we will do when the meal and the last handful of fruit are gone. Until I no longer smell like prey, I cannot range too far afield and a bowman needs both arms to pull and hold the arrow.

The weather holds hot and fine for four or five days, and instead of seeking better shelter, I spend my time setting snares, my hands smeared green with crushed leaves to conceal my human scent. I hope that feeding Guapo well will hasten his recovery and we can move down to lower country.

My first catch is a young rabbit, so small I feel ashamed to take it and stun it with a blow to the head. I do the job badly, and the bowman finishes it with a casual rap when it comes to struggling life in our camp. I am kinder and less squeamish after that, although it is easier to find eggs, young birds, and greens.

Meanwhile, the bowman lies by the fire at night and in the sun by day. His deepest wound oozes foul pus. Guapo has me wash it often, mostly, I suspect, because the icy water numbs pain.

In Misericordia del Mar they would have searched it with a red-hot iron, but I only have the point of a war-arrow, and I've seen the job done. It took four men to hold the sweating, screaming patient down. Guapo will not agree to my tying him down and trying.

The hollows around his eyes grow deeper and darker as the days pass. He fingers and pulls at the two pouches at his neck constantly, one the coyote totem he had lent me when we first met, and the other the one he has kept hidden from me until now.

One morning after an exhausted sleep, I awake to find he has not called me for my watch. The baby is wriggling in his soiled clothes, having cried himself out. I clean and feed him, and make food for the two of us before I try to rouse Guapo.

The bowman won't wake and his skin is hot and dry.

The stream is becoming gritty with stone dust from the glacier above; game is growing warier; and plant food is becoming less abundant. Neither the man nor the child can be left alone, and they are no company for one another. I must make do with what is in sight around me.

I sit in the thin shade of the bushes, putting cold leaves on Guapo's forehead and humming to the lightly-drugged baby. The bowman rouses once to tell me the pouch at his neck must be taken to the cold fires.

I promise, crazed with fever though he is.

He falls asleep and will not wake. Toward dawn on the fourth night, his breathing grows hoarse and loud, and as the first sunlight breaks over the shoulder of the mountain, the Old One's traitorous bowman dies.

Raising my head to the sky, I howl softly for the dead. No one and nothing answers, not even the jaguar. Nothing, except my son, hungry and dirty as usual. Eventually, I scrub my cheeks with my fists and put him to my breast. I have little milk and he complains.

I make myself boil a quarter-pot of meal, sweeten it with berries, and force myself to gag down every mouthful and lick the pot clean before I scour it with sand and leave it to dry in the sun.

As vultures circle high overhead, I strip the corpse: clothes, stained and smelly though they are, two pouches, bow, arrows. I take the cord from the bowman's braids, hesitate over his ornaments, his lump of gold, then take those, too.

I am sending him naked and empty-handed on his journey into the dead lands, but I have so little, anything might be the difference between life and death. I will make offerings when I can, and raise his son.

The vultures start landing in the nearby trees, eager to feed. I must gather enough wood to send Guapo on his way properly. If there are any watchers, a large fire may deceive them into thinking there is a large camp here or even a wildfire.

I will hide once it is burning well.

All day I lift, pull, and sweat. As the last red of sunset fades, I light Guapo's pyre. The flames rise and I can smell burning flesh. Child in the crook of my arm, I open his pouches. The one I once wore holds a tuft of coyote fur; the other, a scant handful of witches' eyes.

I toss pouch and fur into the fire to call his spirit-guardian to guide him one last time. Perhaps the trickster can provide the goods I cannot spare. The witches' eyes I pour into my palm and count. There are an even dozen, eleven dull and gray with age, plus one that is still dark and vital.

On an impulse, I put that one back, hang the pouch around my own neck, and toss the rest into the fire. The pyre explodes in hungry white flames that lick at the zenith and obscure the stars.

The white flames will call the fuego fantasmas. I know it. My son in my arms, I run. Bow case rattling at my back, I am forced higher and higher by acrid smoke.

It is some time before I can stop and see that the screen of bushes before our camp has caught and is burning fiercely. At least those flames are of natural red and yellow.

Most of what I salvaged has gone with Guapo after all. I almost am not sorry. Sitting on a stone outcrop, still as the rock itself, I watch as the white ones drift down out of the sky.

By dawn the fire has burned out and they, too, have gone. I go down to the blackened, blighted place, sweep up the ashes with a pine branch, and cast what is left of Guapo and of his goods and my camp into the stream, then it is done.

I will never speak his name aloud again. I search for the kettle and the gold, hoping they at least would have survived the flames, but the flare from the witches' eyes has seemingly destroyed everything. I have no goods but what I stand in and carry.

Those, and a promise to go north.

I have done enough fool's work.

To find some vantage point to study the lay of the land, I scramble down slope, intending to find my way to some sheltered place, and then, as the weather permits, south to the warm lands.

I am tired of being cold.

By afternoon a fine, cold rain is drifting across the mountaintops. I head down into a valley, move through a world ghostly with fog. Stumbling up and down invisible slopes, I am unable to pick a direction or choose a sensible course, too driven to stop and wait the weather out.

The high woman's scream of the jaguar sounds around me in the mist. I trip and fall, hard, on rough stone, landing awkwardly on my hands and knees to protect my son. Stunned by the enormous pain where my unpadded bones struck rock, I cough to fight the sick dizziness, and taste blood in my mouth.

I've bitten my tongue.

A gust of wind tears a hole in the all-surrounding gray. In front of my face is a single trembling bunch of sweet grass, its blue flowers beaded with dew. There is nothing more between me and the rocky bottom of the valley.

Shivering, I crawl back from the edge, get to my feet, sober. I must make peace with the jaguar spirit, sacrifice, cleanse myself, seek a new path for my life.

The best I can do is a small mouse, caught in its last careless moment, too far from its hole. Building a fire takes a long time in the damp. Spark after spark blinks out. When one catches, I crouch, fan a pinch of my precious dry herbs into flame.

I build a cone of sticks over the fist-sized body, then burn it whole. Passing my son, naked, four times through its smoke, I hope that the angry jaguar spirit will relent and that the coyote's child will be safe.

Unable to capture anything else living, I bury my mother's copper sun under four heavy rocks, three in a triangle and a fourth on top. Then, I touch the earth, lift my hands to the skies, flick my spittle into the flames, and ask the fire to protect me.

It is the simplest charm, the first one children learn to do, giving up some childish treasure to amend some child-

105

ish fault. I can only hope it is enough. My mother's sun was dear to me. I have nothing of hers left but myself.

All that night the white whirlwinds of the fantasmas drift across the sky, high above me, going north against the wind. I shiver and watch, silent child cradled against me, lost in my own grim thoughts. I need a place, people, some plans for the future.

Sleep. Sleep, now.

By next morning the weather has turned warm and cloudless. After that, all day, every day, the sun beats down and every living thing races to complete its growth before winter cold comes again.

Against all commonsense and not knowing why, I, too, turn north. The first days are difficult but I fall into a steady rhythm of walking from dawn to near noon and from noon until near dusk.

I pick and gather as I go, and, although I grow thinner, my muscles also grow harder. I do not mind the slow flattening of my belly and the corded look of my legs. There is no one to see how unfeminine I had become.

One day I go down a long slope broken here and there by deep green mounds of bearberry bushes and find I have come into the valley of a river so placid and slow moving that at first I think it is a lake.

However, as I make my way along it I see the water has cut its way down through the hills. The valley's flat floor is a flood plain, covered with short grass and herbs because everything is ripped away by the flooding river each spring.

It is easy walking on the spongy turf and I go into a slow jog, then a faster, and finally a run, until I nearly overbalance on a slick patch of leaves and sit down, panting, laughing.

The silent, plump baby bound against my belly looks up at me with black, inscrutable eyes. He is a very quiet child, seldom crying although my mothering is more often rough and ready than skillfully tender.

Sobered, I return to walking.

North.

There is a making upon me to do the bowman's will. I would never choose this mad course yet I am going. At night fantasmas stream by overhead, like migrating birds. My dreams are filled with flowers of cold fire that blossom and fall to ashes. I awake at false dawn and set my course by the last stars.

Day by day I walk north crossing scorched swathes where spiky shoots push up through the new grass. I guess they are burns from lightning strikes until I see white fire, distant but too near, again.

Whatever it is rises from the ground into the sky and is gone, leaving its trail to blow away with the clouds. I crouch low, like a frightened mouse. I wait a long time before hastening on my way, carrying my silent child.

I hope I have not been seen. If I have, I want to be as far away as possible from this place as soon as I can. I drive myself on into the night and sleep cold and hungry. I cannot turn back. I must go on, although fear is my constant companion. The eyes in the sky are not friendly to me. To Guapo, perhaps, but not me.

Summer days are long, but in the north the season itself is short and ends abruptly with heavy snowfalls. As it is, only the long, slow sunlit days assure me that I am not too late. Not yet. I can see the season changing as the plants rush to flower, to seed.

Thinking of doing more than going north like one possessed, I seek out a birch grove. Fresh-cut bark would be best, but not wanting to leave the slightest sign of my presence, I take a stiff curl dropped from a fallen trunk. I use a sharp twig and spit-wet soot to make a rough map and a note or two each evening. The crude materials permit no more.

What I would give for a half sheet of parchment, so much more durable than paper, some ink, a pen. I sew my record into a leather packet with a flap, doing my best to make it watertight with tight stitching. Rather than any totem sack, I wear it on a cord around my neck, proud I am literate.

Walking, suckling my son, I often think of when my lady Mercedes taught me to read. At first it amused her to teach, and afterwards, when her eyesight grew poorer, I diverted her.

What books she had were mostly descriptions of the region and records of the town's past generations. I looked on Misericordia del Mar with new eyes the day I understood it was named "Mercy Beside the Sea" because after the dark night of the shipwreck the rising sun showed them sweet water and green hills.

My lady was very proud that her family had been one of the ones that arrived then, not the taller, darker outlanders who the books said came down from the hills in the colony's second winter. I look at my large, brown hand feeding another stick to the campfire and smile sourly.

Knowing that it is foolish, I sit on a rock in the middle of a wilderness, with no one to talk to but the baby in my arms who looks more like his coyote-faced father every day, and recite as much as I can of what I know. It is not much, but the music of the words soothes me.

I miss the sound of familiar voices, the comfort of belonging, of being owned and thus valuable and cared for. I shove a stick deep into the fire, scattering sparks and ashes. Grief and fear made me foolish before. Better a slave than dead, and better free than either.

Slave. Slave. Slave. I can almost hear a voice.

Night-blind from gazing into the flames, I look into the darkness around me and poke the scattered coals together again. Night thoughts are no reason to go cold. All the same, cold as it is, I cover the embers with ashes early.

I grow more furtive, like a hunted thing that scents the dogs. One evening when I sit cradling my son, my campfire still unlit before me while I wait for the last clouds to foretell the weather, I see a thin thread of smoke bisect the sun's red disc.

Rocking the baby, I watch. A natural fire usually spreads quickly. This neither spreads nor goes out. It sends a message although it is not meant as a signal. There are men there.

Eating a cold supper, I hide myself well before rolling into my blankets to sleep. Women do not come into the hills. Not if they have any choice. If traders catch me, some will use me mercilessly and the rest will have no stake in defending me.

I am no match for most of the men in wilderness craft. My safety and my son's depended on their not knowing there is anything to look for. I move whenever it is possible to move, in daylight, by moonlight, and sleep when I can. I keep the boy slightly drugged, which means I am slightly drugged myself.

There is no help for it.

It is with great relief that I top one huge, slow-rising hill late one evening, fantasmas streaming overhead like luminous clouds, eyes hunting for strands of smoke, and see a hemisphere of pearly light against the northern sky: the cold fires.

I have come to my journey's end, fulfilled my promise even though I did not want to. Once I cast the witches' eye into the flames I will be free to go, south, toward the warm lands, and find a home.

Inside the white fire stand towers, near invisible. I think them a mirage until I see the fantasmas doubled in one and then another and realize the huge forms reflect so perfectly it is hard to make them out.

Flattening myself against the ground, baby in the crook of my arm, I study them. The shapes remind me of the great shipwreck off the coast of Misericordia. Throwing anything into the fires will not go unremarked and being remarked will be dangerous.

Will it be enough if I just leave Guapo's sack with its remaining witches' eye on the ground and go away? I know that was not what he meant. He said to take it to the cold fires. Not near. He wanted me to throw the sack and its single witches' eye into the flames.

Flat on my belly, I braid a sling from a hank of my hair. As a child I could hurl a pebble a fair distance, although my accuracy left much to be desired. The fires are a much bigger target. Fulfilling my oath means I have to get within my range.

Close to the dome the ground is covered with thickets, seeded with the first witches' eyes that I have seen in a long time. Seeing them, I know I must be quick.

On my hands and knees, my son swinging at my belly, I feel the air drawn to the fires whisper past me and see the flash of small things drawn into the flames. I take a deep breath.

Whatever the bowman did, whatever promises he made, I have no business here. Brushing the hair back from my face, I fit the witches' eye, still in its pouch, into my sling. I tuck the baby, secure in his blanket, under a bush, and stand.

There is a swish and rustle. I crouch, instantly, the witches' eye still in my sling, and look and listen. Nothing. But I heard something. Hidden by the dense foliage, something moves, very slowly, stalking, stalking me.

It may not know where I am yet.

Pfft!

I stare at the running streak of blood down my forearm and at the dart, striped like some giant wasp, black and yellow. I pull the venomous thing out, drop it. Everything goes slow. I fall onto my side, trying to reach my son. My arms and legs twitch, indifferent to my will.

My son wails, struggles to free himself from his blanket.

Stung again, I am unable to see anything other than the second black-and-yellow dart pumping its venom into my arm. Fool, I think, as darkness takes me before whatever hunted me arrives. Fool.

I awake in a circular room with hard, smooth floor, walls, and ceiling. White fire runs through everything, yet I am chilled through, huddled in on myself and shivering. I must find warmth. I crawl toward the nearest wall. It hisses at me.

Slowly and painfully, I back up. I can see the bruises around the stings' swellings on my arm. I sit up, and cough with a wave of nausea. My tongue is like a scrap of old leather. I am have nothing but my shirt and skirt. No pack, no boots, no totem, no map.

No baby.

I call until my voice is a harsh croak, then collapse on the floor, exhausted. I sleep, then wake to find I have no choice but to back into a corner, pull my skirt up, and leave a puddle like an animal. Not much later fear and pain make me make another contribution.

I squat as far as I can from my mess and wait, shivering, as oozing milk stains the front of my shirt. My son will be hungry. I keep offering him my painful breasts whenever I doze off, and waking with a start when no eager mouth accepts them.

The woman who eventually comes, walking through the wall as if it were not there, looks enough like Guapo to be his sister: short, dark, thin-lipped and dour.

I wonder if he sent me to his kin as he died. It would have been a proper thing to do, but it was not like the man I thought I knew. Embarrassed, I stand, brush down my skirt, fumble for some polite thing to say.

She gestures me forward with one hand, never glancing at the stinking mess, then takes my wrist and leads me into the wall. It hisses and sends a chill over my skin. We go along a featureless tunnel, through another wall, and into another room. There she lets go of me, dusting her fingers with unconscious distaste.

The room is filled with many glittering things, some of them beautiful, but none obviously useful. There is nothing of mine in it. "Where is my baby?" I say.

The woman shakes her hand in negation, though whether to say she doesn't understand or she won't answer I don't know. She motions to me to strip and I try her own gesture on her. No. Her thin lips narrow further and her hand goes to her waist.

Weapons have a certain look about them, comfortable to the fingers and hard on the eye. Piece by piece, I strip to my bare and dirty skin before she is satisfied.

Covering my crotch with my hands, I hunch my shoulders and wish for the modesty of even a small piece of cloth. It is not a polite reception. It is the way masters treat slaves. The woman waves me back, back, back into a narrow upright tube.

The door closes and a waterfall pours in. I fight to escape until I see I will not drown. There is an opening in the center of the floor where the water rushes away in a swirl.

The sun-warmed stuff streams over my body, drums on my head, releases all the odors of sweat and dirt and rinses them away.

Seeing the dark dirt peel from my feet, I rub one foot and then the other to encourage the process. Then I scrub my armpits and groin with my fists and look to get out. I can't.

A wave of foam goes over me, leaving me gasping, straining to keep my face free. Then the water begins again. There are several cycles. They strip the dirt from my hair and the calluses from my skin. I will be as soft of hand and foot as any lady and just as unable to walk the rough paths of the wilderness.

Numbed by the pressure and the sound, I appraise the bony body and hollow-cheeked face reflected in the wet wall. Never a beauty, I have become ugly. They will not value me much, will put me to hard labor.

Perhaps think I am not worth feeding.

The flow stops, the runoff from my hair dripping down my back, trickling into the crevice of my buttocks, down my legs to pool around my feet. I shiver, cold. "Let me out?" I whisper. They must have some use for me or they would not have washed me—unless they clean bodies before they are dead.

"—Let me out!" I slam both hands against the door.

It is a man who opens it.

My hands fly up and down to cover myself as I look around for my missing clothes.

Indifferent to my nudity, as if I am a dog, he throws a shapeless sack of a cloth dress at me and leaves. It was blue before it was washed many times and very clean. I draw it on and sit on the floor to wait, cradling my head in my hands.

Much later someone shoves an olla of water and a dish of corn and beans through the seamless wall. I drink the icy water slowly. The beans and corn are tasteless: no salt, no peppers, no tomatillos. I eat them anyway. I need food and this is what there is.

Then I wait. I surmise they are puzzled. They expected Guapo and got something quite different. A woman and a child, without the man. On that thought, I wonder, Where is my son?

I start calling again. "Ah-yah?" There is no answering cry. I invoke my spirit, but cannot feel its presence. I am alone as I have never been alone before.

They are punishing me, perhaps, for not properly caring for the bowman. I did my best. The things I took, I took to save his child. Even they went in the flare from his pyre when I cast in the witches' eyes.

Two or three uncounted and uncountable days pass. I sleep, find where to ease myself, bath in the rushing water, milk my painful breasts, and am fed when it occurs to someone to feed me. I have no idea if the sun rises or sets or where the moons are in the sky.

Late one evening I wake, groggy and cold, on a broad hillside above the cold fires, childless and angry. I think, I must go back, but the frigid air brings me to my senses. I could die here. Indeed, that may be what they hope.

While I was trapped, the first hard frost has come. The leaves are black and withered, and there is ice in the cracks in the stone. I have nothing but the thin cloth dress they gave me, which does not keep out the wind.

All I can do is huddle myself together in the hollow beneath a boulder. I lie all the darkness long, hands in armpits, knees pressed against my chest, and curse those who had left me, ill-clad and ill-prepared, out of doors at the beginning of a bitter autumn, curse until I am too numb to care.

There are sparks and smoke from the campfires on the other side of the great bowl from me. I fantasize walking unseen, warming my hands at their fires, drinking from their cups. I am not dead yet and not invisible. The men are as dangerous to me as ever.

I am very near sleeping into death. The gate of the dead lands gapes open for me. If I want, I can enter. I need do nothing but wait and float up into the river of stars. I sleep, and, sleeping, do not dream.

The morning sun is well up in the sky before I wake, and higher still before I can think well enough to realize I must make fire. Not even food takes precedence over the need for heat.

I've seen fire made as a child, but seeing and doing are quite different things. Raveling coarse thread from the hem of my dress, I loop four strands over my great toe and braid a thin, strong cord. I loop the result around my unprotected neck to keep it safe. Its touch makes me wonder what has become of my totem.

I will replace it if I can. I have offended the jaguar and cannot afford to do so again. Searching along the side of a stream I find a punky branch and a broken stream cobble. My search costs me legs wet to the knee and I can no longer feel my feet.

Bit by bit, the dead lands are claiming me, dull as I am. I need one thing more, I think, frowning at the ground. My two hands, stone and punk, sketch the proper shape in the frigid air.

A stick. For a fire bow.

It is a slow, hard climb up the hill. One that I finish on my hands and knees when I fall into what I seek: a bush, with straight, stiff, supple limbs. I blink and straighten up. Exercise has warmed me. I look around, wondering why I wanted to be here.

Finally, slowly, I break and pull a branch. With stiff hands, motion by motion, I make a loosely-strung bow. Looping a pointed stick into the cord's slack, I press its tip against the punk and drill.

The sun warm on my shoulders, I go at it in mindless earnest. When the pile of hot wood dust darkens with heat I lean forward and breathe, very gently. I see a red glow, smell burning resin—it goes out.

I drill again.

And again.

And once more.

Finally I drill on and on, crying, my tears let run down my cheeks lest my hands be damp—

A spark.

Scrap by scrap, I coax the red glow. It buds, blooms into a handful of fire. If I had the talent I might see my fate in its freshly-kindled flames. As it is I only know that its heat means life.

I hold my gray hands as close to it as I can stand, see the color come back into my nails. For this night, at least, I am going to live. Seeing ruddy firelight through my lids, I wonder if it is a sunset or a sunrise for me.

A bright flare of anger comes from deep, deep within me. I have been robbed of so much. Childhood. My proper name. The dignity of a wife. Motherhood.

They, whoever they are, hidden behind their walls of fire, sailing across our skies—yes, I am sure of that—will have to defeat me. I will not yield. I am sixteen and I will not yield.

Having fire, I have to devise a way to carry it with me. I make do with two pieces of softwood in which I scrape matching hollows. Coal tucked within, I bind them together with the fire-drill's cord.

Deprived of air, it will burn slowly. I tuck the improvised nightglow against my bare skin at the waist of my dress, where I can't ignore it if it becomes hot. I tuck a few blocks of wood into a bundle of twigs and look for shelter.

Under an overhang in a stream cut I build a small, smokeless blaze. As the last red-gold of sunset fades I turn one side, then the other, to the heat. I put my hands against the small of my back and stretch as my dream-jaguar stretched. I am too tired to do more than curl up around the bed of coals.

I am climbing steps toward the light, every muscle in my body sore with effort. I can smell wine, and grain, and blood. A jaguar coughs.

Wake.

My fingers touch the wooden container tied at my waist, but it is not hot. Overhead cold stars watch me dispassionately.

Weeks of travel from security, if Misericordia, with its dying old woman and knife-wielding priests, is security, I look into ashy coals cradled by round stones, and see nothing but what is there.

The spirits know me. They will speak in ways I understand. All I need do is listen; all I can do is think. If the bowman was one of those who dwell inside the cold fires and if they recognize my son as Guapo's and if they have claimed him as their own, can I accept that—

No. I am not sure my son was taken. He may still be lying in the thicket, killed instantly, or left to suffer with hunger and die of cold. It is unlikely that is still living if he was not taken, but I must know. I have to go back.

I know where the fires are by their light in the dawn sky.

It is not hard to find where I forced my way through the tangle. I reach the spot where I was taken. I look for the spot where he must have been, hands sweeping the ground to find what my eyes might not see. There is nothing but the baleful glitter of clustered witches' eyes.

An ache in my head grows from a dull pain to an agony that makes my vision blur. It hurts to look up at the bright sky. I close my eyes a moment and listen to the hiss of leaves in the breeze.

I wake in the same blind, seamless room as before or one identical. Wrapping my legs with my arms, I rest one cheek on one knee. I can wait as long, longer, than they. That is the message of my ordeal in the cold. I am strong.

The woman who comes is not the one I saw the first time. This one stands, silent, until I get to my feet of my own accord, then walks off, wigwagging her hand, Follow, follow.

I do, awkward on glossy floors that never knew the sweep of a plasterer's hand or the smack of the settling baton.

She opens the door to a room. Metal, shiny and spiky, gleams everywhere.

I back away, but not quickly enough. My head explodes with pain and I fall to my knees, blind with agony. "No," I say, and, "Listen."

Masked people seize me, fit me into a metal frame. They do things that should be painful but are not, their masked faces lifeless. Corpses who breath, I loathe their unclean touch. Better to die, cold and alone, and wander the earth forever, than to be one of these cursed dead.

Toward the end one of them goes out and brings a baby in. It is my son. Baby fluff shaved, his naked skull looks frail and vulnerable. I can see the pulse in the soft spot at his crown. He seems quiet and healthy, although a white one-piece garment hides his body.

It is like the ones they all wear, men and women alike. I understand then that he is theirs, his fate out of my hands. They have told me what I came to learn but the price is high, very high.

Trapped in unresponsive flesh, I wish I'd known up on the mountainside, for, like Guapo, they have made me less free than any slave. I can feel them move this hand so far. Twitch that finger. I close my eyes. They open them and make me look where they will.

Yet I know, despite all they have done, I can resist. Must, for I want to live. To live I must seem strong and stupid. There will be times when I am on my own. I will wait for those moments, stealthy as any slave.

They will not watch all the time, otherwise they would never have let the bowman nearly die of exposure. Guapo the Fool, believing the voices in his head would guide him safely, had very nearly killed us and his child.

I wake in the same kind of room they've put me in before. Again and again, I stand and sit, speak and am silent, at their command. When they are satisfied I am trained, I awake in the middle of the endless plain, a pile of gear beside me, the knot under my scalp at the nape of my neck throbbing.

This time, they have made sure I can't come back.

Naked, I sit at the center of an enormous circle of rustling green beneath an overarching dome of blue, and cry until no more tears will come. Only when I am dry-eyed do I respond to the nudging in my mind, dress, make everything else into a pack, and begin walking: south, south by east, then east.

Days go by and I see nothing but the changing sky, the waves of grass rising and falling in the wind. There are not many birds or animals, and they go unmolested by me. They gave me rations. I eat when I am prompted to, mumbling tasteless, crumbling bars until prompted to stop.

When my shirt becomes dank with sweat, I walk bare-breasted, chest and shoulders smeared with earth against the hot sun. My boots fall apart, the hide worn to flapping shreds, and I cut others from my skirt. When those wear out, I go barefoot. My feet grow as hard as any pump-slave's.

They are not very interested in me, checking in once or twice a day to move a hand, swivel a head. I am, I suspect, used for training.

Turning and wandering through I am sure is all one vast sameness to those looking through my eyes, I make my way east into the mountains and find the stream and the cave where I spent the winter.

They have sent me far enough south that it is still summer. I sight in my landmarks and climb. After three days searching, I come to the four-stone shrine of my mother's pendant. I open it.

The turn of seasons has corroded the copper sun to blue-green. Nothing but a nugget pounded smooth and thin, and shaped into a hollow with punches, it crumbles as I try to scour it at a streamside with sand. It releases, among the shower of aqua corrosion, one bit of sky blue that I snatch from the water rippling over gravel.

It is a turquoise bead, finely carved into the likeness of jaguar woman's head. The full lips turn down at the corners into a stylized snarl, while the empty pupils of the eyes are cut through to the channel for a cord.

My bundle, freshly plundered, gives up a side lacing to hold the bead. I wish I had known what was hidden within the copper sun, but my mother would never have told anyone. She may not have known, herself.

Jaguar woman is old, older than the fuego fantasmas. I hide her in leather, whipped round, hang her from my neck. Men will kill for my bead. An unblemished pale blue, it is worth more than I am.

I come down out of the mountains and head west, intending to go south into my own country without going near the coast. Slowly the land grows harsher, the bushes thornier, the grass patchier. I wake one morning to rise, awkwardly, and look around me for the benefit of whoever is staring through my eyes.

Scarcely taking time to gather my goods together and conceal my camp, I set off in a new direction, one I have not chosen. I go straight east, toward the sea, through the great dry.

Any deviation for any but the most obvious reasons earns me a throb of pain that blinds me with tears. The hard skin begins to wear from my feet. I am, again, a thing.

I hate it.

Once I understand that each day ends at some sort of water source I become as feckless as Guapo. I make no effort to use what craft I have, even though my watcher does not spy on me constantly.

Having convinced me to obey, he sets me going like clockwork, and goes away for hours at a time. It would be easier to follow the contours of the land than to march in heedless straight lines, if the punishment for using commonsense was not so painful.

Still, my captor sets no tasks actually beyond my strength to accomplish, does not compel me to injure myself in any serious way—although he does come close—has, in short, some care for his hapless tool.

I become tolerant if not trusting. It is not until I am on the very path I fled down with Guapo that I realize that my rider intends that I return to Misericordia.

There, on my knees, retching with pain, I fight him with all I have. If my lady has died her heirs may send me to follow her. If she hasn't, my time will still be short. Lady Mercedes was old.

I struggle while the shadow of a single, stunted bush moves the width of my hand. I lose. I am, after all I have done, a slave.

Struggling to my feet, licking the acid tang of vomit from my lips, I go down the path I fled up so hopefully a year and more ago. I stumble down to the water gate, closed as it should be, and ring and ring at the bell before one of Lord Xavier's guards comes, lance in hand, to investigate.

It is Tonio, and he knows me. Even through the grate of the watch-port, I can see his eyes widen. He unbars the gate, pulls me in, and closes and bars the way again without questions. How much of a threat can one lone woman be?

His hand on my arm, I pass the open kitchen door, see the white flash of startled eyes and hear a rising babble, but Tonio pulls me past.

We walk onto the smooth, cool tiles of the main house, then without a pause into the estate office, to face Lord Xavier. He is sitting in a low-backed chair, wineglass at his elbow, lap-harp across his knees.

There Tonio stops me and we wait.

A single plangent chord hums through the room as, pick in hand, Lord Xavier plucks at the strings idly, displaying his white fingers against the inlaid wood.

I take a deep breath.

The flourish of saffron-yellow lace at his throat matches the candle-flame, and the scent of roses in the sunny garden almost smothers the smell of the expensive spice used as dye. Lord Xavier has come up in the world.

The fragrances are too strong to be pleasant. My nose wrinkles. I brush at my face to keep from sneezing. Tonio knocks my hand down.

"What is it?" Lord Xavier says, putting the lap-harp aside. It softly rings a dissonance, knocked from its tuning. He places a finger on the strings and glances at Tonio with incurious eyes.

Then he sees me. His mouth opens and the lord gapes like any lout in the street. Recovering himself, he asks the obvious question, "Where have you been?"

"North," I say, hands knotting and unknotting in the folds of my skirt, "he took me north."

"Who?"

"One of the Old One's bowmen."

A vertical line creases the fine high brow. While everyone called Leon Ildefonso the Old One, the servants did not use the nickname to their masters' faces.

The watcher stirs within me, curious.

"My lady?" I ask, as if distracting my Lord from his displeasure.

"Well," he says shortly.

I mask as much relief as I can. At least I will not die immediately. "Well," I echo softly, as if I am pleased— which I am, or I ought to be. She was always kind. I have, perhaps, not valued that enough. In this past year I have learned some hard lessons, but none hard enough to make me willing to die for her comfort.

Leaning back, Lord Xavier places his fingers on the arm of his chair, considering where to begin, but somewhere in the shadows of the room behind him cloth rustles, and he says abruptly to Tonio, "Take her home."

The guard touches my arm and I back away politely. I wonder at the Lord's lack of curiosity until the fire leaps a little and reveals the pale oval face of the black-clad woman in shadows behind him.

Her fingers stroke the blown glass quinta on a table at her elbow. There is movement inside, gray ants swarming to feed on what are I hope are dinner scraps. The ants prefer meat, and they have no objections to eating it helpless and live.

Her dark eyes examine me, oddly incurious, like those of an insect or as if I were an insect, which was the more likely. Hers is not a generous face. Its eyes and lips are narrow, and its wide jaw set too firmly for a lady.

I hope my expression is not revealing, for I am out of practice. Whoever she is, she is not Lord Xavier's wife. His first wife, that is. I have been gone over a year. Perhaps this proud, cold woman, hands crusted with rings, is his second, come with new wealth and spices from the south.

Bowing and backing, I wonder what other changes there may be. It is plain, that with more pleasant occupations on his mind, Lord Xavier has concluded I am his aunt's problem, not his.

I stiffen knees gone weak beneath me. If she still has her health, my lady's questions can be far more penetrating than my lord's. She prides herself on knowing her household and she certainly knows me.

The order being given, I am hustled out of the door, to walk the length of the town half-naked, only my ragged blanket around my shoulders, hiding my even more ragged clothes.

Tonio ignores my questions, so intent on getting me to my lady that I fear she is on her deathbed despite Lord Xavier's assurance. I, tired, mouth sour with vomit, and fearing interrogation, am not nearly as eager as Tonio.

The cool shadow of our portal passes over me then drops behind my back like a like a bar of cast-iron. Only one servant comes to my escort's hammering at the main door. One is enough.

"Dolores?" breathes Celia, before she turns and began running and shouting, voice unintelligible with echoes. They lead me in to my lady, filthy and foul-breathed as I am.

"Child, she says, and gestures.

I am no child, not any more, but I kneel so she can look me in the face, her test for truthfulness when I was. I feel her wrinkle-rough hand take me by the chin. She stares into my eyes, long and hard, as if she can see the alien watcher looking out.

But she sees nothing. It is just old age, feeding its eyes on the flesh of the young. She sees nothing but what she imagines must have happened to me. The awkwardness of my greeting is assumed to be emotion, not my hesitation at unheard promptings.

Seeing that tears hang on her lashes, I smile as tenderly as I can. I am relieved she does not question me long before she sends me off to my room, which is clean and orderly, waiting for me as if she'd known all along I'd be back—or as if my things would do as well for the next young servant who took her fancy as a companion into death.

Sitting on the narrow frame bed, I look at the jagged crack in the wall that has to be replastered each spring, and cry the easy tears of exhaustion. I feel the watcher leave me and roll, dirty as I am, onto the mattress worn hollow with the shape of my own body and sleep, not even thinking to pull open the covers.

Accustomed to rise at first light, I awake earlier than the rest of the house. I take myself down to the irrigation tank in the garden for a bath. This early, the path is cool, smooth, and all too familiar beneath my feet. I carried many buckets of water from here as a child.

I look forward to having a real bath later in the day with much pomp and heating of water to fill the servants' porcelain-tiled tub, but it is going to take more than one washing to get the grime from my flesh. The soles of my feet are black with ingrained dirt and smooth dark half-moons lie under all my nails.

There are other changes, too, from the girl they will remember. I am lean and hard, with muscles down my thighs and arms that I will have to dress to conceal, and exercise alone in my room to maintain. I remember my first escape far too well to ever willingly be so weak again.

Today I can, running and hiding, distance my Lord Xavier's men, if my unseen rider will let me. The presences let Guapo escape death, maybe they would let me too. I need some hope in my heart.

Scrubbing between my toes with my bathing stone, rinsing and rinsing, I see the water cloud with dirt. I rinse my head under the tank's infall and am back in my room, working at the tangles in my matted hair, before the house begins to stir.

As I smell corn batter browning on hot iron and hear the cackle of chickens let out of their coop, Celia's shy face peers around the edge of the door. She mimes surprise that I am awake, then comes into the room and takes my comb from me.

I lean back in the chair as her fingers loosen every strand down to the scalp without breaking a one. My lady's hair-dresser knows her trade. Intent on the worst of it, she works for all of five minutes before her curiosity bubbles over in questions. "Was it very bad?"

I take my time over a reply. Celia sounds stupid, but she is just naive. Someone I might have been if I had been luckier. We are the same age. "Bad," I say, my voice rough with memories. "I don't really want—"

"To talk about it?" she says, making another soothing stroke, then lifting the mass of my hair as if to weigh it. She brushes again, mind on her task. "That's sad. No adventures?"

"A few." No, I wouldn't have been like Celia. The life I was born to would never have left me so unsophisticated. I sit back straight, face calm, quite proper, as I have been taught.

That I am so much like a lady is entirely owing to the fact that I am a slave. Free, I would never have risen so high as to ever have a body servant do my hair.

Combing done, Celia uses an oiled cloth to bring up the gloss and begins brushing again.

Answering questions, yes or no, as the fancy takes me, I start to tell her about the cold fires. Agony flashes through my head and tears spurt from my eyes. "Ah," I gasp.

Celia takes my sudden tears to mean that there are things too painful for me to remember. She tries to distract me with what we might have for dinner, who has sent to ask about me.

My headache fades as the presence relents, its point made.

I know her better than it does. Celia's granny-tale-nourished imagination will flesh out the scanty information I have offered and some of her guesses will be shrewd.

The kitchen will have a good story tonight. Even though the tale my lady's hairdresser will not be exactly true, she will capture the essence better than the one within me can anticipate.

Starting on the local news, Celia lifts the sleek mass of my hair in both hands, pins it up, and adds a head cloth. It is knotted and folded high, as if to cover a chignon I do not have: stylish at home wear.

The lady in Lord Xavier's house is indeed his second wife, his first having died abruptly and conveniently birthing a stillborn girl, freeing my lady's nephew to marry a well-connected lady from Los Tegues.

"Ah?" I say.

Lord Xavier is now the agent in Misericordia for his wife's family. Celia thinks the family will soon begin to spend part of the year in Los Tegues, leaving the quinta here to produce fruit and vegetables for market and as an office for the spice business.

I sit very still, as if unwilling to delay her grooming even by a word.

Tongue momentarily still, Celia tucks the last loose ends out of sight, teases out a few tendrils, winding them around her finger so they curl. "There," she says.

Wordless, I admire her work in the mirror. It has been so long since my hair has been up that my neck feels chill and vulnerable, but to look at me I might never have spent time in the wilderness. "Beautiful," I tell her.

She smiles. Oh, she knows her worth, that one.

My hair properly dressed, Celia sorts through my wardrobe and finds nothing sufficiently grand for me to make my entrance to the kitchen in.

Combs, cloths, and brushes in their box, she is about to slip out the door to get one of the cast-offs my lady has given her, when I reach for the faded blue I would have worn on any ordinary morning. "This one," I say.

I don't want coddling and curiosity. I don't want to seem favored. Work dress donned—it hangs loose on my hard body—I go down the stairs with Celia, her light chatter providing a cover for my silence. "—and then he said, and then—"

The sight of my fellows, gathered at the kitchen hearth, bowls of mush balanced on their knees, grumbling their way through the same jokes, complaints, and well-worn compromises, I've heard so many times before makes me wince inwardly. Tears come to my eyes.

They look up and go silent.

Then they make me welcome.

Summoning a smile, I try to show my gratitude that their good manners keep them from babbling excited questions. I will repay their courtesy with the hard currency of tales and adventures, although not today.

Life is safe and pleasant here, but it is also boring. That I went away and came back again may be the most exciting thing that has ever happened.

After filling my bowl at the pot of boiled coarse-ground corn, I help myself generously to the honey. How long has it been since I'd eaten anything really sweet? I wipe my eyes with the back of my wrist.

Spooning away, eyes on my food, I say nothing until I hear the silence. I look up to find them all staring at me. "It's good," I offer. "Delicious."

"It's mush," says Emilio, the gardener's boy.

It is wonderful.

"Lady Mercedes will see you as usual," says Isabel.

Mouth full, I nod. My first task every morning had been to read to our lady. I hope I remember what a printed page looks like.

I take a third helping, excusing myself by saying I had no supper the night before.

Emilio and the stable boy, who had never gone a whole day without food in their lives, gawk. Celia's hand flies up to cover her mouth and she shoots a glance at Isabel, cook and manager, who flushes, embarrassed.

It was late when I came and it hadn't occurred to anyone to offer me anything. It hadn't occurred to me to ask. I've gone to sleep hungry often since I had left here. I empty my third bowl and go upstairs.

Although I am used to being hungry, I see no reason to tell them that. They failed in hospitality and my lady will be angry if she hears of it. I will not, of course, tell her. They will see that I do not lack again.

I knock softly on the heavy door to announce my presence and push it open without waiting for a reply. Lady Mercedes is up and dressed, but she is wrapped in shawls as if she is cold.

She is an odd figure on this fine morning when the pigeons are already ruffling their feathers in the warm dust of the garden. In the brighter light of day I can see how the veins have risen in her hands, and the crevices and netted wrinkles of her skin hold stale cosmetics.

Also, she is not as clean as she had been, or my time in the wildness has sharpened my sense of smell. I open the shutters wide to air the room, and she blinks at the sunshine.

Placing my stool and her chair in the best light, I wonder who read to her while I was away. Lady Mercedes' own eyes are too poor and Celia is an uncertain reader, jabbing her finger at the words like a farmer using a planting stick.

"Good morning," I say as I always said.

My lady doesn't reply, she never did, but she piles her shaky hands one on the other, and looks at the three shelves of the bookcase, intent on the treat of selecting a new book.

Normally we read them one by one, top to bottom, left to right, in order as they are shelved. "I'd like the natural history," I say. I read that when I was so young I could barely remember the pictures.

The old woman jumps and her lips part in a withered "o." "Yes," she says, as her eyes look me over speculatively, "that would be nice." Her eyes narrow thoughtfully, considering the change between us. It comes to me that her other servants have also become a shade less respectful, although no less fond of her.

The natural history is a large book, its stiff, creamy sheets bound in fine red leather and clasped with metalwork. Her great-grandfather wrote it, and his bold hand fills pages bordered with illustrations painted by his eldest daughter, who if not talented had been precise.

I lift the bulky volume from its place of pride, sit, and prop it on my knees carefully. As a young girl I heard, more times than I can count, the story of the maid, dead decades ago, who dropped it and blunted one corner.

A curious immortality, I muse, and open the book. "A Detailed Description of the Plants and Animals of the Lower Ocotillo River," I announce, "as observed one hundred and twenty-seven years after the founding." I settle into the low, clear voice that will let me read page after page.

My reading is a counterpoint to the rippling water of the fountain in the garden. I marvel at how much I never noticed. Not that having the lords' names for all the plants and animals would have done me any great good, since I would still have had to call them what Guapo had called them, but the descriptions of habitats and habits would have helped me many times.

The sunlight creeps along the floor. I turn page after page, while my lady nods in her chair. When my voice grows rough with strain, she rouses herself and dismisses me, ready to begin the day, checking the household accounts, conferring with her nephew, making her daily trip to the market where, so long ago, she bought me.

Carefully placing a marker of white leather and shelving the book, I wonder what she will do if Lord Xavier takes his new wife back to Los Tegues. Lady Mercedes has never even visited the neighboring town and she has become old and set in her ways.

Grown careless, too, for she neglects to assign me a task, an oversight that would never have occurred before. As it will never do for me to be seen to be idle, I go to the kitchen, and ask Lupe, the cook's assistant, for something to do. As I chop and scrub, scrape and peel—dirty jobs that I will be relieved of as soon as my lady notices—I, and whoever is within me, listen to the dull chatter of the staff.

In a big house, the same things are done by the same people day after day, subject to the slow cycle of seasons. A pot broken, a tool needing sharpening, a spoiled jug of milk, all are fuel for endless recrimination and conversation, yet welcome as variations in the routine.

The year turns like a calendar wheel. In summer food is saved for the winter. In winter the tools are prepared for the summer. There is something to be done all the time, nothing to be wasted: not scraps from the kitchen, not rags from the clothes.

Water, most particularly, must be conserved. Every drop must serve at least twice. Animal waste goes on the vegetables and human waste on the flower gardens.

The aqueduct supply is limited in the best of seasons and each lord or lady must pay a share for the public pump-slaves and assign others from their household to fill their private cisterns.

This morning, it is Emilio who is trying to get out of doing a stint on the treadmill. It is an old drama and the lines of the actors are well-worn, still I can feel the querulous pressure of the watcher in my head as I never felt it on my trip south: look there, look here.

By their different curiosities, there are two, one interested in how the house is run, and another, interested in how we speak among ourselves. That one prompts me to ask several stupid questions before my fellows' reactions make him—or her—or perhaps it—stop.

Days and weeks go by, and some mornings I can pretend that I never left. However, my lady is failing. Fearing her death, her servants maneuver, one by one, to join Lord Xavier's household.

Now the evenings the old house on Chanter's Way are often too quiet for my comfort. I become the household storyteller, reciting my own versions of what I read for my lady and the few staff that are left.

It seems to me that the glitter of the witches' eyes across the mantelpiece is more baleful than I ever noticed before. I am marked for death. They like death in Misericordia, as long as it is not their own.

As autumn comes on, Lord Xavier spends more days in Los Tegues than at home and takes his servants with him. I think it will not be long after my lady's death before he abandons the town his family helped found.

Lady Mercedes' ancestors' shrine will be left to the indifferent care of priests and her family's great houses will melt in the winter rains or shelter grain and animals.

No one says anything of the changes to come to the Lady. She is an old woman and deserves that much consideration. No longer what she was, it may be that she does not—or will not—understand what is coming.

The apple trees bow low under the weight of late fruit; the grapes are almost ready to be brought to the presses. Now most of those who serve Lady Mercedes are comparative strangers, servants come from other houses of the family to work for a day or two, then returning to their own places, safe from the threat of following her into the dead lands.

Most nights she and I are alone together. Stiff and near-blind, she may live years after every vestige of control slides from her once-capable hands. I tend her as I always have, knowing that I will never be allowed to find a place anywhere else.

The sweet-smelling cup will be pressed to my lips and I will walk up the steps to her pyre after she dies. Fear flutters within me like a wind bird in a cage. So close to death, I feel leathery-skinned, ancient.

I no longer have my woman's cycles. Those who lived within me have, one way or another, permanently or not, put an end to that.

My mind as barren as my body, for there is no point in dreaming of the future. I cannot make another attempt to escape unless I am certain of success, for, captured, Lord Xavier will send me to wait in the dead lands for his aunt's death.

My only hope lies with my unseen masters.

Nonetheless, every dawn, on silent bare feet, I exercise using two heavy account books from the now-unused office downstairs as weights. I grip the knobby, well-worn leather with sweating fingers, then run in place until the sweat rolls down me.

It helps control my terror.

Lady Mercedes ceases to leave the house and garden. Some days she does not leave her bedroom. I have to substitute for her, going to the market, carrying what business there is to my Lord Xavier, behaving as if she still acts for herself. I learn a great deal in my newly granted autonomy.

So do the presences within me.

With my new freedom, I attend to one thing that weighs on me. I stripped Guapo before I sent him to the dry lands of the dead and, ignorant, I sent him with the witches' eyes. I can do nothing about the latter, but for the former there is a remedy.

One afternoon, I go past the bone pits where the unknown dead, human and animal, are tumbled into the earth without ceremony, to the place where the spirit merchants squat in front of their wares.

There I buy Guapo clothes and food, all made of paper and papier-mâché, and fill a grass sack with wooden ingots of silver and gold. If he has been poor in the spirit world, now he will be rich, and my funerary debts discharged.

In a sandy wasteland splotched with ashes, I set a fire and feed my offerings into its flames. I implore the spirits to see my gifts reach him, despite their lateness, despite the poverty of the ceremony, despite my not knowing his true name, and "despite any curses that might lie upon him."

Then I scatter the ashes.

Standing there, the wind still sharp with smoke, I think of my lost son. Perhaps I should do this for him, also. He will never know me. But, if he is not dead, it would be ill-wishing.

Shaking tears from my eyes, smoothing down my dress, I walk back. I have little money left, but I have established that I can roam outside my usual ways without being stopped.

But I try not to think of that. My true self only lives in some hidden corner of my skull. For the moment my body is wholly in the possession of beings that are not kind. They play with me.

Alone, I am made to stand stock still, one hand extended, while someone practices closing and opening my fingers without my volition.

In company, I suffer many a skinned knee when it tries to walk me through some obstacle and a few blistered fingers when it makes my hand reach for something hot in the kitchen.

There are other people in Misericordia who lurch and jerk as I do when I am operated. How could I have not noticed for so many years? I know some by sight. One or two of the Lord's clerks. Two or three of traders from the south. A farmer who comes into town with his cotton. There is always the odd stranger skulking through the marketplace or watering his horse at the trough along the main road.

No one says anything to me about my acting peculiar, but then, at my lady's orders, no one has ever pressed me to talk about my ordeal at all. I have changed in obvious ways, having become tall, narrow-waisted, and fuller through the hips. An experienced woman might guess I have borne a child.

Wondering if there is a polite conspiracy of silence, I see the town I have known since I was a child as if for the first time.

Witches' eyes are embedded in its walls, roll in its dust, and are heaped in baskets in the marketplace: glittering lenses that turn dull and lifeless in a year or two and are renewed as the houses are.

When we sit in the garden after supper, the night river of stars is marred by wandering lights, by plumes of smoke and fire, by silent explosions.

Even in the daytime, as I shop and run errands, silvery pinpoints in the sky catch the sun, close but never close enough to see clearly what they are.

135

And whenever there is anything of the slightest interest, there are always the fuego fantasmas, hovering, before, behind, alone or together.

Every morning I awake missing the grasslands, the deserts, the mountains, places where I was truly alone. At night I go to sleep by imagining that is where I am.

My lady grows more withered and bent, another black gap appears in her fine white teeth, and wattles hang on her thinning neck.

Whenever I come in to wake her, I stand a moment to see the rise and fall of her chest. I have a horror of touching her dead flesh unexpectedly, as if old age is a disease that I, too, might catch.

But if I find Lady Mercedes dead in her massive bed I may have a chance to escape. On that thought, I gather a few things. A flint. A sharp steel knife. A set of sturdy boots that fit well. Nothing I don't have another reason to have.

However, choosing her own way as always, my lady dies little by little, requiring me constantly at her side to read, to talk, to embroider clothes she will never wear, to count the drops of drugs that bring neither healing nor relief from pain.

The days of my life are being counted out by the old woman's heartbeat. I am tempted to steal small things and sell them for money. I need a water skin and have no excuse to take one. I need food and have no reason to hoard more than sweetmeats.

My lady's thriving household has almost ceased to exist, yet there are too many inquisitive servants and guards lent by the day or week for me to do much more than I have. It must be unimaginable to anyone that I will do anything other then my duty.

When Lord Xavier himself comes into residence in his aunt's home, waiting for the inevitable and gaining credit as a dutiful nephew, I am trapped. Every waking moment fear flutters within me. At night I dream of dying.

In the early afternoon on a fine, hot day when the sky is pale and the shadows dark under the motionless apricot trees in the garden I am sitting by Lady Mercedes when her sleeping face suddenly slackens. I say, "My lady?" She does not answer. I hold my fear-damp hand to her nostrils. Nothing.

I know better than to allow the body to cool. Called from a glass of wine, the doctor touches the side of her throat, lifts an eyelid, then packs his case methodically, his job done.

He looks at me a moment and decides not to speak. I am, after all, only a slave, and I will not be long in following her, but I do wonder what he might have said if I were a real person.

I pace and shiver in the dry heat, listening to the wind among dust-whitened leaves, whispering, death, death, death to all the plants left unwatered as my lady's household fell into disarray. I am nothing. No one. One of the dead.

Pacing, in an agony of helplessness, I see Lord Xavier coming and know what he has come to tell me. My presence makes me bend my neck in graceful acceptance and holds my face as smooth and calm as something carved.

All I, the real I, deep inside, can do is wonder how much the saffron to dye his falling yellow cuffs of lace cost, and if he will wear a fresh pair for the funeral.

Lord Xavier speaks of it as a great reward that I will go with my lady.

"My Lord. When," I ask.

"Tonight," he replies.

I am not surprised.

It is too hot to delay and the material for the pyre has been gathered and waiting this month and more. I mouth appreciation of his courtesy in telling me personally.

I go to the woodshed, open a bag of sweet spices and sift them through my fingers. Lord Xavier has had time to be unobtrusively thrifty. I am deeply distressed that my ashes will mingle with such cheap stuff.

Stupid with fear, leaning my head against the cool adobe wall, I struggle to think. It is not done yet.

First, I should go and pay my respects to Lady Mercedes, and, after I have selected clothes sufficiently grand to be burned to death in, distribute what goods I have to my fellow servants.

I pick up a handful of dry rosemary and crush it to dust, as I look at the gate to the street. Pain stabs my head and I go, blind with tears.

Washed and dressed, lying on her bed, my lady looks better dead than she has alive for some time. The heat has puffed her skin so that her wrinkles are softened. If the burning were left until tomorrow she would become grotesque.

Miming kissing the swollen, be-ringed hand, I go to dress and take my time at it, as one might expect of someone about to spend eternity in what they select.

Although brown or gray are customary for a slave, black and blue are the death colors. I choose the fine dark indigo my lady has just given me. I knew when she gave it that it was the dress she intended that I wear forever.

A silent Celia brushes, braids, and binds my hair into a crown of plaits like the elegant lady I am not. A last gift of status, appreciation—a last kindness.

We have nothing to say to one another. She, pretty, young, and valuable, has been transferred to Lord Xavier's lady, then loaned back to this household for the past several weeks in anticipation of this day.

By her white face I know Celia has not enjoyed per-
forming her last services for Lady Mercedes, cleansing and
dressing the dead. Still less, perhaps, dressing the hair of
one so soon to die.

She will go back to her new mistress after the days of
mourning have passed. There will be a husband, and children, all the fine things her limited experience allows her to
dream.

Darkening the rims of my eyes, coloring my lips with
sweet-tasting salve, Celia sees to it I am ready to play my
part, to carry my head high in pride if not freedom.
"There," she says, approving her own work. I turn away
from the mirror.

But meeting Lord Xavier's guards in the main hall, I see
from the expression in Tonio's eyes that he had not noticed
I how I changed during my time in the wilderness. I hear
his muttering that it is a waste to Roberto.

Roberto shakes his head.

About to journey into the dead lands, I am sacred now.

No one will speak to me unless I speak.

I am alone in my mind, too. Wondering if the watchers
fear feeling me die and have abandoned me, I lean, one
hand on mud-plastered wall, dizzy with terror, then I realize that if they will not help me they will also not be there
to hinder me.

Now is the time when I must act. Once the funeral feast
begins I will never be alone again. Not even, my lips quiver
with anger, in death, if you choose to believe the priests of
Misericordia. I don't.

I go back upstairs, as if to see my lady again. I will have
to flee in a long cloth dress, without water, with little that
will that will help except what I can steal right now. My
fingers fumbling in my lady's things, I ignore the corpse on
the bed.

Her sewing kit contains the lens she used to aid her failing sight, two small sharp knives, a scissors cunningly packaged in a flat leather case. Cord. Needles. Pins. I tuck the small box into my pocket. Easy to say she gave it to me to carry in the dead lands if anyone notices.

Slipping my sturdy boots on my feet, I remind myself to walk with short elegant steps so my skirt will cover them. They were not made for the long, straight toes of anyone used to being barefoot. There is no chance I can find better in the house.

The water clock chimes once.

Perhaps I will slit the toes to make them easier on my feet. I can shorten the dress with scissors, needle and thread. With the lens I can make fire more quickly than with the flint, but only in the daytime. I still need water.

The water clock chimes twice.

Leaning on the sill of the window I have often opened and closed to begin or end a day, I look over the failing garden. I hope the dark shadow on the seaward horizon means a storm.

The water clock chimes thrice.

I touch the hidden bead at my breast. A jaguar wind will howl at the crowds in the plaza and pound the funeral fires with rain. I stare, willing the clouds to darken, climb the sky.

The water clock chimes four times.

"Delores?"

Closing the window, so that the dead may rest in darkness, I go downstairs. I give away my things with complete indifference. My fellows do very well. My lady was generous to me.

Taking my place in the funeral cortege, I am dismayed to be joined by the familiar mental pressure of a watcher. Feeling a perverted eagerness, I am sure that it is none of my usual watchers.

My wide blue skirts arranged around me, chin up, face calm, I brace myself against the jolt as the mules pull the wagon into position. In a rush, the house servants that once were my fellows pile armloads of flowers about me as if I am as dead as Lady Mercedes.

Celia breaks the taboo by placing a single, dead-ripe apricot in the palm of my right hand where it warms me like a little sun. I love apricots, and now one, ever-renewed, will accompany me into the dead lands.

Lord Xavier tosses an embroidered badge of his house into my lap, and my stiff, cold left hand closes on it. I hold it up so all can see how I am honored and valued. About to be robbed of my life and perhaps my afterlife—for who knows what thing is in my mind?—all I have is dignity.

Western sky flaming with color, I stare between the ears of the cream-colored mules and listen to the jingle of harness. We go down Chanters Way and turn onto the broader road that leads to the temple and the burning platform by the sea. There the dark eastern sky is before me.

The witches' eyes in the walls we pass seemed live with sunset fire. Piled behind me are the spices, discreetly adulterated with herbs, for the pyre. Three loads of wood follow in farm wagons. We rumble like thunder as we roll.

I can feel my the perverted thing in my mind looking and looking as best it may without turning my head or moving my eyes. It had done this before.

If I am too restless they will administer the soothing drug early and I will ride as horizontal as my lady, unable to see or feel. They will avoid that, if they can, for it is thought more fit that servants accompany their masters as alert to their whims in death as they had been in life.

Once in a long while some old fool or young idiot will elect to be burned alive undrugged to show concern for his master or mistress. On that thought, I have my idea.

141

My chances, poor though they are, will be nothing once I am fuddled. If I fail, my end will be agonizing and a disgrace, but long ago my father told me when I cried over some childish terror, "It is foolish to cry from pain you have not yet felt."

By the time we reach the temple plaza sunset has faded. In the windy darkness the torches stream sparks, popping and cracking. The mules twitch uneasy ears and shift their shoulders within their harness. Walking at their heads, the drover touches them up, runs beside them.

At a smart trot we sweep through the spectators, jolt to a halt at the foot of the wide steps. I slip the apricot into a pocket and accept Lord Xavier's hand down. He bows and I curtsy. It is the only occasion in his life when he will show honor to a slave.

Touching his sleeve, I whisper to him that I wish to set the torch to my lady's pyre. He draws back as if my breath were foul, disdainful expression saying no before the word can reach his lips.

I lower my eyes, seeing one of his clerks come forward to whisper at his ear. Lord Xavier's expression changes. He forgot the honor that would accrue from my willing, undrugged death.

As Lady Mercedes' male heir, normally he would fire his aunt's body, step away, and make a speech about the glories of her family. His family. Funeral speeches are an opportunity for an ambitious man to jostle for political position and political position means opportunities for a family of traders. But a servant willing to die undrugged is an even more powerful statement of the virtue of a clan.

He can speak afterward, if he chooses.

I, of course, will say nothing.

"My Lord?" I whisper.

Lord Xavier gives his gracious consent and turns his back on me. The commander of his guard roars the news to the crowd, which shrieks with glee. No matter if I die well or badly, I will give them a better show than they hoped for.

The wind gusts, the torch flames flatten and rise again as the lines of lanterns dance. The wind presses my dress against me, and I fold my hands against my breast, feel the hidden pouch that holds the turquoise token of my mother's spirit guide. I am the jaguar's, I can be strong.

Praising my loyalty with wine-sour breath, one of the priests scuttles to me, and, shielding it from sight, silently shows a tiny box. I look at the man's anxious face, see how little stomach he has for his job, and nod. I feel the small sphere roll into my palm. If I have no luck I may want it very much.

With glances at the ill-omened sky, Lord Xavier's guards surround the body with wood, heap the dusty bags of spices at head and foot. They pour oil over the whole, thin rancid streams that drip and run over the dark, heat-cracked stones.

I sip the proffered cup of wine. It is drugged after all, if not heavily. It tilts to my mouth a second time, but I do not drink. A third, and I swallow only own saliva

One priest watches me as the others mask and drape me in a robe like their own to show I will perform a sacred function. That done, they touch my hands and mouth with salt, honey, and oil. I will speak nothing more in this world.

"Begin," says Lord Xavier.

Men bearing flambeaux run up the steps.

The crowd screams approval.

Taking the funeral torch, lit from the temple fire itself, from one priest, I feel one next to me release my arm. My body seems very far away from me as I ascend the long stairway, the flame of my burning brand streaming away in the wind.

Once on top, oiled stone slippery beneath my booted feet, I pause, feeling the pill in my clenched left fist. Wind whips my priest's robe so it snaps, and I turn to face the dark sea of humanity, my fluttering torch showering sparks.

The crowd makes a sound as deep and animal as the rumble of the gathering storm, and heat lightning stitches the sky. A whip-crack of thunder follows instants later.

I am to kneel motionless at my lady's head amid the common firewood soaked with cheap, stinking oil, light the pyre, and breath in the flames. Eventually my charred bones will burn with the rest.

Compelled by the eager presence in my mind, I swing the torch once, to make it burn brighter, and there comes a great gust of wind, smelling of the sea. My hair bursts free from its coils, lashes my face.

Down in the plaza, the lines of swaying lanterns rock, the rope on which they are hanging falls, and oil swamps their flames. The plaza goes black, for the flambeaux have been blown out. Another gust; the torch in my hand gutters and fails. I am alone on the top of the pyre in the dark in the first splatter of rain.

A brilliant flash blinds everyone. Thunder booms.

I see the priests huddled at the foot of the stairs. They will be anxious to get the pyre burning before the wood becomes soaked. A sulky, wet smolder will not burn two bodies cleanly. One stands forth, and gestures at me.

My mouth ritually sealed by the salt, honey, and oil, my hands dedicated, I go down the steps into the lightning-startled dark to get another light from the sacred fire.

I drop the pill and put my hand on the small knife I carry for household work. Knife hand concealed in the folds of my skirt, I go to the waiting priest with the spare torch, hidden from the hundreds of eyes in the plaza.

Thunder roars on the far horizon, then lightning splits the sky overhead. I see the priest look up at the sky, eyes wide and fearful. Everything freezes an instant before the tremendous noise and the darkness arrive together.

He is the same height as I and I stand on the step above him. Something deep within me snarls, and, one hand driving the blade up into him, the other takes the torch from his grasp.

I swing it, once, and drape his arm across my shoulders to assist his dying body up the pyre to my place at the head. The crowd mutters its disappointment that I have apparently fainted as I settle him, very decorously, among the wood.

Straightening his outer robe, I pull his hood down to his chin, then close his hand on the torch and help him light the pyre before him.

With dignified haste I back away from the roar of flames and go down the steps and into the temple, merely a priest returning to his position by the sacred fire on the inner altar.

There is no one in the rain-splattered colonnade, although I can hear voices further in, where the high priests must have retreated out of the rain and wind. Almost silent to ears deafened by what has gone before, the rain begins.

I glance over my shoulder, but the red glow of the pyre holds steady. Bad oil burns as well as good, and both will float and flow on water. There is a snake of flame feeling its way down a crack in this side of the platform. Fire must be rippling down the steps on the other. I hear screams from the crowd. My lady's departure is going to be spectacular.

Hands cold as snow, I strip off my boots and priest's garment, roll them tight, and tuck the bundle into my bosom. There it becomes an fat old woman's bust, fallen to her waist. I already have blisters on my toes, so I hobble convincingly.

Hands knotting my loose hair into a bristling shrew's knot, I almost stumble on a pile of wine jugs. I take two empties and trot away, a household slave returning home after a late donation to the feast.

Rain hisses on the paving stones, and I turn into a narrower side street, drifted with sand and unpleasantly gritty under my soft feet, but giving good footing. Wet, the empty jugs are slippery and heavy, and I juggle them awkwardly.

I stop to rebalance them. I must look ordinary. Head bowed to keep the downpour from my face, I wish for the water skins of my first flight, then tell myself I am ungrateful. If things went as planned I would be dead by now.

It will be the better part of the night before the priest is missed, and if he has not bled too heavily before I got him up the steps they may not make the connection with me.

The ashes from hundreds of pyres have stained the stones too dark to show blood easily and the rain should wash the steps clean. Already the street I am on is a muddy stream flowing to the beach.

I turn again onto the ceremonial way. No one with any sense would stay in the side street. The great way is lined with basins filled with wood and oil, flames spitting and smoke streaming in the rain.

Throwing the bundled priest's robe and my useless boots into a hissing bonfire so large and hot it still burns fiercely in the downpour, I hurry on. There are ward-fires all over town tonight. Childless ghost women prey on children and my lady lost hers.

Filling the wine jugs with water at a horse-trough, I am on my way, bent like an ancient crone under my burden. I need to be a long way away before morning. The priest's body may not burn cleanly as my lady's.

Since I was forced to return, I have said as little possible about my adventures. I did have to say that Guapo took me out as I came in, by the trail near the woodpiles. There are guards there, now.

So.

This time I must leave by the highway over the main causeway, and head south toward the cities, like a hundred, a thousand, runaways before me. My stride lengthens and my back straightens as I go toward freedom.

Cold rain soaking my clothes, balancing two heavy jugs, I still feel anticipation at the names Los Tegues, Orocan. They say the alcalde's house in Los Tegues has doors of beaten silver and the temples of Orocan are roofed with gold.

Not that I will be going so far along that highway, but cities are still places to conjure dreams, at least until lightning turns the landscape black and dazzling white and blinds me again.

One hand trailing on the high curb, I walk along the deserted road. It is easy walking even in the dark: the paved way cuts across the land like a ruled line. Toward the middle of the night, the storm grumbles down to nothing. The air grows still.

At the first hint of dawn I scramble into the scrubland by the side of the road with my two heavy jars and find a convenient thicket to lie in through the daylight.

With plenty of water and thorn bushes to shield me from the sun, I am in good shape. Tomorrow, at night, if my luck holds, I can return to the road and refill my jugs at one of the horse stations.

Meanwhile I sip a little less than the comfortable minimum and watch. There is traffic, but I see no unusual haste or parties of armed men. Most travelers are official and pass without speaking to one another.

Traffic is rare enough that I have, for the first time since my escape, time to think, and I do. No one seems to be looking for me, yet. They may not know that the wrong person died on the pyre. They may be looking for the priest, not me. They would be very discreet about that.

There are rumors that the temple rats come into the brothels and wine shops in disguise, perhaps true enough to delay a serious search. I cherish a spark of hope that I may get away, have a life of sorts. Meanwhile, the sun is warm, but not too warm—

It is mid-afternoon when things change.

I have been free of the presences since the priest gave me the pill. It is a shock to feel one—strong, new—moving my head to see where I am, then lifting a jug and have me drink very deeply. It makes me eat Celia's apricot, too.

On my own impulse put the sucked pit in the sewing case, safe. I want that token of a kind gift. Vision blurring, I strive against the presence's will that I stand, look about, let it see where I am. I could die for this thing's amusement.

I press close to the earth, cheek against the coarse debris of leaves and twigs I am resting on, and wait, limbs twitching with the other's will that I rise, show myself. Finally I force myself further into the thicket. The womb of thorn branches around me defeats the watcher, and it leaves me.

When the moon comes up, pale and thin, sailing behind thin, fleet clouds, I crouch, crawl, and carry my water jugs to another place of safety, nearer the road but more hidden. There, exhausted, I sleep, arm around cool clay.

In the morning I see traders with heavy pack-baskets strapped to their shoulders and a lady, traveling with her servants going north, toward Misericordia. Couriers pass in both directions.

But my eye is drawn to the lone horseman who comes from the south. It's not yet noon, but his horse's head hangs low. He has ridden it hard and he only rides slower now because the animal is near faltering.

The rider reins to a stop and begins rubbing the beast down directly across from my hiding place. He takes his time, looking up and down as he works, until the long road is empty to the horizon in both directions. Then he leads the horse toward me as if I am standing up and waving at him.

Ridden, I think.

He stops in front of me.

Supine, deep in thorn thicket, I look at his scuffed boots.

"Get up," he says.

It is a grim, harsh voice and I obey it.

He looks me over with icy eyes and I wonder if Guapo looked so cold the night we met. Plainly this one is not pleased to see me, and how can I blame him? I don't want his company either.

I brush the dirt off my dress, check the cords that bind my wine jugs together. When I am presentable, he says, "Come," and walks back toward the road, leading the horse. Shouldering my burden, I come.

There is no question of my status. He is a master; I, a slave. He will ride and I will walk. South. Back to wherever he came from. We have trudged a dreary league or more before it occurs to him, or perhaps he is prompted, to tell me his name is Tomás.

"I am Luz," I say shortly. The priests' men will be look-ing for Dolores if they come looking at all, and I chose that name as a free woman. It is what my child's vision was: light growing in darkness and the mask of the jaguar.

The horseman looks at me with the unfocused stare that tells me something else is looking out of his eyes, and then he shrugs and lifts the reins.

His stallion, fine-looking despite dirt and sweat, has a long tangled mane and tail, both rippled from a recent braiding. When we reach the first roadside shelter he waters it sparingly. He does not groom it.

Then he pulls a dress and head cloth from his saddle-bags, along with a face mask of the kind ladies wear to pro-tect their complexions. Wordless, he holds it all out to me.

Turning my back, I strip and don it all. It is a fine dress, though not so fine as the one I took off, the mask is worn but clean, the head cloth almost fashionable. Now I appear a passable servant to a lady of the poorest sort, the kind that would keep as rough a retainer as Tomás.

"I want to be past the town where I spent the night as fast as possible," he says.

Folding my indigo gown into a pad for my shoulder, I nod. We have been in and around the town itself, not further north. None of Tomás' contacts saw me. I was visiting a sister or some such thing. We were never this far north.

He walks the horse off. I stride after. Tomás soon settles to the best I can do. He has a sharp eye and stops often to water the horse and me, both sparingly, the short stops of someone in a hurry.

Himself, he does not drink, does not sweat. It is not Tomás' first long journey in daytime heat.

As the sun gets higher, I walk mechanically, mind's eye seeing another world. Always—my left foot on the highest step, my right hand rising toward the gap of light between drapes, smelling blood, burned grain, wine—I come back to the dusty road, and the sweat-dark stallion's side.

I am bitterly disappointed each time.

Nonetheless, with my vision's return, my heart is high and my pace eager. Some of my happiness is the simple joy of unfettered movement. I have yearned for life beyond my lady's house and the well-trodden paths of Misericordia.

We make good time and by mid-afternoon we enter the outskirts of Los Tegues. I look around me with suppressed curiosity. The place is less impressive than I had expected.

And less safe, too, for unlike Misericordia, a large area of the town is outside the wall, vulnerable to casual raiders and probably lawless, given its twisting and turning sprawl of alleys.

Stopping before the double-handled hanging vase of a wine house, Tomás goes in. I stand, hand on the hot leather of his metal-decorated saddle, hoping he isn't going to spend the stifling afternoon drinking while I wilt in the sun.

But Tomás returns quickly, breath fruity with wine so new it is almost grape juice. He has bought a loaf, which he stuffs into a saddle bag after tearing off one rough, dry hunk for me and another that he holds in his teeth. He hand feeds that to his horse.

Eyeing the shop awnings billowing in the steady sea breeze, he waits for the two of us to finish chewing. Done, I blot the sweat on my cheeks with my ragged mask. Then he mounts and we are off again, without a word being spoken.

Tomás rides. I walk. The horseman is a tight-fisted bargainer, unwilling to waste a single tarnished copper. First he sells the jugs I stole to escape. He gets us everything we are likely to need, especially a change of male clothing that I don in a thicket not far out of town.

We are well away south on the great road before the second rush of traffic leaves town in the cooler hours. Our slow gathering of supplies has left plenty of people who will vaguely remember they saw us in town, but probably not when or maybe even what day.

Our alibi established, I and the horse walk until full dark, with only the occasional pause for a little water. Tomás, riding, does not drink.

One or two wagons loaded with goods drawn by straining oxen pace with slow solidity in the center of the road while we pass them on the outside at twice or three times their speed. I look at them with interest, not having seen many of their kind.

They would have come from further to the south or east, where the massive beasts work to advantage, for slow as they are, in well-watered country they can forage on the roadside grasses and thrive. Horses need grain, which means either money to buy along the way or cargo space that does not earn profit.

When the first stars come out in the east, Tomás leaves the highway, and cares for his stallion as I pile my pack and his saddle-gear. Then I sit watching him as he fills the horse's nosebag with grain, tosses me bread and cheese, and sits down to eat himself, one long day done.

Without a fire and a quarter league out in the desert we are near invisible to travelers although I can still see where the white road cuts the darker sand of the desert. I count a few stars, and yawn.

"Sleep," Tomás says, and I wrap myself in my blankets, stiff and smelling of their previous owners, and tumble into dreamless oblivion, helped, perhaps, by the thing in my head. I have not a fear in the world, although there are many I would have, had I been free.

Tomás pokes me awake at false dawn and tells me to wake him if anything moves on the road. With that he sleeps until the bright edge of the sun rises in the east. I keep watch, but nothing moves on the road, not even couriers.

The horseman slept dressed, and doesn't stop for breakfast, so we are back on the paved way and moving in about as little time as it takes to reach it.

I find my legs have stiffened and I move slowly, waiting for the muscles to warm up. He seems comfortable with that, not pressing either me or the horse.

As the day gets warmer he waters the animal thoroughly, gives me another hunk of bread, stale and tough by now, and takes one himself to eat as he rides. Mouth full, I walk and wonder in silence what is to become of me.

Whoever he is, Tomás has better nerves than I, for I jump and look behind me in panic at the distant drumbeat of a fast rider. "Messenger," he says, reaching down to grip my shoulder so tightly I can feel the bruises start.

Obedient to his hand pressure, I pace slowly on my way, someone who has come a long way, and has a long way to go. The messenger thunders past on the margin without a glance.

Tomás lifts his reins, telling the horse to pick up its pace. Whatever it is, it has nothing to do with us. For all my lady's prestige, a slave missing from her funeral does not rate a courier.

Near noon, we leave the road for the sparse shadow of a patch of greasewood, out of sight of the road but not so far away as to be suspicious if anyone should choose to follow our trail in the dust.

Here Tomás opens a small flask of half-soured wine, flavors our water, cuts a hunk of bread, a hunk of cheese, and adds a hard strip of dried meat for relish. The stallion gets a scanty feedbag, mostly to keep it from lipping the salty greasewood leaves.

Tomás finishes first, pulls his head cloth over his eyes, and, without a word to me, settles for a nap. I creep into the brush to relieve myself, find getting the pants down awkward, and then crawl further in until I can see the way we came through a screen of stems. Arms around my legs, I sit, watching.

The horse, nosing around the edge of the bushes, considers me for a moment and goes hip-shot for a nap itself. After that nothing moves in the noonday heat until a party of men come trotting along the verge.

They are looking from side to side as they come and stop to consider where we left the road. While they are conferring, I slide back into the thicket and out the other side. Tomás pulls the cloth off his face as I emerge and says, "How many?"

"Five and an officer of the wall guard."

He grunts and gestures me back into the brush.

I go.

The guards' horses have trouble in the soft soil, for they all ride carelessly, not bothering to find the firmer areas or even to stay well positioned in the saddle when their steeds stumble. Their horses are streaked with sweat and in need of a rubdown and a watering. The men stink of cheap wine and strong liquor.

Tomás, head cloth draped around his neck, rises to greet them.

"Have you seen a woman," asks their captain, "dressed in fine dark clothes, tall, and forbiddingly handsome?"

"Not since I left Los Tegues yesterday," Tomás says dryly. "And she was too expensive."

The men snort, sounding like their geldings, which are milling about, tossing their heads and nipping at one another, restless in the presence of Tomás' stallion, which is willing to give them trouble but hampered by its feedbag.

I can see their shadows against the cover of leaves above my head. If they think to look, if I move, they will see me.

The officer dismounts and asks Tomás to step in the dust.

The horseman does, not too quickly, not slowly enough to be remarkable. Apparently his print is close enough to my own in size that no one sees the difference between the two in the powdery soil. They see the trail of one, where there were two, one on the horse.

I smile grimly, face against the dirt.

Remounting, the officer rides off followed by his grubby troop.

Tomás appears to calmly resume his midday nap.

I flatten out, chin on arms, watching the clouds flee the wind and the shadows grow. It seems that we are exactly what we appeared to be, with no reason to fear anything. I admire his nerve.

Still, when we resume moving, the horseman does not return to the road. Instead we strike out across the barren waste, mouths dry and eyes itching from the salty dust that drifting on the wind so that I, turning to look behind me, cannot see our trail, only streamers and twisting veils of dust sliding along the ground.

Tomás sits his horse like something carved and I follow as if pulled on a string. The going is much rougher, so I can't judge how much distance we cover, but the plants become scarce and salt-crusted ground has become clean dry sand long before we top a dune and see the sea, restless with some distant storm.

I look north and south, try to figure out where we are, but there are no landmarks, just a blue curve of coast and waves capped with sun dazzle.

There were maps in my lady's books but they were seaman's maps. Most of the interior was filled with information about various ports and calligraphic variations on "Unknown & Unexplored."

The tide is going out and the damp beach gives firm footing to the horse and to me. Cooled by the endless wind, we can go quickly. Our trail will be erased by the incoming waves. By the time the sky over the sea is a dark blue we have come to an apparently deserted village in good repair. "No one here?" I ask Tomás, surprised that adobe structures so sound seemed deserted.

"Out of season," he says, swinging down and leading his mount under cover. Nonetheless I am glad to see he enters every building, ducking in and out of the low doorways before he returns to where I am unpacking for the night.

Looking at my hopeful arrangement of stone-hard bread and sweaty cheese he says, "Wrap it up."

I obey.

"There's plenty to eat better than that. They harvest shellfish here, but it's too hot to move them to market this time of year."

I tie the final cord and follow him down the beach to a tumble of weed-slick rocks.

He shows me how to spring the purple-shelled ovals free and starts back to the huts, saying, "Bring some weed. *This* kind."

Hand full of his sample, I look at his straight, strong back, and do as he says. It's not hard work but I am tired and hungry.

Head cloth full of my dripping harvest, I go back to find Tomás hasn't been, as I expected, idle. He is squatting, fanning a growing blaze under a pot with a little water. The utensil is far too large to have been in his saddlebags. I am about to ask where he has gotten it, when I saw that the fishers had left a pile of them, too heavy and cheap to be worth stealing.

Seeing the direction of my gaze, the horseman says, "They take the shellfish to market live, packed in weed, in kettles, ready-to-cook."

"Oh," I respond. I've never heard of such a thing. When we wanted seafood in Misericordia del Mar, we went down and bought it off the boats drawn up on the beach. No respectable cook would have served something prepared by someone else's hands. It took two servants with poles to carry the huge jug in which live saltwater fish were brought to my lady's kitchen.

Tomás grins at nothing at all.

He probably thinks I am an idiot.

So much the better, if true.

He pries the crisp flesh from the shells and I follow his example. Everything I gathered barely covers the bottom of the pot. We eat it all, soften hunks of stale bread in the juices, and eat that, too.

Smothering the fire with handfuls of soft ash, Tomás rolls into his blankets, and I into mine, and we sleep without setting watch. I, for one, don't dream.

The level rays of the rising sun in the east wake us. I roll over and get to my feet before my body completes a sharp protest. I am sore and stiff from the walking, and chafed from the unaccustomed clothing rubbing at my thighs and crotch.

Tomás rolls his blankets ready for packing, then stretches and begins stripping.

I watch and look away, uncertain if I am to follow his example or what. Squatting, I fumble my own bedding into order in time to look up and see his lean figure splash into the surf.

Every itching spot and filthy smut conspire to make me pull off most of my clothes and follow, entering the water some distance away from him with my too-large man's shirt hanging modestly almost to my knees. Beneath its cover, I scrub myself with handfuls of soft sand until my skin is pink, almost raw.

The water is warm, but you cool rapidly when you leave it for the brisk wind, and I am glad to put on the well-worn dress and to once more be a woman.

I wind my frayed head cloth in a turban around my head, spread my wet shirt and pants to dry in the sun, and lay out my indigo gown to air and lose its twisted wrinkles. I am unwilling to bury it in the sand, and the horseman has said nothing about it.

Better, I think, to take it with me than to leave it behind and confirm our trail for anyone who might follow. Besides, I may need good clothes wherever I am going. Thoughtfully, I fold it up and pack it.

Also, I want it to remember my lady's joy when she saw how pleased I was with it. It was the finest thing I had ever owned and it had not occurred to me at first that she was giving it in anticipation of her own death. She wanted me to look like a proper servant in the dead lands.

Watching Tomás swim and dive, I build up the coals of last night's fire, thinking to toast some of the cheese, but he wades out of the surf with clusters of green snail shells and we roast and eat those.

They are less good than the shellfish of the night before, still, I eat everything in my bowl and a second half-helping by the time Tomás finishes the everything else.

We clean and clear all traces of our presence from the village in total silence. Even the horse's dung is carried into the surf in one of the flat harvesting baskets. Tomás rinses it with a casual shake and returns it to the pile, ready for use. In a day or two, even a good tracker will not be able to tell we have been here.

That done, he saddles his stallion and rides off down the curving beach with me following. The tide is coming in and we go on the soft sand, speckled and splattered with foam like spit. I wonder that we do not go where the water makes the sand firmer as we did yesterday and ask Tomás.

He looks down at me and says, "Jellyfish."

I ask a silent question.

Tomás points out into the water, and adds, "They sting."

Hoof beats muffled by the dry sand, we labor on, spending twice as much energy to make half as much distance as we did the day before.

Presently the tide begins to go out and I see stranded globs on the hard, wet margin. Recognizing the fruit of the sea, I bend to pick it up. They are edible. I know, I've seen them dried in the marketplace at Misericordia.

"Don't," says Tomás, lordly on his tall horse.

Backing away, I step on another kind. I have been walking barefoot for speed and comfort and think I had cut myself until I sit down with a thump and see my foot is whole. "Ah," I says, tears I don't want to cry streaming down my face.

Tomás curses, vilely.

Not that it makes any difference. Plainly, I am going to have to ride his stallion. The sand is far too soft for us to ride double. Already the stallion's head droops and the animal takes every opportunity to doze, hip-shot, head hanging.

Tomás hoists me up, hands around my waist, as gracelessly as possible, and we set off down the beach again. We make better time that way than we did before, since his long stride eats up the ground, and I, for all my exercise in my bedroom, am not as hardened to days of walking.

Soon my foot is grotesquely swollen. Locking one knee around the saddle's high cantle, I give myself to the rhythm of the moving animal.

Presently I enter a state where I am neither awake nor asleep, but dreaming with eyes wide open, the spirit of the seabirds calling me. I fly above toy figures on a beach, the stiff little horse, the woman in a dress gray from dust, the man in seedy, travel-worn brown. The dotted line of their trail stretches across tan sand, beside azure water and foaming surf. In the distance, a gold-roofed city sits like an eagle in a cliff-protected nest.

The horse stumbles and I come to myself with a jerk. There is nothing in sight but sea, sand, and a lavender haze where the sky meets them.

My foot is shapeless, the toes sticking out like some odd embellishment. The pain lances to my knee every time the horse steps and the tears run down my face no matter how I try to stop them.

Giving up the effort, I sit, crying noiselessly, remembering the mechanical playthings they sell for the festival of the dead, a skeleton mounted on a skeleton horse whose hooves are pinned to painted wheels. You turn the crank and the thing walks and walks, yet never leaves its wooden base.

Tomás, who has been intent on the way ahead, looks at my foot, jerks his stallion to a stop. He draws his belt-knife, so quickly I have no time to react, and slashes the length of my instep.

I jerk and cry out, furious.

"It'll split," he says, grimly, resheathing the knife and leading the horse off again. "A clean cut is better."

Now I ride watching the fluid ooze out of the cut and drip from my toes. There is surprisingly little blood. The pain slowly passes until there is only a throbbing in the cut made by Tomás' knife. He has left the sole of my foot whole so I can walk again as soon as possible.

By the time the eastern sky is dark and only a hint of red and gold can still be seen in the west, my foot is near-normal size, although I cannot stand on it when I slide down the side of the horse.

I fall to my knees and retch with the pain.

Tomás walks the stallion away, leaving me where I lie.

Dinner is hard bread and lukewarm water. There is nothing to build a fire of, and the brisk wind whips the day's heat from my body.

Rolled in my blanket, I spend the night moving from position to position, trying to ease my foot. I am comforted only by the thought that since I would plainly be riding again tomorrow, it would not be so great a disadvantage if I were sleepy.

Towards dawn I limp a little distance away and relieve myself, pawing a hole in the loose sand and covering it like any animal.

Then I stagger into the warm surf and sit, letting the sea wash the oozing cut while the first flush of dawn appears in the east. It is beautiful and, exhausted by pain, I do not care.

Tomás rises and makes no pretense about emptying his bladder before he resaddles the stallion and leads it down to me. Evidently we are going to have no breakfast.

I submit to being heaved aboard and we are off. I don't know how to measure how far we have come, but I know it was a long way for a man, a woman, and one horse in so few days, further, perhaps, than anyone would normally bother to look.

As the day wears on, I become more cheerful. I am hungry and thirsty, but I make no complaint. For all the distance we have come, the pursuit, if pursuit there is, will have to be very close behind to find any traces of us.

If they have figured out what happened, then it is possible the priests roused the towns to seek out the killer of one of their own. Tomás may know something I do not. The presence within his head may be urging him on, but he seems more brisk than worried.

Now the beach is rimed with the broken lace of dried foam and weed. I can smell the dead sea-things in the tangles, rotting. That curbs my appetite for a while, but does nothing for my ferocious thirst.

I see the first thin patches of grass crowning the dunes with relief. Grass needs water. Tomás walks, the horse walks, and I sit in the saddle, nursing my foot, lulled by the stallion's easy stride.

We pass pale meadows where long leaves trace arcs and circles in the sand, geometry that is erased by the same wind that creates them. White and black birds dive into the sea in great splashes of creamy foam, only to reappear and struggle into the air, sometimes with the bright prize of a twisting fish, more often not.

Padding down the beach on four paws, empty-bellied, I sniff the air for prey. My nostrils curl with distaste. The barren sand, too flat and empty to conceal anything, is overlaid by the sharp smoke of fires, the stench of uncovered ordure, and, fainter than those, the pungent scent of spices.

"There," says Tomás.

I look where he points: a line of cliffs against the southern sky. I squint, trying to pull details out of the haze and distance, but my eyes blur and water in the fierce light, and I look at the man instead.

His teeth are bared in a smile of success.

I try to look pleased.

"Orocan," he says.

We have come to the greatest of cities and can lose ourselves in its multitudes. The towns could never enter its gates in force and the religion here is not that of the North Coast. The priests cannot claim me here. I am safe.

Glad Tomás is looking into the distance, I allow myself to feel relief. The ordeal is over and I am to see a place I have been hearing about since I was a child.

Perhaps I will become someone's maid, work my way up to owning a stall or a shop. That may interest my watchers so they leave me alone. On that thought my happy mood passes. Inside, I am still a slave.

Closer, I tell this is no city of golden roofs and silver doors, or if it is, it is an uncommonly dirty one. I can smell it even at a distance. Misericordia is far cleaner and it is not all that clean.

Tomás unslings the water skin, drinks deep, then passes it to me. I finish it down to the last drops dripped into my thirsty mouth. There is no reason to stint. However it smells, Orocan will have water and food.

Tomás touches up his horse.

I plod after him, suddenly downcast. The jaguar vision has brought back the wide sea of grass under a boundless sky, the smell of the wind from the mountains, and the absolute freedom I have lost.

It is near dusk when we come to the sea gate, passing noisome heaps of garbage on the beach where the scavenging clouds of small brown birds have given way to the nighttime rustlings of rats and the snakes that hunt them.

A single guttering torch burns at the grill-barred entrance. The man who sits idly flipping his knife into the pounded clay floor does not seem surprised to see us. He opens the gate, then lifts the torch high to study my face, and says to Tomás, "You've done better."

"Done worse," says Tomás, and, lighting a second bundle of fat-dipped reeds, he leads the stallion through with the air of a frequent visitor. The horse shakes its head, then follows obediently. It has, indeed, been here before.

Disliking the gate ward's inquisitive gaze, I pull my head cloth around, masking my face. Once more, I am imprisoned by the eyes of men.

The steep tunnel switches back and forth as it climbs inside the cliff, the smell of old trash occasionally diluted by wind through slits cut through the face of the rock. By day the place must be tolerably lighted, but at night the single flame Tomás holds high only emphasizes the gloom.

We pass great bundles of rubbish piled along the walls. Not until one curses us do I realize these are sleeping people surrounded by their possessions: a chipped pottery jug encircled by an arm; a lump of bread, its crust spotted with mold, clenched in a fist; a child, eyes glittering fever-bright, bound in its mother's shawl.

My heart thuds in my chest. What we will do if they turn on us for our whole clothes and water bottles? What if they think we have food?

Tomás seems unalarmed.

Perhaps these lowest of the low are so broken that they are no threat, or perhaps, I think, as we come to the top of the climb and I see a second barred gate, they are constrained by their privilege of sleeping within the city even though they have no housing.

At the top there are three guards, all absorbed in a game on a board. Two of them welcomed the interruption. The third, the winner I guess, looks mildly annoyed until he sees Tomás' face and laughs. "Got another one?"

All three laugh. It is not a pleasant sound and the stallion twitches its ears.

My escort nods, face neutral. They joke and try to peek under my hooded head cloth then paw through what little baggage we have until they are satisfied we have nothing of interest to them.

One gives my thigh a firm squeeze in passing. Knee around the cantle, I can't pull away, but my annoyed jerk does show him my scowling face.

The guard grins at the displeased horseman. "Hard times, boy?"

My guide grunts and puts the stallion into motion. Hoots and suggestions follow us as Tomás strides and I ride away from the guards. I can see the angry set of Tomás' shoulders, but he says nothing.

We go a good distance through darkened streets, and when he raps at the broad door we finally come to it is with nothing but authority.

I look at the heavy wooden leaves studded with the square heads of iron bolts. The town gate of Misericordia is not so heavy. What are they defending against?

A viewing panel swings open, and a wary brown eye rolls at us an instant before we hear the groan of a rising beam. Tomás leads the horse in and goes to help rebar the door.

My hands flutter like birds, clasp themselves against my breast. The place is a prison, and I am inside it. The thing within my head awakes and soothes my panic.

Wherever this is, and whatever is to happen, this is where this presence meant for me to come. I can hope it had some purpose in doing so. I can also hope it means me well.

Tomás leads the stallion close to the door and lifts me down. I feel the slimy filth of the courtyard under my bare feet and wish I had forced my boots on. I limp and wince my way into the light of the hall brazier and wait, not knowing where to go.

I stand there a good while before I realize that the servant has already gone off about his business and there is no reason that Tomás should come back. There will be another entrance from the stables.

Limping down the rough flagstones of the hallway, I pass this house's duende, which stares, eyes rolling. The first room I enter is the junction point for five different passages besides the one I come from.

One hand on the wall, swollen foot poised on its toes, numb with fatigue, I pause, unable to choose. In the dunes I could have sunk down, wrapped my clothes around me. Here I need to find people, and do whatever they think proper before I sleep. I will just rest a moment.

The odor of food rouses me. I follow my nose until I stumble painfully down a flight of steps and face a well-banked hearth at which three large kettles bubble lazily.

As in any quinta, they have soup and mush for the night staff and early risers, and a pot full of hot water ready to boil for cooking. Tomás is there, busy with a spoon and bowl. "You took your time. Get lost?"

I numbly shake my head and accept a bowl from the scrawny serving maid. Filling my belly with the hot savory stuff, I revive enough to look around.

Wits sharpened by the food, I see the girl, sitting feeding the fire stick by stick, is not so much scrawny as simply very young, all knobs and angles and long bare legs.

She looks at Tomás with hero-worshipping eyes and he pays not the slightest attention to her except when he empties his bowl and jerks it at her in token that he wants it refilled.

It almost hurts to see how her eyes caress him. I was never been so young, self-deceived, or so full of dreams. I could envy her.

The girl brings the dish, slopping full, and I can see her wince at the overflow onto her hands and the table.

Tomás describes her habits in one long physically impossible phrase and she returns to her stool, chin quivering. I see the man look sideways, satisfied at her distress.

Brooding on Tomás' petty cruelty, I finish my bowl, then look to her for more. It is good in the way of soups that cook forever, enriched by whatever extra meat or vegetables the household has, the pot perpetually on the simmer, never empty, never full.

She doesn't see me.

"Hey," said Tomás, and jerks his chin, pointing without pointing.

The servant, her cheeks wet with smeared tears, comes and takes my bowl and refills it, not quite as generously as she did his, then retires to her place without ever looking me in the face.

Just as well she did not see my sympathy, I think. That might have made it worse. Dip my spoon again, hiding my face with my head cloth, filling my ravenous belly.

When I put my spoon down, immediate hunger satiated, I examine my foot. It needs hot water, soap, and bandages. "I need to wash this," I say to Tomás.

He looks up from his bowl, eyebrows one black bar, and jerks his head at the maidservant.

She doesn't wait for me to ask her, but gets to her feet and begins assembling things. I might have had the water any time I thought to ask for it. There is a jug kept warm in the ashes of the fire.

Clean cloths and soap are stored somewhere near the outside door Tomás must have entered by, or so I guess from the horse-scented draft through the kitchen when the girl goes to get them and leaves the door curtain draped back.

Tomás reminds her of her omission with an elementally nasty mouthful.

Dodging the spit, the girl kneels and began cleaning my filthy bare feet before I realize what she is about.

She freezes, twisted, waiting for a blow, when I jerk away.

I relax back into her reach. The servant looks up and we see one another clearly for the first time.

She has beautiful sea-green eyes in a broad-cheeked face, spoiled by a raised scar above one eyebrow and a mouth that droops with unhappiness, or perhaps mostly the late hour.

Maybe this night shift is her punishment for some fault or perhaps she is here because of the man she idolizes. My expression is noncommittal, yet the girl peers, surprised, at my face, and I wonder what she sees there.

I have not seen myself in a mirror for days, but I know Tomás has grown steadily rougher and wilder in appearance. Perhaps I too look wild and dangerous. I hope not. Better not to be noticed, to show nothing.

For all I was treated better than she, I know there is, in truth, little difference between us. We are both slaves. I am astonished when she puts a finger to her lips as if I had been about to say something.

She bows to her task, wiping off the filth with a damp cloth and soap, then putting the injured foot in water so hot I grit my teeth to stand it. She dumps a whole cake of precious salt into the bowl, and I sit, drowsing as the mixture cools and draws the poison from the wound.

Tomás gets up and goes out without a word.

I'm surprised, then I laugh a little inside myself and at myself. Apparently I have been getting Tomás' best manners.

Sometime later, the girl wakes me from my sitting sleep with a touch and a whisper. She leads me to a shelf bed, padded with clean rags and straw.

I crawl onto it indifferent, for the moment, to the unknown house, the city, and the strangeness that lurks in my own head. Retreating into myself, I climb the fire lit stairs of my vision again and again until I sleep.

Awaking in an enclosed, unfamiliar place, a presence crackles alert in my mind. I lie in bed, sorting through the sounds in the nearby kitchen, eyeing the slant of a dusty sunray.

The noon meal must be in progress. They left me alone a long time, perhaps because I have no place in their routine. Not wanting to confront all those curious eyes unwashed and unkempt, I lie still and wait.

I draw my knee up and feel my foot. Stiff and scabbed, but the swelling is gone. I sigh and lie back, longing for a bath, clean clothes, even just a long drink of cold water.

My shyness is reinforced by exhaustion. After all I underwent on my journey north with Guapo, I feel this time I should be hard and vigorous. The trip south has been nowhere near as difficult as that to the cold fires, and instead I find it an effort to move at all.

I could even sleep again, if my bladder was not so full. A thought occurs to me—the house is not an elegant one—and I roll off the bed to find I am right.

Beneath the shelf is an unlidded chamber pot. I position it and squat. The my overworked leg muscles are so stiff that I have to hang on to the edge of the bed to use the thing properly. I slide it back where it came from and lie down again.

Smelling its staleness, I listen to the clatter and shouts from the kitchen. They are bringing in wood and the cook is angry at the mess.

I wonder where Tomás is, then think of Guapo, who could have been a worse man than he was. As long as I could think the boy was with his father's people, I was not sorry that was over. I roll over, face away from the door, buying a second or two if anyone comes for me, smear my tears with my fingers.

By the behavior of the guards at the gate, Tomás came often, bringing women. Was he stealing slaves? Or was this—I twist and sit upright, sorting through the clues—a brothel?

Looking at my dangling feet, I sink back down. I am a tall, bony slave woman, not a skilled courtesan; certainly not valuable enough to seek me out so specifically or bring me such a distance.

Or perhaps I am intended for something else altogether. The thread that ties the two men together and to me is the presences. It may be nothing pleasant. I need be in no hurry to discover it. Too tired to think what to do, I slump back into sleep.

Presently the shadows began to lengthen again. No one is going to come for me. As happened the night before, I am expected to make my own way around the house. It is a curious state to be in, neither servant nor guest.

I rub my bare arms, comforting my fear-rough skin, and nerve myself for the trip to the kitchen. When I limp through the door, none of the people by the hearth is familiar.

But, however the girl of the night before became scarred, it was no accident. Every face that looks at me is marked in the same way.

Seeing me, startled expressions give way to hoots of laughter that bring the cook bustling from the larder to order me fed, cleaned—graphic gesture with hand and nose—and clothed.

Not, I gather, in that order. I scurry out after the bath girl, followed by catcalls and whistles. "Ah, my beauty, come, let me put on your saddle!"

Sinking gratefully into the deep tank, I soap myself over and over in gallons of steaming hot water. Then, because I am unfamiliar with their way of bathing, I have to face the outraged bath girl when she returns with towels.

I calm her by helping her bail and scrub and refill the tank. Then I wash, dry, and polish the tiled floor alone, under her mollified eyes. Done, I understand her anger. It's a backbreaking task. I don't think I have ever had to do a household task so physically hard.

My reward is that the girl helps me assemble an outfit in which I won't look ridiculous and that no one will recognize as once being theirs. The old clothes are drab and sturdy, but luxuriously clean and fragrant with lavender and sage.

Back in the kitchen I have a meal put in front of me without a word. It is bad luck to look greedy in a strange household, and I should wave it away, once, twice, but my stomach says yes, and I may not be here long. I should eat while I can.

Not until I have emptied a third bowl of the ubiquitous soup do I realize that Tomás too is at the table. He looks at me and nods as if I am a distant acquaintance it is inconvenient to acknowledge at the moment.

I feel my ears heat and, feeling foolish, polish my bowl with a crust of bread like a child, just to have somewhere to look. I saw the truth of Tomás already. Without a word, he has made it plain I am a parcel collected and delivered, no more.

With nowhere else to go, I go back to the cubbyhole where I slept, only to find my bedding heaped in a basket by the door, the final wisps of mattress-straw burning on the hearth, and the floor damp with mopping.

The clothes I brought with me and my cherished sewing kit are gone. All I have left is the apricot pit in the totem bag around my neck. It was a friend's gift, and if it has no power, it holds good wishes.

Hoping to find some place to sit, I follow the passageway out, walking slowly. My foot doesn't flex properly because of the scab on its top, and favoring it strains the leg.

Opening one door I hear a rustle and chirp from the dark, shiver, and close it. Birds' feet, dipped in heart's-blood, can scribble the future for the priests to read. The foretelling is not a joyous event if you are a slave. It is a slave's heart's-blood that they use.

The next door opens on the blackness of a great stair smelling strongly of damp and faintly of long-dead things. I close that and limp faster, toward a wedge of sunlight on the foot-hollowed tiles.

A breeze stirs my hair as I step outside.

The place cannot properly be called a garden, although a few pleached trees throw a flickering shade. This is where the household washing is hung to dry and the maidservants sit, picking over vegetables and sewing.

Beyond the shoulder-high enclosing wall is empty sky and the ocean far below. The view is so overwhelming that I wondered they waste it on slaves until I see there is another shelf above.

That will be where the masters take their ease.

Great stains on the cliffs show where Orocan's filth has been dumped for generations. From where I sit I hear the rush of water released from washing and rinsing tubs or perhaps from bathing and sanitary facilities.

Here someone has diverted bath water to these inter-
woven shade trees. I can smell the perfumed soap, see the
bubbles among the roots. Touching the trunk of one, I
wonder if the masters even know this arbor is here.

Sometimes slave quarters are completely unknown to
the masters, and as long as the house runs, none of them
will come here. My lady would never have tolerated so
loose an arrangement, but Lady Mercedes built and main-
tained her own fortune.

I was a lucky child. It is hard to think that but it is so.

Nourished by the rain of water and debris from above, a
thicket grows along the cliff foot. In the distance, something is tossed. An explosion of small brown birds rises and
falls upon it. Like some senile old man, the city squats in its
own ordure.

I watch the sea and the sky. I wait. I will eventually find
out why the presences want me here, in this disappointing
city of legend.

The wind changes.

Wrapping my head cloth across my nose, I wonder what
the masters do, not so very much higher. Burn herbs, perhaps. I edge around a fold in the rough-hewn rock. Braziers
stand in the corner, ready to be emptied and shined, their
ashes probably saved for soap making.

Big bunches of lavender and sage swing, drying in the
shade of the arbor. There are small bouquets of mint and
parsley, ready for the pot—

I jump.

Tomás has touched my shoulder. One look at his unfocused eyes and I know whatever I am to do next has been
told to him and not me. I follow him.

No one pays the slightest attention as we leave. Three
maids pass with heavy baskets of wet clothes, on their way
to collect the dry things. Two cook's assistants sit in the

shade of the portal, scaling fish, as in a posada of the poorer sort.

In the streets, many of the people, dazed and blank-faced, are obviously not free. Tomás is not an escort to dispel fear, but, there being no better choice, I go where he goes.

The city is divided into two parts, an upper and a lower, by a natural split in the cliffs on which it is built. We entered at the lower gate of the lower city. Now we are walking toward Orocan's upper gate.

A narrow bridge spans the gap to what is, at the highest tides, a separate island. Whoever controls this bridge controls the upper city. A few axe-blows to the cables—

Legs shaking at the prospect of crossing the airy structure, I shudder as my escort grips my shoulder, in warning—or even threat.

He pushes.

I step out.

The flooring booms beneath my feet, and I set my eyes on the great stone plinths at the far end. Step, I tell myself. Step.

I nearly fall when my foot hits solid ground.

Tomás looks me over with a grim smile.

To gain a moment to compose myself, I feign looking around me, and then I really do. The two support pillars are carved from a wall of living rock four or five times the height of a man, absolutely vertical, and so polished that it shows a dim reflection of the two of us.

The path turns abruptly out of sight to the right.

Tomás starts me up with a shove.

There is a narrow stair cut up and through the rock, lighted only by slits in the cliff-face itself, although there are empty holders at intervals.

We come out of the stone throat onto the highest plateau. Wind whipping our hair and clothes out sideways, I stop and stand blinking in the bright light.

Here is the Orocan of stories.

The houses are roofed with copper, silver, gold and precious stones. Glazed tiles, I guess, seeing the vivid colors in the clear morning light. Squared and leveled by the hand of man, the platform where we stand is part of the cliff itself.

We pass the walls of splendid quintas, but there is no sound of children playing, nor of wood being chopped, no smell of fireplaces, nor of food. Nothing but the strong sea wind, the light, and the buildings built into the living stone.

The place is filled with things not-quite-seen and not-quite-heard, a buzz of sound that might be the rushing air, and might be spirit voices.

When we pass some potted trees and I see the drying splatter on the paving stones that says they have been watered recently, I sigh in relief.

I nearly don't see the first person we walk by, she is so still and so intent on her task of planting seedlings in one of the giant urns that line the road.

It is her yellow and blue headscarf that catches my eye, fluttering in the chill wind. Seeing us, she draws its tail across her face, and works on, hands stained with earth that must have been carried here by the basketful.

Presently Tomás looks around him like a man seeking a route not often taken. When we come to a corner house, its white stone walls crowned with sapphire tiles, he turns off the main way, his pace quickens. Tomás is anxious to see the last of me: that is plain.

Entering a narrow tree-shaded street, I understand why we saw so few people. We were on a ceremonial avenue, and it is too early for anyone to be going to the lower city, which must hold the markets, the storehouses, the craftsmen and women.

In leaf-dappled shade, the high city is just waking up, stretching, and tasting the first meal of the day. Its menials have already crossed the bridge and perhaps returned, too.

We come to a tall gate, stone posts decorated with tiles, its white metal panel decorated with enamel and what I take to be brass but might be gold.

It has a snarling jaguar head in the middle of its design. I run a forefinger down its curling tongue. It is like being licked by the metal. Something inside me shivers, pleased.

Tomás strikes a gong, once, with the stick chained by it.

The door is not opened immediately and the man who finally does open it does not look like a servant. His clothes are far too fine and he carries himself with arrogance.

Without a word, he looks a question at my escort, and I think, Not one of us. Unbound.

"Here she is," says Tomás, and walks away without ever crossing the threshold.

I do not look to see if he glances back. I know he won't. It is the measure of my desperation for human warmth and caring that this, this entirely predictable event, hurts.

The unbound man gestures me in and closes the gate with a complicated mechanism that lifts and lowers a heavy weight at the pressure of his fingers.

The courtyard, as clean and bare as the city outside, has plants in whitewashed jars and jugs, here splashy red and yellow zinnias, there the spires of purple tillats. Surprised by my shadow, a flight of butterflies rises as high as the surrounding wall and is swept away by the sea-wind.

The man leads me through empty, whitewashed halls to a room, shows me in and closes the door. There is no sound of locking, but I turn about, looking at the solid walls, as if he had locked me in.

I am absolutely alone in this unknown place. I have been in worse. Not often have I been in better.

The room's walls are textured by the round stone hammers that flaked it out. What furnishings there are were carved when the room itself was carved: a bench; shelves; an undercut block of stone that might be a base for a duende no longer here.

Of the earth, it is a proper place for me. I sit down, search for a watcher in my mind and find none. In that moment of freedom I find nothing more to do than to yield to overwhelming sleep.

Curled on bare stone, I dream of climbing endless stairs toward a bright, cold light. When my empty belly awakens me, the sun has moved so far that I think it will scarcely be seen as rude if I at look for someone of the household.

Perhaps I have been forgotten.

Opening the door, I call softly.

There is no answer.

I go through room after empty room and pass several stairs leading down to some lower story. At the main gate, I tug at its bar, but it is too heavy for me to lift alone and its clever mechanism defeats me.

There is nothing but silence anywhere. No furnishings, no clothes, no food, no water, just echoing rooms. There is a smaller, locked door, sunlight hot on its metal panel of leaves, but I can see nothing through the cracks around it but darkness.

I shake it gently in its frame, and disturb nothing on the other side. Perhaps it opens into another house, then, or courtyard or storage space. This might be the way the man who met me and Tomás left.

Finding my way back to where I was, I seat myself, clasp my hands in my lap like a fine lady. That which lives within me knows where I am. I rather wish it did not.

There may be people all around this house, but they cannot get in. I stare at my interleaved hands. I have not been this alone in a long, long time. It is pleasant to think freely.

There are not enough ways in and ways out for so large a quinta, even if it is deserted now. There must be others that I have not found.

The walls are more than thick enough for passages within them—someone may be watching me now through some peephole in the rock. With that thought, I stand, move restlessly around the room.

I am hungry, thirsty, and so terrified it is a relief to feel a presence in my mind prompt me to rise, go to one of the stairways, and stare into the darkness. It wants me to go down.

Touching the bag that holds my bead and token apricot pit, I do. When absolute darkness closes around me, I half turn back, wanting a torch. But there is nothing in the house, not even a piece of furniture that I could break and burn.

Down a dozen steps, make a quarter turn in a corner, then down another dozen. Intent on counting steps and landings, I soon lose track of the flights, but there are many.

My eyes see hallucinations of the dark, faint light, here, then there, then nowhere. I stop, panicked, and press my cheek against the rock, taking deep breaths of its scent.

I am the earth's.

Calmer, I resume descending until the walls are damp. Now the stairway seems to breathe, a breeze shifting in, then out, then in. I must be close to the level of the sea, with no way out but the many pitch-black flights above.

Pausing again, cheek against stone, I listen. There is something, perhaps far away, that I am hearing through the rock. It could be the ocean. Could be some huge drum, or some enormous machine.

I reach the bottom. There is still no light. My heart races and my head swims. The tunnel slants down slightly, pushes me forward step by step. Presently the footing grows slick, the stone worn smooth. I wonder who—or what—went this way so often. I slow, sore fingertips against the wall.

Behind me something pants, huff, huff, then again, more softly. Not sure if what I hear is real, I stumble, fall forward onto my hands. I can see the pale vague outline of my own stinging fingers.

There is true light ahead.

I walk slowly out of darkness into gloom, then into shadow. The walls are rough, ragged natural stone. Nearly sun-blind, although I am in the shade, I stand in a green and gold forest of ferns under a patch of blue sky that I can cover with my hand.

The footing is uncertain, chips and slabs of stone that tilt every which way, some teetering precariously and others mortared together with the dark humus of generations of plants.

I sit down, rub my legs, remembering my vision, which could be of the climb back up. The jaguar has claimed me and I will have a home, however, meager, in the afterworld.

Having won a true death, now I must win a true life.

Thirsty, I test the shelving rock, climb a bit, awkward in my dress. There should be springs higher up. I strip off, tie my dress around my shoulders. I am able to use my arms, although my legs are tired.

A good distance off the ground I come to a wide ledge covered with soil and plants. The lushness of the vegetation suggests water. I hunt until I am sure there is no open source I can reach. I sit, legs over the drop, back against warm stone.

Moved by an impulse, I draw my apricot pit from my totem bag and tuck it deep into a seam of earth. Then, muscles trembling, I make my way slowly back to the ground. It is easier to climb up than down. I take great care.

After pulling my dress on again, I hunt the dry floor of the cenote for the few hollows where rain has puddled. I lap the water from them and wish there were more.

The light begins to fade and it grows colder. Too exhausted to climb the stairway again, and not sorry to be out of easy reach of my keepers, I huddle myself in a niche in the wall of the well.

I dream the women, eyes drug-wide, falling, to shatter on the stones at the bottom. Waking with a jerk, certain I am falling myself, I lie, panting, in the relative commonplaceness of my recess in the rocks.

Something nuzzles me.

Rolling over, I know what I see cannot be real. White, with turquoise eyes, the biggest jaguar that I have ever seen stands watching me. The rough tongue licks my scabbed foot, once, thoughtfully, then it gathers its hindquarters and sits down. I grip the totem bag at my neck and am very still.

Its eyes are on a level with mine.

We look at one another until it sighs and roughly shoves me over for its own place in the niche. I settle against its warm bulk and wait, breathing its feral scent.

Compelled to touch and stroke it, I find the reason why it has sought me out hidden by the stiff fur at the base of its skull. The skin overlies a knot like the one at the nape of my own neck.

We are both enslaved.

The next morning the pair of us set out up the long stair in the dark. Knowing the distance and my destination the climb seems shorter. I stop at the moment I have seen so often in my visions. The light streaming through the half-open door—a beginning or an end?

The jaguar nudges me to get on with it. The hard climb leaves me glad to finish, sit down in the sunny courtyard. The jaguar sighs and settles down to watch the butterflies on the flowers.

Eventually, thirst and hunger drive me to search once again, opening every door in the hunt for some creature comfort. Even if I can manage the mechanism and lift the bar, I fear going out into the street. Where will I go, who will I ask for help?

Hungry too, perhaps, the jaguar follows me everywhere. When I give up, it sits down and says, "Whuff!" disappointed.

"Whuff!" I say back and it eyes me speculatively.

Beneath the imposed control I can see it is as wild as I am, and I am very wild indeed. Those who presume they control us are very foolish if they think we do not think for ourselves. It has tasted my blood. Let its watcher's attention waver and I might be nothing but living meat.

I circle through my prison yet again. The cat comes with me, sniffing and pressing against things. The house must have been richly furnished; it is still very beautiful.

Something moves beneath my hand.

I slide back the panel I have not tried before, and find a colonnade facing the sea. Water trickles from a green sea-serpent's mouth into a basin with pearly octopi writhing on its bottom. The stone-work is like frozen sea-foam, white and shadowed purple, with long-clawed crabs peering from the waves, and shells in clusters and garlands.

Cupping my hands, I drink the water. It is sweet, so sweet. The jaguar noses beneath my arm and laps. Far below us, the gulls scream as they search the shore for plunder. I lift my hair in my hands, comb it with my fingers, feel the wind and sun on my neck.

This rich, rich quinta must once have been full of life. Now it stands empty as a pestilence house, left to be scoured clean by the sun and the wind. Yet the seabirds have not roosted here. There is only the wind, and that whispers too softly for me to understand, but I guess that people come here often.

Whether they stay is another matter.

Toward evening I am mind-slaved again. I go back to the front entrance. My hand is guided to the mechanism that can lift the bar at a touch of my finger. It is hidden beneath and behind the arm-thick iron, something smooth and subtle from the oldest times.

Opening the heavy gate, I check that I can get back in—the jaguar brushes past me—and close it behind me. The pale, blue-eyed jaguar lashes its tail, once, twice, and crouches like a dog, waiting. It, too, has no choice.

I hoped that I could move unseen through the dusk, but the gloom of the east-facing windows deceived me. It is still golden evening in the high city. People stroll the streets, at least until they see me and my companion.

Seeing us, they flee as fast as they can without running, without any sound of alarm, as concerted in their action as a flock of startled birds.

In a state of clarity, induced, perhaps, by thirst and hunger, the world appears to glitter with aliveness. I can smell the jaguar pacing beside me, the flowers on the garden walls, and the salt rot of the sea blown inshore by the breeze, all at once and separately.

The watcher prompts. I go back the way I first came for a distance, then turn and climb a different, higher hill, its stone cut with steps set deep enough in the rock that it is not so bad that there is no handrail, although the sea-wind lashes my face with my hair.

I am well up the zigzag stairway before I realize I am being followed. The silent, heavy-laden crowd has baskets of fruit and bread, joints of meat, jugs that might contain water or liquor.

181

The jaguar beside me snarls at one prancing feather-cloaked man, then staggers, chastised by its controller, before coming to heel again, and pacing on beside me. I put a hand on its back, steadying it, and myself.

The dancer gives the wrist-rattles he wears a single shake and leaps, forward, back, all around the jaguar, the stiff plumes of his wings hissing in the steady wind. One broken tip pinwheels in fluttering counterpoint to his efforts. Sweat beads and runs on his arms.

I wonder if he, too, has a lump at the base of his skull.

We come out on a broad area, leveled and paved. There is a unobtrusive building overlooking the sea, so skillfully designed it takes a sharp look to see that it is not part of the cliff itself.

At the edge, I look down at the different shades of blue in the ocean. At the crests of the waves, foam burns with sunset fire. The wind lifts and tosses my unbound hair into a nimbus, lashes me with it, plucks it seaward.

I step back, resisting the pull. It would be easy to jump. I store that observation for some future, and much worse, time. I have no illusions that my riders share my morals. There may be hard choices ahead.

Prompted, I go into the building. There is a crook-legged stool and a leather drape for the door, which I untie and let fall closed. Following me, the jaguar noses it aside, pushes its way through and settles in a corner, like a hound at its master's hearth.

I sit listening in the dark. People come forward, place their burdens in the building's porch, and leave. Someone chants, once, twice, seven sacred times, then comes a whispering that might almost be the wind, and is not. Another chant, punctuated by responses from the crowd.

The jaguar stares at nothing; so do I.

When it is full night and very still, I go out and take a loaf and some fruit for myself, a grease-slick joint for the jaguar. It crouches in its corner, tearing at the cooked flesh, while I sit on my hard seat, eat, and worry.

The day's events have told me more than I want to know but not enough to save myself. I have become a goddess embodied. Living gods have short life spans. I have not come so far, done so much, to be an avatar and then a sacrifice.

I want to feel my hands coated with clay as they build a pot, to have a husband to care for me, to be among people who know me in all ways, good and bad, perhaps even to have another child, although I know that is unlikely.

Serving the whim of the unseen things in my head that have nothing to do with the earth, the wind, the fire, the spirit animals is dangerous for me. The true powers often punish the impious in subtle ways that they may learn lessons.

I am, through no fault of my own, ignorant. On the verge of tears of self-pity, I bow my head in shame. I did better than this in the past. I eat a piece of bread I do not want, out of hard-learned habit: good times do not last.

The jaguar nuzzles its bone around the floor, licks its chops, then shoulders aside the leather drape and fetches another joint for itself.

I peer around the edge of the drape, sniff, listen. There is incense burning not too far away. The voices come and go on the breeze. But no one and nothing is stirring across the empty plaza, blue with moons' light. I pluck a little roasted bird from a basket, tear it apart with my fingers, thinking.

If the watcher sees me as a counter of one color or another sliding here and there on some vast game board, I am safer. If it does not credit me with being unique or with being able to act of my own volition, I am safer. I must be ready for any opportunity. I may have little time to make my way to freedom.

Having eaten what I can, I return to the jaguar house, arms laden with food for the animal and myself. My presence makes no objection and offers no suggestions.

Will the one within answer questions if I ask in the shaman way, casting the bones or the pebbles? Perhaps it depends on what presence is there.

That moment when I stared over the cliff edge made plain to me something I did not want to know. I do not much care if I live. There are worse things than clean death.

Among my people my spirit animal would have been called to protect me. Everyone would chant to destroy whatever it was that had attacked me. But here, nothing can be done about the evil that threatens to seize me.

As I unbar the gate, the jaguar brushes against me. It is all hard muscle and coarse fur, a wild thing as familiar with me as a house cat. It is what the presences want it to be.

Watching it, I wonder if I surrender myself to their promptings will I become what these people believe I am? I shudder, knowing I am a fraud and my masters are not kind.

I must escape and take the jaguar with me. My spirit will expect it. If there is a way, the means lie in the well where I met the jaguar. I will descend again at dawn and search for an exit. I am too exhausted to begin tonight.

But next morning feather-cloaked men and women come and place the marks of slavery on me. The chains are gold-dipped silver and the slave-brand colored wax, but I am property.

The one thing I have that a slave would not have is the heavy necklace setting the mask of a jaguar at the base of my throat. From the weight, it is nearly pure gold, fine and soft, not something made to take much wear.

I remember my vision of wide-eyed women falling down the hidden well. Sacrifices. These people fear the jaguar wind, smashing sea against land, leaving the fields

salty and worthless. They think a human death will appease
the spirit of this place.

In truth, if they turned the city's back to the sea, made
the cliff pleasant with gardens and balconies, there would
be nothing they could not abandon to the wind and reclaim
afterwards.

I am a foolish, fuddled prisoner of fools. The only thing
that cheers me is the jaguar and for all I know, the blue-
eyed beast spies on me for them.

In pale morning light they walk me to the high place
again, and chant for a long time in a language I do not understand. The jaguar curls up and goes to sleep in the sun.

I want to join it, since my legs ache. Instead I look at a
distant mountain that trails a plume of snow or smoke.
Snow-capped, symmetrical, it makes me uneasy.

Around me, the show goes on, this time without an
audience. The colors of the dancer's feathers are different. I
have no idea about the chants. I wish there were drums, not
just high wailing.

Everybody walks me back to jaguar house, chatting in-
comprehensibly. Several of them obviously enjoy my not
being able to understand. I note their faces, that I may remember them.

When I ask that they bring me my clothes and gear, I get
a pitiful collection of bits and pieces, none of it mine. I give
it all back. My lady's sewing kit, which is what I hoped for,
is gone. It was a pretty thing. I am not surprised.

My jailers settle into a routine, coming at odd hours on
alternate days. There are apparently colors and chants for
each time of day, all determined in some manner I don't
know, perhaps casting sticks or stones, perhaps examining
sacrificial entrails.

On the days they will not want me, I methodically
search the upper city. I go down street after street, trailed
by the white jaguar, and see the houses are tightly packed,

hidden behind walls and gates. It is not a city to escape into.

Followed by my padding, silent escort, I come back each evening to the dwelling with the jaguar mask on the gate, where, all night, a guard stands outside. That honor means I cannot don ordinary clothes and walk away. By day, of course, I am imprisoned by everyone's eyes.

And always, whatever directs the jaguar can turn it on me if it wishes. A most fitting death, should I commit some heresy. I am held tightly. The very wind of the heights whispers fear, stinks of blood.

My best hope is the stair within the house itself. My legs are too sore to make the climb down—and up again if necessary. I cannot waste my chance if there is no egress. They will watch me more closely still if they know I hope to flee.

The jaguar cannot have been living in the well. There was no food, little water, no sign that the animal was there for even so brief a time as a day. It had to have been released to join me.

There must be a way in and out.

The half-understood jokes when I passed through the main gate from the seashore seemed cruel then, and sinister now, even when they can only kill me. My spirit has a home and I, a name. My vision, the climbing up toward the light comes to me—comes more and more often.

I do not have much time.

They hold a ceremony every other day for seven days. I walk the streets of this high city with fine cloth sliding on my skin, the weight of gold chains heavy on my neck and wrists. They dance, they chant, they return me to the jaguar house.

The weather continues fine. By day the city is a riot of flowers and awnings and flags fluttering in the wind. By night I can see lamps, candles, and grill fires everywhere, for people not only eat out of doors, but high ladies prepare dinner with their own hands. It is a happy time of year, as long as the jaguar wind does not come.

I eat my own cold suppers alone. Ever so often, the ground shivers, like a mule bothered by flies, and there is a strange smell on the wind, as if the earth is frightened.

In my bed, almost asleep, I wake when everything shakes, hard, for just a moment. The jaguar screams like a woman in pain. I get up and dress, expecting visitors.

They come, not as quite as they had before. There are babies in arms, wailing, among them and children, so sleepy they stumble as they walk. The adults awake, intent, swarm around me.

The ground quivers, again, and again, as if something stirs beneath it. The white jaguar, seemingly indifferent to the crowd, follows at my side unrestrained.

We walk in a loose group without any particular order and are nearly to the place where I crossed with Tomás before I realize that the top of the Well, if that is where we are going, must be in the lower city, not the upper.

Of course the real ceremony would be a thing for the common people. It costs the aristocrats virtually nothing to appease the superstitious: a captive, fed and housed for a few weeks, some fine clothes, some precious metal—and even that must be recovered, for I saw none in the pit. It is a very thrifty way of dealing with the mob.

It will cost me my life.

Alone with the jaguar I have passed this place and never noticed these towering piers. In passing, I touch the woven metal cables they support, the metal walls. The floor plates boom underfoot. It's all salvage from the oldest people; riches beyond calculation.

I would have crossed a bridge far less substantial had I known or even guessed it was the escape route I hunted for so long and fruitlessly. Perhaps the watcher in my mind blinded me.

Now there is nothing to do but hold my head high, keep my face expressionless, and walk firmly toward my fate. If the spirits will that I die, I will. If I am to live, I will.

Unable to see for the people on either side of me, I hear the strangled snarls of the jaguar, trapped behind me. I keep moving, leaving others to cope with the beast—if they can. There is no reason I should aid in my own execution.

Besides, I have no confidence in my own ability to handle the beast when it is already fighting the controller in its head. By the screams behind me, not all of them animal, there is blood shed before the jaguar bounds past, sending people staggering against metal walls which boom and bow—and on into the lower city.

She will be stopped and reclaimed.

Having crossed, the group forms up, me in the center, a half dozen feather-cloaked men before and beside me, their arms interlinked, caging me.

As we pass to the drone of a flute, people stare and follow, abandoning whatever they are doing, calling strange words to one another. To my ears they are cruel sounds of derision.

The plaza where the crowd stops and spreads out is on the inner curve of the cliff and not much like the one where I was before. Its stone paving has been scoured clean by the rain and sun, and probably by the hands of slaves using fine sand.

Looking back and up at the gleaming houses of the high city, I wonder which bright roof I have been sheltering under. Within in its high-walled courtyard, I could not look here, or I might have guessed much more than I did.

The place of my sacrifice, if that is what this is to be, is far more impressive than the black-stained stones before the temple in Misericordia del Mar. Inset in its center is a great bowl of sections of obsidian. Its empty bottom opens into a deep shaft.

This, then, is the Well of the Maidens. The sight is everything one could hope for of a legend. Expecting to be urged toward the opening, I tense, prepared to spoil their ceremony if I have the chance.

Instead, I am relieved of my chains and yoke and seated on a chair placed precisely on an inlaid sun. One by one maidens come forward and drank from the rim of a huge silver dish held by two men.

Seeing the reluctance beneath their bravery I wonder who will fall tonight. Nothing is offered me. That means something, but I am not sure what. I touch the soft gold of my jaguar necklace. Surely they will not spoil that.

When all have drunk, the women space themselves equally around the edge of the pit. We wait in the golden, fading light. People keep looking at the women, then at me, and I understand I am supposed to do or say something.

I have no idea what.

The crowd that presses around us begins to shove and mutter. The feather-dancers go through them, swinging their whisks for order, but there are calls for the sacrifice to begin, calls I can understand.

The mob surges forward and those nearest the edge have to struggle to keep their footing. It looks as if many will be forced into the pit if I do nothing, so I stand.

The silence is instant, except for the half-smothered wails of some infants. "Bring me a bowl and six straws," I say. Someone will have to die, but there was no reason the choice cannot be fair.

They bring what I requested, and I break one of the straws slightly short, and leave the rest the length of my little finger. I put the straws into the silver bowl they used for the drink, wiped dry but tarnished inside by some drug, stir them about with my hand.

Then I wave to indicate the two men should take it to the women waiting in all their finery for death. Forgive me, I think. I cannot see how to save you all.

The two stop by the first women, lift the bowl so high she has to strain to reach in, and pull it away as soon as her fingers close on a straw. She hides it in her hand. One by one the other women draw their fates.

Then I step forward, majestically, and open my own clenched fist to show they should do likewise.

They do.

The selected woman stands, numb, with her short straw, until one of the men takes it from her and replaces it in the bowl, then goes around the circle collecting the others, after casting one long straw into the gulf.

Without further preamble, the first woman steps over the rounded edge to slide to the empty bottom of the stone bowl and fall from our sight.

The crowd gives a deep sigh of satisfaction. No sound comes from the depths. It is done. The wind howls softly.

I open my mouth and close it as the two men move the bowl to one of the remaining five women, raise it up, and lift it away after she has made her choice. They go to a second, a third, until finally another woman displays the short straw, hands it back, sees a long straw discarded, then steps off the rim.

One by one the women are chosen and die.

It seems that I have only decided the order of their death. Standing there, surrounded by too many people to run, I feel firm hands seize my upper arms and move me to the very edge, rounded by the hundreds of feet that must have hesitated there.

Someone calls a question in the language I do not understand.

There is a ritual murmur back.

They call again.

And the murmur comes again.

A third time.

The crowd parts to reveal my jaguar bound on a litter, teeth bared in a helpless snarl. I can see her muscles bunch and flex as she fights to free herself. They tilt the litter and slide it over the edge with its unwilling passenger. The jaguar gives one long, wild scream, amplified by the deep shaft in the rock.

Abruptly it is cut off.

There are only echoes, eerie ghosts of my own primal terror. I can feel the soles of my sandals flex on the edge of the drop, smell the wine-scented breath of the two men who hold me, and know I stand not the slightest chance as they thrust me forward. My skirts blossoming around me, I slide down the steep curve, over the edge of the lower opening and fall—

No!

—only to bounce in a net stretched across the pit. Stunned by the force of the drop, I lie until the mesh contracts around me and I am pulled to one side of the Well like a netted fish.

This high up the walls of the shaft are finished in a pattern of arched openings separated by narrow, fluted columns. Further down I can see it is rough, left natural. I am hauled between two of the pillars and dumped onto the cold stone floor like any fisherman's catch.

It is Tomás who rolls me unceremoniously out of the seine.

Smelling blood and crushed greenery, I stare at his well-worn boots, his jacket, his cold, uncaring face.

Humiliated by the urine that streaks my legs, shaking with reaction from my fright, I am still able to think. They are not done with me. The goddess must be seen to live again, at least some of the time.

I get up.

Tomás drapes a feathered cloak over me, so I look presentable, then hustles me up a flight of stairs, through a door, out onto the plaza. Robe heavy on my shoulders, I walk out into waning sunlight and waxing moonlight, and raise my arms.

The crowd roars.

I stand, proud and whole, until feather-cloaked men escort me to the prison that is my home. As a reward of sorts, perhaps, someone returns my gear, including the sewing kit. I tuck that into my clothes, intending never to be parted from it again.

Left alone, I look down the dark stair, think of the carnage that must lie at its bottom, and wonder if the last goddess was surprised when there was no net. It seems unlikely she died of old age.

For two days I am left completely to myself, locked in. I grow restless with hunger and my head aches. I am being ritually purified, perhaps, rendered less potent after being inhabited by the goddess. I stare at the wall, at the sky, at the garden—being boring for the presences.

Stretching my muscles, testing myself, I think. Even if the stairway does not go to the Well of the Maidens there will be streams and underground pools, and, at this dry season of year especially, before the rains begin, empty passages cut through the soft stone by water.

In fact—I sit and stare at zinnias red as blood—Tomás' stallion splashed through fresh water streams and reached the sea gate in the base of the cliff. In one way or another, that water came through the cliff.

On the morning of the third day, the gate is unlocked. I feel no alien curiosity in my mind: a sign, perhaps, that nothing is to happen today. I must satisfy myself that the stair from this house leads to the foot of the Well of the Maidens. The proof will be the bodies of the women and the jaguar.

With no clear plan in mind, I put on more clothes than I need and sling a full wineskin full of water over my shoulder in a repurposed sash. I have no food, and two days have blurred the memory of my terror at the edge: I need to get moving.

I could go out into the city again, seek out the plaza surrounding the Well of the Maidens, get my bearings, and even get food. But now, when the inhabitants of the city are satisfied by the last ritual and I can walk freely, now is the time to go down into the earth.

Making sure my grudgingly-returned sewing kit is in the pocket I used it to make, I set out, lighted torch in one hand, a bundle of unlit ones tucked under my arm.

Making my way down, I wonder where I was at each stage of my first journey. It is easy to see things my hands did not tell me. The shaft is square, rough-smoothed but not finished. From time to time there are variations in color where the natural stone changes or where mortar was forced into cracks.

Today, I can smell the sea.

Knowing the depth and the soundness of the stair, I descend at a steady pace and find myself in the lower tunnel much faster than I remember from my first journey.

Halfway along the level stretch I smell the somber stench of death. I press my hand to my mouth, knock out my torch, and wait until I can see in the dimness.

I am in no hurry to see the horror that will be there. Head cloth lifted to cover my nose I am torn between horror and hope. Maybe the smell is something else. Maybe I have the wrong well. Maybe—

The women's faces, bright finery, and drug-dulled fear swim in my mind's eye. Only the net has spared me their fate. Reluctantly, I go forward, come out into sunlight, and stop. It is the bottom of the Well of Maidens.

Thrown by the curve of the bowl at the top of the shaft, the women have fallen into the center of the pit, become a shattered mound of bone and meat and cloth. Butterflies and flies rise from it in irregular clouds as the sated give way to the hungry.

Foliage veils the limestone walls in green. High above, high enough, perhaps that those on the plaza cannot smell the death stench, I can see a single patch of cloudless turquoise sky.

There is no sign of the jaguar. Perhaps I was not the only survivor. Maybe, she, too, fell, safely bound to the litter, into the net and was carried away to be used another day.

I turn around, thinking, looking, wondering where she was when Tomás and I first came to the gate of jaguar house. There must be another way in, one they released the jaguar from on my first night.

It may be barred, but one certain way out is better than two hoped for, and however it is closed it may only be designed to confine an animal. I laugh at myself, and cough from the stench. I didn't figure out the mechanism that lifted the gate above; I was shown. I didn't see the bridge; I was blinded.

The easy way to die is do nothing.

Backing away, I find a rock to sit down on, crush a leaf in my hand and cup it under my nose. I was not wrong in thinking the Well a pleasant place when I first saw it.

Its lower walls are thick with ferns rooted in all the natural irregularities of the stone, like a garden, although now they are dappled with blood to more than my own height. Any passing shower will wash them clean, as it must have often before.

It is a sobering consolation death had taken the women without hesitation. No one need come and check. I can see nothing of the stonework at the top of the Well, which means no one standing there can see me. I am unobserved.

Moving around the edge of the bottom, I push aside the drapery of fronds, looking. I turn in the wrong direction and so I am two-thirds of the way through the circle and about to quit my search and rest a moment before I find the tunnel.

The opening is not even deliberately concealed, just a darker break screened by drooping foliage. I step into it, and see its floor, crusty with sand, is dimpled by the pugmarks of jaguar. I follow the trail, although my torch is beginning to flicker.

I must know what lies here.

There are empty cages lining the tunnel, still stinking of carnivore's dung. I smell her warm, live body before I see her, fur streaked with some unguent, her turquoise eyes half-closed in daytime doze.

She rises unhurriedly and comes to the bars of her cage, then licks my hands with her rough tongue.

Putting my hand on the latch, I pause and consider. With her with me, I may be protected against casual interference, but I cannot become anonymous, just another former slave seeking to make my way in the city and the farmlands around.

Also, I have no way of controlling her, and it may be that her controller can observe me as mine can observe her.

There is little good that could happen to her, and I am sorry for that, but I will be fortunate if I save myself. I leave the gate closed.

As I turn away, she gives a long sigh and settles in her straw again, her dappled hide blending into its dim gold. I touch the bead at my throat, but that does not comfort me.

I must hurry. At any moment, someone may enter my head and check on what I am doing. The passage winds from side to side, sometimes narrowing to little more than a

wide fissure in the rock, then broadening out to a something comfortable for three or four abreast.

Finally it becomes a cavern that domes upward. Slabs of
stone fallen onto rough rock show the underground chamber is the start of another natural well.

I can hear the sigh and whisper of the sea long before
yellow-green reflected light begins to dance along the
walls. I dowse what's left of my torch against the sandy
floor and tuck the stub into my bundle.

I may still have to go back. This is the place to set a
guard or two, or for there to be some living space for the
jaguars' caretaker.

Creeping along the wall, ready to flatten against the
stone at the slightest unnatural sound, I see nothing but
rock walls and floors littered with the debris of past storms'
fury.

Climbing up and over a sill of mortared stonework and
down a series of ledges that make an irregular stair, I find
myself on the shore, amid the stench of the city's garbage.

I am free.

Behind me the cliff wall is inset with a stone mask of a
jaguar, warning enough even for those who cannot read.
There are tiny figures of people to the north of me, near the
door of the lower city, gathering what they can from the
tide wrack and Orocan's refuse.

Slipping from shadow to shadow, I leave the forbidden
zone. There are a dozen or so scattered scavengers out after
the tide, gathering weed to dry for fuel. Slave's clothes look
like slave's clothes, and that mine are of expensive fabric
will not be obvious from a distance.

Once among some rocks, I rise up and work my way
down to the shore. There I bundle seaweed over one arm,
and mimic what I have never before seen done, until I
round a headland and am out of sight.

Then my walk becomes purposive.

I don't abandon my dripping armload, the smallest thing may mean the difference between life and death, comfort and misery. Walking on the hard, wet sand left by the tide, I try to remember what I know of what lies further south.

Between joy at my good fortune and my own thoughts, I have forgotten the watcher in my mind. I am surprised to feel the nudge; whoever-it-is is astounded.

My head swivels involuntarily, then I turn in a full circle. Seeing nothing but sea and cliff and sky, I throw down my bundle of weed, pick it up, then stand motionless and uncomfortable in the glare of sunlight for a long time, resisting the pressure to return north.

Muscles straining, I stare at the straight line of the horizon, the glitter of sunlight on the waves, the dark specks of the fishing birds hunting trough and crest, and think of absolutely nothing but standing here, in this place, with the wet sand drying on my clenched toes.

A long time later, a different presence releases me from my rigor, lets me stretch and ease the pain of long-abused muscles. When I begin walking south again there comes a suggestion I turn north.

I ignore it.

The suggestion comes again, more insistent.

Still I ignore it. I haven't forgotten the pain they can inflict, but the worst they an do is kill me and whatever means they chose are likely to be less terrifying than falling again and again into the pit never knowing if today would be the time no one rigged the hidden net.

Whether it is the degree of my resistance, curiosity, or simply that it will be difficult to restore me to my place as goddess without my cooperation, the presence leaves me alone for the rest of the day.

With long, determined strides, I walk south. In late afternoon, I make a fire in a safe place, using the slanting rays of the sun and the lens in my lady's sewing kit. With fire and in concealment, I can spend the night in relative comfort.

Wading into the surf, I use my loosely woven head cloth to net finger-long tiny fish. Split open and baked on a hot rock, freedom's food is as good as anything I ever ate.

Rolling myself against the stone wall of my shelter I sleep until the cool half-light of false dawn wakes me. Awake, I set myself moving as quickly as I can.

The watchful presence will take advantage of any hesitation to turn me north, so I walk south at the tide's edge, one foot in water, one foot in sand, one foot in water, one foot in sand.

I watch my left toes print themselves into the sand again and again, walking, walking. Pausing, I look at the single line of footprints that dots out my track. Seeing them, I walk further into the surf where my feet will leave no prints even for the time between tides.

Where am I going?

I have been a child, a slave in Lady Mercedes' household, then subject to Guapo and Tomás by circumstances, ignorance, and timidity. The only choice I chose to take was to go back for my son.

My eyes constantly search the ragged rim of cliffs and the level line of the sea for any observer, but there is no one, not even the one that lives within.

I cross the first stream of sweet water, pausing only to drink my belly full; I cross the second stream without even bothering to drink; and also I cross the third, although three is a lucky number. I must not do anything predictable.

When I come to the fourth stream, shallow and winding its way across the beach, I stop and find a flattened pebble the size of my thumbnail, mark it with a scratch on one side, and flip it. Scratch I go up it, plain I go on. It comes up plain.

Fingering my scrying stone, I go on, wondering if I have the nerve to bring off what I have in mind and if it will amuse some one of the presences in my head sufficiently that it will cooperate.

If I have understood anything at all about those who watch me, then my ability to entertain is what may give me a chance against them.

In the marketplace at Misericordia, black skirts draped over their wide-spread knees, a half-dozen or more old women wait to tell your fortune, and mend it, too, if it turns out badly.

Lady Mercedes made fun of them in public; in private she sent her kitchen maids for advice. Offering as much commonsense and simple medicine as anything else, the brujas probably do more good than harm.

I am a striking, if not handsome figure, tall and stern. I, and the knot at the back of my head, know more about the world than many. I have my reading to help me too.

Without consulting my stone, I take the first small stream that offers itself, and gather fresh-water crabs and sand-cress for my supper. Away from the beach, I soon find a hollow in the dunes, start my handful of fire, and sit nibbling cress while the shellfish steams between two pads of seaweed. I come to a decision: I will be a wise woman.

Busy thinking of chants and bits of ritual I can weave into a convincing whole, I eat, bury the remains of my meal and of my fire, and move off to find another place to watch the wandering stars and sleep.

When morning comes, I walk south again, thinking of how to evade too-direct questions, how to answer the unanswerable, when to tell good lies. Long used to watching my surroundings while thinking of other things, it is growing dusk when I look about me with my full attention.

The land is becoming one with the sea. Tall marsh grasses obscure the horizon, the distant bitter wail of the

gray and white seabirds has given way to the nearby chat-
tering of the speckled chits that run up and down swaying
stems, their beady black eyes watching me, incurious and
unafraid. I am too big and different to be a rival for their
tiny kingdoms.

Now I camp for the night, rise at first light and walk on.
There is no reason I know to hurry but now I eat my only
meal at noon and that is often cold. I am confident in my
intuition and heed its urging to make haste and leave no
trail that men alone can follow.

The presence checks on me only twice a day now,
roughly an hour before dawn, when the cold and the fading
of the stars has already awakened me, and an hour or so
after sunset when I am settled for the night.

Otherwise I go about my business unhindered.

I am seldom uncomfortable with the cold or heat, and
rarely need more than an hour to dig, catch, and prepare as
much as I care to eat. My biggest problem is the flies that
rise from the bogs in a black, stinging mist that follows me.
The land changes as I go, and always as I go I look for any
sign of others' passage.

Days go by, and I do not grow careless. I know the
heart-shaped prints of the marsh deer, and the long curves
of the four-eyed sea snakes come ashore to hunt turtle eggs.
None of them are what I fear and hope to see: the sign of
other human beings.

Alone under the high, blue summer skies, I am, in a
way, the happiest I have ever been. I savor the air, the water, the food, the strides of my strong legs, experiencing
every moment, knowing that this cannot last. Nothing does.

It is a bright afternoon, with enough mist in the air to
promise a cold evening, when I see it. Time was, when the
half-slumped hollow in the beach sand that marked the end
of my isolation would never have caught my eye, let alone

called me to turn aside and crouch over it: a such little thing to make so much difference.

Someone walked here barefoot the evening before when the sand was wet. Whoever has a small foot, with the big toe well-separated, may sometimes have worn sandals but did not wear boots. I judge it about twelve hours old. A child's, or a small adult's.

I look around me, smelling the wind, watching the dip and fall of birds over the marsh. There, the flutter of chits disturbed enough to fly, but not to flee in haste. I drape my veil over my head, check that the hilt of my knife is both hidden and ready to hand, and go to make my first appearance as a wise woman.

The person who crouches, digging clams from the sandy flat is somewhere between a girl and a woman, and does not take alarm when I step from the grass and stand watching her. That tells me they see strangers here. I am not entirely pleased about that, but I have already revealed myself.

She stands, wiping muddy hands on muddy dress, and lisps an inquiry.

I respond in confident tones. I ask where her village is, although what I say does not matter. We do not speak the same language. I have not understood her question or she my answer.

Her eyes seek the jaguar mask on the necklace at my neck.

In the days alone I have become careless of covering it.

When she taps the base of her own throat in inquiry.

I cover the jaguar with one hand, and my eyes, briefly, with the other: this is a thing not to be spoken of rashly.

She nods, apparently satisfied, gathers her digging stick, two baskets, the board she was kneeling on, and signs I should follow her through the tall canes clicking in the breeze.

The path is as narrow as a game trail, wide enough for one carefully placed foot after another. I take care to step exactly as she does. I can smell the green depths of the bog. It would be easy to die if one strayed.

The village is a cluster of huts woven from the reeds, seemingly ramshackle and hard to distinguish from the surrounding marsh. The girl hangs her two baskets from a pole outside one door and goes to another, bends forward and calls softly. A hoarse voice answers from within, then clears its throat and speaks more plainly.

We go in.

The interior is plastered with mud, decorated with scratched and painted designs and figures, making the whole tight against the searching wind. For all its outward appearance this village is not much less permanent than Misericordia with its grand adobe houses that melt in the winter rains.

The weathered man who stands to welcome me is not really very old, perhaps ten years more than myself, but his face is seamed and lined with days spent baking in the sun, squinting into mists, and being chapped by winter cold.

He is near naked, wearing only a piece of soft leather passed between his legs and looped over his belt before and behind. Braided into a cage of fibers, a witches' eye is hung around his neck.

It is the first I had seen in a long time. The coast I came down was free of their baleful glitter. Had I stopped earlier, I might have remained more free, but this seems to be the place I am destined to be.

He is not surprised I don't speak his language, and having listened to my short pleasant greeting, he switches to mine, and we converse, slowly and simply.

The girl who has brought me is his granddaughter, Mist. He hesitates just long enough to tell me that she has, as I might have guessed, only just chosen her youth-name and has not yet been vision hunting.

Mist, I think, and wonder why she picked something so ephemeral. I would not have thought it a propitious choice and perhaps her grandfather did not either.

Eyes on the necklace at my throat, he inquires, with civil indirection, if I have powers. I say I have, although I am still learning how to control them. He is pleased at the answer and I am glad I didn't tried to claim more. Honesty established as the standing between us, I relax a little.

The headman asks what he may call me, and I say, Cat's Child. He nods as if he had known it beforehand. He offers his own use-name, Eye of the Sea, then, settling to his haunches and gesturing to me to do the same, he discusses where I might live, a polite way of inquiring if I am going to stay. Their wise woman's house is vacant, he adds.

I ask if she is away.

No, she died the previous winter of a coughing that she could not heal. He names the others that died on his fingers, for I cannot believe he has the number correct at first.

I look at the huts, room for nearly three dozen people, and count who is here. Although some would be off hunting and others gathering, their numbers seem sparse.

"How many are you now," I say, glancing away politely.

"Less than twenty," he answers.

"And the coughing? Is it still among you?" I fear the wasting disease that comes with bloody spittle. It is incurable, although with great care, a patient may live a long while.

"No," he says. "It took all it could, the season after the traders returned from the island."

We look at one another, it not being necessary to say what a disaster this was. Many of those I can see are young children, and even they have been set to work, for every stick of firewood, bundle of reeds, and string of smoked fingerlings moves the group a bit further from cold and hunger, and this is summer.

I explain that I have little skill as a healer. My talent lies in prediction and farseeing. Looking at him, I expect to see disappointment on his face. Instead Eye of the Sea's eyes blaze with interest and he begins to press me more closely.

Puzzled, I explain again that I can sometimes see or know things at a distance but that I have as yet little control over what I see. I regret my skills are not more useful. I want to make the matter plain beyond any doubt despite any barrier of language. Once again I expect disappointment when I pause.

But the headman nods to himself, obviously exceedingly pleased, then stirs his tiny pot of fire and throws a pinch of strong, sweet herbs upon the coals. The tent fills with the fragrance intended to carry gratitude to the spirits, whatever ones they honor. I will need to know. Beyond that there is still some threat or uncertainty here I do not understand. I must find out what.

Wondering if Eye of the Sea is one like me, I watch him carefully as I will watch him from now on. It will be seen as no more than the proper attention owed a headman, and I must be certain. My time in Orocan has taught me one harsh lesson. You must learn as much as you can as fast as you can and not waste opportunities.

I ask what the village is doing for a healer. Eye of the Sea says they pay several man-loads of dried fish a month for Mist to go south and study with another village's wise woman. His granddaughter shows promise as a wind-witch, and perhaps she may marry south one day and they, in turn, send a daughter north in exchange.

An alliance, I think. That hope, at least, goes some distance toward explaining the odd choice of name. Perhaps it is considered suitable for a wind-witch's student in the village where she studies. Perhaps her teacher picked some-

thing weak to guard herself against the child's innate un-
controlled powers.

They sacrifice in the Well at Orocan to the jaguar wind
that comes in the stormy years in the warm months of
summer, driving water against the sea-cliffs until stone
shudders and cracks, crumbling into the wild foam. How
much more terrible the storm would be in this flat and de-
fenseless land. A wind-witch would be a great asset.

I nod in my turn, and murmur something about its being
a sensible arrangement. To avoid tempting evil spirits, I am
not too congratulatory. I wonder aloud if I can find someone who will help me direct my talent.

Eye of the Sea shakes his head. He knows of no one in
the marshes. Indeed, if I stay here and can tame my talent
to see worthwhile things, like where the fishing is good and
if there are raiders up the coast, I might make myself and
the village stronger and richer. New people will come from
the other villages and they will bring much-needed skills
and talents.

"But you will be welcome in any case," says Eye of the
Sea, resting strong hands on muscled thighs. "It is hard,
with so few hands to do the work, and although children are
welcome, someone must tend them. They can only do so
much for themselves. They must be children while they are
young or they will never be strong adults."

I dip my head in agreement, though my own life does
not make me sure it is so. They need full-grown people.
Even a barren woman with no talents would be as useful as
many a man here. As it is, I am very valuable.

Sitting cross-legged, resting my elbow on my knee and
my chin in my hand, I feel the pressure in my mind. If
whatever-it-is is going to cooperate then now is the time for
it to offer me something to give Eye of the Sea in earnest of
my talents. I wait, silent, to see if it will.

The vision comes. It is as if I stand above the earth on a high, invisible cliff. I can see the tiny wrinkles of the waves crawl up the beach and the dark shadow in the water that is the fish, feeding in the sea-grass.

Unprompted, I lean forward and begin to draw in the clean sand decorating the hut floor. "There is a place that looks like this, where the coast comes in and in again, and then goes out next to a huge rock of white and gray."

Eye of the Sea nods.

"There are fish there."

The headman doesn't bother to nod a second time. He is out the door, calling to the men and women scattered around the village.

The great net, heavy and stiff, woven of grass, is kept in the roof of one hut, where I guess the smoke of the fire protects it from insects and other pests.

They lift it down, placing their shoulders, one by one, under the huge roll as it slides off the beams. They jog away, preceded by excited children. I follow, carrying empty baskets with the rest of the stragglers.

We climb the last low dune to find the children already in the water across the mouth of the bay, and the seine unrolled on the beach, its handlers preparing to walk it into the surf. The headman waves his arms and the children began to move as the mesh floats out onto the waves. They clap the water with their cupped palms, producing rhythmic smacks that are very loud even on the beach.

Eye of the Sea leans sideways, one ear under the water, and smiles. "The fish are coming," he said. Everyone begins to sing. I can see the net handlers moving more and more slowly, and the headman calls to first one then another. He waves his arms vigorously and they walk toward each other, closing the purse. Wading waist-deep through an ebb and flow that glitters with escaping catch, I look at Eye of the Sea.

"The net will burst," he says, "if it is too full."

"And the gods will punish you if you take more than you can use," I say sternly. The headman stares at me. I have never heard myself use that voice before.

The handlers came up the beach with the waves, chanting, using the surge to push the net higher on the beach, then bracing themselves to stop it from being sucked back down.

I am proud I had been able to bring them this moment—yet I do not believe this was what Eye of the Sea had in mind. There is some other reason he is so eager for me to stay and I must know what it is, and soon, very soon.

This place is not so far from civilization as it looks, for south of here, past the Salt Marshes, the jungle begins. The jungle that trades parrots, monkeys, and dye-root to Orocan and north.

Fish are tumbling, flashing silver as the handlers tow the seine onto wet sand and open it. The haul leaps frantically as eager hands reach in and begin stunning and gutting.

Every adult bends to their task and the children run up out of the sea to thread the carcasses onto reeds, sides opened out so they are two flat fillets joined at the backbone.

I stoop and take one fish up. I have not seen the like before. It is the length of a hand, silver on top, white on the bottom, with a dark gray line down the side.

Flopping and twisting in my palm, it leaps free, to lie writhing, salted with sand, until it wriggles down to the wet margin, is seized by a retreating wave, and departs with a flash of sunlight on its tail. I rub my hands together and smell them.

"Come again," says Eye of the Sea, softly, at my elbow.

I look sideways at him. He is speaking to the fish.

When the headman crouches to the work, I crouch, too, watching his hands, doing as he does. Everyone does, laughing and joking, brown hands slippery with fish blood and scales.

Only when the sun leaves the sky do we scoop the last of our catch, whole, into baskets, and carry it back to the village, to finish the gutting by firelight.

I fall asleep with the rest, deaf to the mob of seabirds quarreling over guts and bones on the village midden, at what I hope is at a safe distance from us.

Sometime toward dawn, I hear howls and yips but whatever they are they come no nearer. None of the sleepers around me gets up, although I see eyes open, and then close, unconcerned.

I go back to sleep. I have passed the first trial.

Next day I turn my efforts to refurbishing my hut, a fine one, a full ten paces across, but in some disrepair. Mist comes to help and to show me what to do, constantly pointing out and naming objects and people as she works.

By evening we have hauled in two loads of fine white clay, replastered half the interior, and I know most of the names of the people in the village and twenty or twenty-five common objects.

That night I sleep in my own hut, stomach full of roast fish and smelling of the fug of sweet grass that fills our clothes and hair even as it drives off the bugs and dries our catch hard and translucent for the winter or for trading. A good day: I have done well.

Yet that first impression of Eye of the Sea, witches' eye watching from its place against his chest, stays with me. I have not found the exile I wished. The presences will be watching me.

The days go by. I do not waste them nurturing my talent, but spend them as the rest do, gathering the fish and birds we will need to survive the jaguar winds and the bitter cold that will follow.

Hands gritty and stinging with the salt we pack ducks in, I wondered how much better the cities would be if their priests had less time to elaborate their jobs. I pack salt onto another duck. It was my good luck that they were wrapped up in their priestliness.

Winter will give me more than enough time to sit, brood, and talk to whatever is in my head. For now, having been given a place to fill, I must fill it well. Even the presences may understand that there are not enough people here to allow anyone to do nothing but study the omens.

The heat turns oppressive and the air is still and heavy. When I go down to the bathing place and find a brisk little breeze whipping the tops of the grass and making tiny whirlwinds dance between the reeds I rejoice, and splash into the water.

Then a presence seizes me.

My joy dies. From high above I see a vast vortex of cloud and winds. Up to my knees in salt water, I look at the oily, irregular heaving of the bay and the pale green of the sky with new insight. I leave without my morning bath. There will be water enough, and soon.

Running up the now-familiar path, I trip, stagger, and run harder, my feet splashing mud high onto my skirts. I find Eye of the Sea sitting inside his doorway, staring up at the sky.

"Storm," he says.

"Worse," I respond. "The jaguar wind."

He looks at me sharply.

"I have seen," I say, and squat and draw my by now customary outline of the coast and an arrow of the storm moving toward us, directly into the bay.

Everything between here and the coast is boggy where it isn't outright marsh. "Will it flood?" I ask urgently. It seems obvious that it would.

He purses his lips, refuses to agree. "It may turn away."

"No," I say. "I have seen."

The corners of his mouth quirk with what might be annoyance. Not many people use that tone to him. "It may not," he agrees, looking out the door at the grass flattening under the hissing wind.

"I have seen," I say the third time.

He looks away, reluctant to listen.

There is no high ground between this and the next village. We have all our winter stores here. We cannot move everything to safety, and if we stay, perhaps we can keep the stilted storage huts safe, and wait out the rise in the water.

But, if the water rises too fast, we may all drown. "We must build rafts," I say.

Eye of the Sea looks at me, waiting for me to explain further, weighing the worth of what I have said, perhaps. Perhaps just resisting unpleasant reality.

"Rafts," I say. "From the cane, and load everything we can on them."

Still he does not respond.

I believe what I saw when I touched the seawater. The storm is terrible and it is coming. There is no time to waste. We must make ready.

Rolling my eyes back up into my head, so all the headman can see is my blind whites, I sag, "Ahhhuu." I tip over so fast my feigned swoon almost becomes real.

I hear the headman's footsteps as he runs away, then his voice shouting orders. Once set into action, he must know more about how to do such things than I. The smallest children are gathered into the raised hut with the preserved food, and we women, with a wary eye on the sky, cut stiff grass and plait extra bindings. The men go to hack the canes.

The sky goes gray-green and the air grows chill. We all work faster, not wasting time looking. I can feel it," I say, chanting, "I can feel it." The jaguar wind is not far over the horizon. "Not long, not far," I say as my fingers fly and the others bend to their work, silent, intent.

Fast as we women braid, we have to sacrifice the communal fishing net for enough cord to bind everything together. I wince as the seine is pulled apart.

If we survive, it will take weeks of work to repair, but a small village, no matter how prosperous, does not make great coils of twine on the off chance that one morning they might be needed. There is always something more urgent to do.

By the time we have bound the canes together and moored them loosely to the food hut, a fine rain is falling and there is a film of water underfoot. Not too many minutes more and the mud will be dangerous for the smallest. The paths to the beach are already impassable. We crowd together, grateful for the warmth of other bodies. Someone begins to sing, and a few others join in.

I have too many things to worry about, and retreat into the privacy of my hood and robe. Lightning cracks a jagged whip across the sky, and everything that can bend flattens in the wind.

It comes.

The huts shudder and sway, and I think of the carefully plastered interiors cracking and crumbling with the stress. Then the real downpour begins.

I can see nothing but the swift play of black and gray clouds and livid lightning, and the silver of water filling the low spots everywhere.

The rafts are buoyant enough to lift all of us, but while they are still grounded the water, warm as blood, laps up between the reeds, making our feet and legs wet. The wind whips away our bodies' heat.

Eye of the Sea leads us in gnawing dried fish while there is still light to distribute the pieces. We will need energy to keep ourselves warm through the night.

It is so dark I think that day will slip into night without our noticing, but when the livid sun does go down it is as if some giant hand placed a bowl over us.

We are trapped alone with the cold, the wet, and the feline cough and scream of the wind. I can feel my companions move restlessly, but there is nowhere to run.

Then the rafts dip and heave, pull free from the mud beneath. I clench my teeth, make no sound. I hear others gasp. If my idea is wrong, there is no longer any chance to change plans.

The food hut is beside us. It is an enormous temptation to climb up into it, to be protected from the unending tapping of drops on head and shoulders, but the structure has not been made to hold more than three or four people at a time, and every gust makes it sway alarmingly.

The smallest children on the rafts, bundled into their mother's, aunt's, or elder sister's clothing, wail a high, thin counterpoint to the wind.

On the edge of the raft, near the building, I jump with fright when something big and dark looms up close to my side. I put a shivering hand up and feel knotted grass and knuckled stems.

We have risen so far off the ground that we are near level with the lower platform of the food hut. There is more than a man's height of water under us.

Not until the sky begins to clear and the light of two feeble quarter moons shines over the marsh do I come up with any useful strategy.

I can see the bright flash of people's fright-wide eyes as they look around at the desolation. There are no familiar landmarks besides the battered food hut and our hastily-constructed rafts.

We float at the center of a vast well of cloud, and its walls, twisting and billowing in unfelt winds, formed our enclosing horizon.

Everywhere there is a shining sheet of water broken only by dark patches of brushes and cane ripped from their footing and woven together by the storm.

One drifts close to me, and I look for something to fend it off. It will be filled with desperate marsh rats and other vermin.

But the men, more experienced than I, are ready with poles and heave the drift away. They stand around the edges to distribute their weight, ready for more.

Still our haven rocks, precariously full, bound to the hut that holds our future for the coming cold. A great barricade of flotsam is accumulating against its windward side.

Eye of the Sea and I confer. Since the wind will be changing direction when it returns, I am for pushing the debris away and retying our rafts to the other side of the hut. The headman is for staying where we are: a second set of knots, made with wet, strained cord in the gloom, may not hold so well as the first.

I think of swimming in the cold, murky water to resecure the rafts and am quiet.

He does not say, although we both know, that one or more of us might die in the effort. I think it worth it; he does not. I do not challenge him. He may know better than I what is possible here and now.

Gnawing and sucking a piece of dried fish, I watch the glitter of moonlight on the heaving flood, and wait in the oppressive calm. I lick my fingers clean and softly chant a song my mother sang. Most of these people will not know the words, but its message of home and peace and plenty may be understood anyway.

It is almost a relief when a gust ripples the waters. There is a buzz of gossip before the wind rises to full strength.

We have passed the halfway point, we can hold out, we will make it.

I have not counted on how much colder and tireder we all are, and how stiff our fingers and slow our reactions have become.

Reed is the first to lose his grip. He and his pole go so quickly that no one can help. We hope that he will fetch up on one of the floating mounds and wait out the storm with the other refugee animals. No one stands a chance in the floodwater: deep, cold, and filled with debris.

There are others forced overboard, torn from clenching fingers and desperate hands. One child slips from its mother's clothes and is lost in the surge without even a wail. After that Gull screams continuously, reviling the jaguar wind by name. The others ignore her, hoping not to attract her bad luck.

The air is a bloody red that heralds the rising sun when the hut lurches free from the mud below and sails before the wind, dragging our raft after it.

Crouching, hands locked on the binding ropes, I hope we are being pushed toward the low hills to the south of us. If we are going out to sea with the tide we will not make it back.

It is cold in wet clothes with the wind clawing at us. Not even the children complain, hungry and tired as they are. The faces of the adults might be made of stone, expression-less.

Now we sit tight together, well centered on the raft. Water sucks and laps at out feet. Not even the clouds ripping to shreds to bathe us in pearly pale light lifts our mood.

With a shudder, we ground, gritty mud sucking at our craft.

I look at the white-faced headman and we both laugh. We aren't going to die this time.

The men drive the poles deep, deep into the quaking mud. We watch debris stream past us, traveling out to sea with the retreating water.

I chant my song again, with a voice so rough it has no meaning except that it may reassure or be taken for magic. We sit close together, and wait.

Small animals creep towards us from the drift-masses that we pole off. Harvest mice. Water rats. One solitary exhausted hare that flounders away at the last moment.

Much of the wildlife will have been swept away and drowned. I drum with the heel of my hand on the water and a few weary mice retreat to their tangled refuge.

Some will sneak past in the dark, drawn by the smell of food, but everything is packed to defeat them. I am willing that they keep their lives, if they can.

Right now we need to feed everyone and to secure the hut somehow. I crawl about, counting by sight, touch, and voice. We are three less adults than we had been. Four, if you consider Gull useless with grief. I don't bother to count the children. We will keep those we have left as safe as we can.

I issue instructions, batter down fear with practicalities.

Surrounded by water but with little to drink, we wait while the skies become flat gray and the marsh vanishes in fog.

Gull screams all the time we are stranded on the sand bar. I bore my own loss with more dignity, but perhaps my child still lives.

It is raw and miserable although we have plenty to eat and, once we set pots out, more cold water than we want to drink. We wait three endless days, watching our refuge shrink and swell as the waters around us rise and fall in response to tide, wind, and the rain that comes and goes and comes again.

When the pale and watery sun breaks through the clouds for good the afternoon of the third day, we gather ourselves together, pole toward the mud flats that were our home, looking about us as we go.

Eye of the Sea and I exchange glances and say nothing. There is nothing familiar. The land is scoured bare in places, whole islands torn out and washed away, and on those that are left the vegetation will have little time to re-cover before winter will be upon us. The migratory fish and birds will go elsewhere.

The food we have already gathered won't be a total loss if the sun tomorrow turns hot and we can dry it again, but some of the more recently dried fish is fuzzy with mold. It might do as bait, if the turbid water settles fast enough for schools of fish to come inshore. We decide we must dis-pose of it, lest it foul what is still good.

We ground the hut and the raft. Scouts prowl about, paddling improvised boats, looking for some flat place to begin rebuilding.

There is no sign of our former village. The huts have been completely swept away and the sandy mound where they were is covered with a tangle of uprooted bushes.

We are able to build a fire to make a soup of sorts from water and fish, although it is not hot enough to dry the fuel to keep it burning through the night.

The next morning Eye of the Sea and I draw apart and confer. Still new to my role as wise woman, I am pleased to be consulted, and have to strive mightily to conceal it. Craving power will be a weakness of mine; I had so little in my earlier life. The headman, used to responsibility, sighs, rubs his face, says, "Shelters first?"

"Dry the fish?" I reply.

"If we can find the fuel," he says skeptically.

We send most of the adults out. What is pulled from the water now might dry enough to be useful by evening. The small sticks and limbs the children are already piling may save our food. They are such quiet children, it frightens me. They will remember this.

Agreeing to build on the high ground rather than wait for lower and formerly more favorable sites to dry, we mark out temporary shelters and space out the fire pits even though there are no walls to surround them yet. We must think ahead, avoid wasting effort.

The women, especially, are displeased that we will be so far from sweet water. There will have to be a rotating team appointed to haul for all. But we will be safer from storm surges.

Our priorities are shelter, fuel, rafts to move things on, and food. When we can we must trade south for more clay cauldrons for water. The fine basket grasses will not grow long enough again this year, so we must do what we can with cruder materials.

Delaying the permanent solution to the water supply means that more energy has to go into solving it day to day. Failing to erect shelters means some might die of exposure. Our supply of food is spoiling but there is nothing to dry it with. We dither back and forth. No choice is guaranteed to be the best one. All is clouded with whether our luck is good or bad.

Finally, Eye of the Sea looks at me and I at him, and we both agree to start somewhere, rather than debate further. "Shelter," he says.

"Yes," I reply, "and a temporary kitchen, near the water. Something we can afford to lose."

Having decided to decide, things go better. By evening, what fuel we have is smoldering under fowl brought down with birder's nets. For that, at least, wet wood is useful, and its heat can dry what we will need through the night. We eat well that night, and have shelter from a passing shower.

All through the struggle I did not make a bad decision. I am proud of that. At dawn Eye of the Sea says only children should turn the smoked food and feed the fires beneath it. The adults will use their strength to find building materials.

We have a bit of luck when we go down toward the coast and find, not far away, a drift of things driven inland by the storm, among them huge trunks of trees. Wood is rare and precious in the marshes: this find is wealth if we can split and cut it. The largest, if we can claim it, is fit to make a sea-going canoe.

At the moment, that one is beyond our ability to handle, but there are plenty no thicker than a strong man's thigh, and we heave and haul to separate those we can from the tight-packed mass. One by one we float beams back to the sand bar, lay the long trunks out lengthwise, and break off the smaller branches to build fires at the points where we want to burn the logs across.

Half the children are sent scurrying to bring water from the hummock's edge to wet down the trunks and keep the logs from catching, while I crouch and coax the coals of the previous night's fire into new life.

I go from place to place, starting the burning, calling to the women to set the racks of preserved food in the billowing smoke, and to the other half of the children to bring the grasses and herbs that will season it.

The fires will fulfill two purposes at once. I have extra fuel, grasses, and herbs pilled near, and stand back to survey the purposeful activity.

I would have had a hard time giving orders, since I do not yet know the women well, but Mist followed me, carrying the tackle, doing as I did, an example to all.

That underway, we reverse roles and I follow Mist from person to person as she struggles to cure the ills already present and prevent new ones. There is a hot bitter tea for everyone and salves for scrapes and cuts.

A lot of time is spent on making the evening meal plentiful and varied, for we find roots torn from the bog and driven in windrows, along with the herbs, grasses and seaweed.

At long last screaming Seagull, exhausted and dosed with a tisane, sleeps, while all around her the world becomes ordered again. I hope she will be better when she wakes, for we need every hand we can get.

Nonetheless, the mere absence of her keening makes the world a better place for the rest of us. Except for those on watch and tending the fires, we sleep, soundly and deep.

The next morning, heavy-eyed and slow moving, Gull silently joins us and is, as silently, welcomed.

We work hard through all the daylight, sunrise to sunset, every day, and in partial shifts throughout the night, always with one eye on the changing patterns of the clouds.

If it were to rain hard again before we can get what we have under cover, we can still lose our hope of survival.

Still, we have hope.

There is so much wood that we can afford to build massive double walls of uprights driven into the ground with horizontal branches between the inner and outer uprights. Thicker than my forearm is long, such walls will withstand most storms, although not, perhaps, the one we had just come through.

We drive the piles as deep as we can, pack the spaces between the two walls with coarse fill, baskets of pebbles and clay from the stream delta to our north.

Later we will build up our island.

Now we erect huts, plaster the inside with white clay, burn it hard with flaming twists of grass. Winter will do to paint and decorate them. Next spring we will build more solidly.

Eye of the Sea remarks he may not live to the time when those huts will have to be replaced, for the true jaguar wind only strikes every dozen years or so.

Even now only the roofs, bundles of reeds bound together in the old way then tied onto wrist-thick arches made of more reeds, are very vulnerable. If we search carefully, we may find enough flat rocks to weight them down, but, for now, reeds are one resource we do not lack.

By the time the marshes have a brittle skin of ice on them in the mornings, we are secure and provided for if the winter is not too hard. We have done well. I am proud of myself, and strive not to show it.

The burning and scraping that will make a sea-worthy canoe from the huge log that we have floated and hauled to the village has been underway ever since the storm. It only requires one person to keep an eye on it.

Serious work on that is a project for deep winter, after we have built a hut over the log. For now whenever the weather is foul the canoe is turned upside down, to keep the inside dry.

The morning comes that Eye of the Sea says the marsh had frozen for good. We stop, exhausted, silent, and spend a day doing almost nothing, roasting tubers and fish in the fire, singing, and sitting, happy, still.

The rhythm of our lives changes to winter.

One cold clear day I spend alone, gathering frosted sand-cress to liven the communal soup pot and to have time by myself to think.

Whenever sun blazes on ice, it reminds me of the tracks across the sky above Misericordia. Here the skies are never marred by white trails and there are no fuego fantasmas.

For weeks nothing has stirred in my mind but my own thoughts. I do not admit, even to myself, that I hope for freedom. Real freedom, such as I have never known since I was child. In some ways, I am child still.

Because I still do not have many of the skills of an adult woman, I often do the work of the men or the children. That will have to change—or I will have to learn things only I can do.

When I can I search the stream banks for precious pieces of obsidian that can be flaked into crude replacements for the metal tools the village lost and has not been able to re-place.

The traders did not send word among the villages to come to the usual autumn meet on Trader's Island north of us. The headman does not make much of it in public. In private, Eye of the Sea worries.

Perhaps they know we will have little to trade in such a bad year, but there are trading partnerships going back a generation and more, and once or twice the traders have given some grudging credit in order that we have tools to survive the winter: this year, nothing.

The biggest trading meet is in the spring, when the glossy winter pelts of the marsh weasels and striped reed-hares bring high prices. Hunting and trapping as always, we let everyone assume our partners will come then, that it was the storm that upset the regular round of things.

The marsh-dwellers all know how little the tools cost the traders, though for us they are expensive. They could afford to be generous this year.

Resentment floats from village to village, so much so that the headman journeys to our neighbors to give and re-ceive advice about what we should do if the traders never send word.

Eye of the Sea and I sometimes spend the evening hours at our own small fire, free to admit doubts and ignorance and explore the other's knowledge.

Occasionally Mist joins us, and we squat together, wor-rying as I remember Lady Mercedes worrying about her estate, but while she schemed for comfort and prestige, we fight for survival.

The days grow shorter and darker and we listen to stories by the fires as our hands work at the hundreds of things needed to replace all we have lost.

I learn how to fortune-tell, refusing some questions, and so giving more good answers than bad. I am learning what I hope will be my true trade and finding it to be a good choice.

During the daylight hours we roll coals in the deepening hollow of the dugout we are making, and scrape the char away before leaving the log lightly dampened for the night. The work could go faster, but we fear a smoldering fire that would destroy both good luck and weeks of effort.

The sun turns, and we celebrate with double rations and a little of the dizzying liquor made from the honey for which we had traded ten man-loads of wood and two of dried fish.

The days grow longer and the larder leaner, and we watch for the first signs of new growth with anxious eyes and flat bellies.

And finally spring comes, little by little, and the marsh melts and turns green. Day after day passes and the traders' messengers do not come.

I am anxious, and not just for the village. I don't want be seen by outsiders. There has been time for this odd happening and that strange occurrence to form a pattern for someone clever.

Following a thought that grew while listening to tales around the fire all winter, I decide to make a solitary expedition south, glad to exercise my skills and reassure myself that I can still survive on my own.

The whole village turns out to see me off, believing that I am on a vision quest or something equally spiritual. It is easiest to let their assumption stand. It is even, in a way, true. I shoulder my bundle and leave without fuss. Most wise women are taciturn and it suits me.

The beaches slowly turn from black sand to gray cobble as the days pass. I weave my way west, then east, then west again about the great mountain range that plunges into the sea, trailing off into steep, uninhabited islands white with birds.

Night and day the air resounds with the grind and clatter of wave-battered stones. Rough water, broken by reefs and shifting heaps of gravel; bad fishing, and so not much explored.

Alone, I am happy in my own company. On the fifteenth day, the sky to the south is no longer the shifting blues and grays of the sea-sky, but a shimmering uneasy white, the sky of an oncoming snowstorm, although the air is far too warm.

I watch for the cloud cover to drift higher in the sky, for fog to come creeping over the churning sea. The air stinks, and the very foam of the waves is gritty, filled with floating pebbles like nothing I have ever seen before.

My vision of light comes every night—a warning, perhaps—and yet for six days more I walk toward that vast, towering whiteness until once again I stand before cold fires.

I am not even surprised. Perhaps shrieking seabirds fly above it, perhaps gaping fish swim below it. But for a human being, it is impenetrable.

Summoning the strange overview that the presence had sometimes been willing to allow me, I find that there is nothing I can see beyond the barrier. Not light, nor dark, nor a blank within the map in my mind, nothing.

Here my world ends and so must my journey. Shivering, I let the picture go, and sink down to rest, to think.

There should be jungle there, for that is where the parrots and monkeys are supposed to have come from. Gold in the streams, they say, and people eager to trade their turquoise, azurite, malachite, and silver.

Obsidian, especially obsidian.

Eye of the Sea suggested I seek obsidian on my journey south, but I cannot pass the cold fires. I rise and turn back immediately. I have an idea that lingering would be a bad idea.

I wish I had not tried to see beyond the barrier. Still, nothing speaks in my mind. Maybe the presences have forgotten me. Maybe the long nights staring into the fire bored them into leaving me for good.

Maybe it will be a cool summer and a warm winter. Maybe.

Exploring the shoreline, I retrace my steps. Glad though I am that there is somewhere for me to go back to, I am not eager to return to the village.

I have lived better, and both the fear of death and the novelty of survival living have left me. I remember apricots. Sometimes I almost wish I had not left my apricot pit in the Well, although I have not seen anywhere it might grow.

Rounding one cape, I come upon a beach strewn with bones: long bones like tree trunks, hipbones with arches like doorways, skulls so large a man could crouch in them and look out of empty sockets bigger than his head.

Vast creatures, mountains of flesh, died here and were stripped by the air, sea, and the gray ants that swarm everywhere. I wade out into the water to avoid the voracious insects.

Further along the tide line is strewn with the rotting remains of other beasts like nothing I have ever seen: things with milky, blind eyes and mouths that opened sideways; delicate discs of flesh like fine lace undulating in the waves; and others so singed that it is impossible to tell what they once were.

Over it all lies a smell so strange it is like taste, like touch—no, completely indescribable. Now I wonder if these are what lies hidden by the barrier of white fire and, if so, who is on the inside and who on the out?

The barrier of cold fires stretched away in what seemed a straight line, but I know from Lady Mercedes' book, *On Navigation of Planetary Surfaces*, that a small section of a very large circle might look straight.

I squat, drawing in the sand, trying to remember the words I mouthed but not understood. Sometimes my memories are willing to yield up their knowledge.

But what I remember this time is too full of unknown symbols for me. I doubt they had meaning to my lady, either, although she did tell me how they were spoken. "All-fah. Bee-tah."

She enjoyed the sound of my voice, a soothing murmur in the high, cool room where she spent a quiet half hour before a busy day. I made a music of words for her, nothing more.

Carefully, I use my forefinger to scribe a passage I once recited and consider it.

There is a hissing, far too close for comfort.

I turn around.

A pillar of burning white is coming toward me. One hand pressed against the wet sand, I get to my feet, slowly. Too frightened—or too wise—to turn and run, I shuffle backward as it advances, the beach steaming where the whirlwind of flames passes.

It looks like a fuego fantasma but I have never seen or heard of one acting like this. Hot urine streaks down my thighs, splatters the sand, as, in a wave of incredible pain, my muscles pull against one another all at once.

Something makes me stand still. Then the thing inside my head uses my mouth to make three distinct sounds like nothing I have ever heard before. "LEAVE HER ALONE!"

The pillar hunting me drifts back.

Shocked, I startle myself when the three sounds come from my mouth again. They are words, I think as I stand locked into place by some other's will. Words.

The pillar flickers, retreats, slowly, down the beach, around the rocks, hissing over the sea, until it is out of sight. Perhaps it becomes one with the distant and unseen barrier.

Released, I sit down on the wet sand with a thud. Hunting has taught me to see camouflaged prey, yet I cannot believe what I saw within the pillar of flames: a human being or something very like one. They are people who do these things to us.

The presence that seized me leaves me as abruptly as it came. I stay, sitting, until one of the many gray ants scavenging the beach nips me.

I wade into the water to make it let go. Looking onshore, I see the sand around the tide line carcasses now seethes with ants where there were none before. They will attack me, if I linger.

Day after day, thinking about the implications of that swift and unexpected intervention, I head back, gathering useful herbs, seaweed, and the occasional bit of black glassy stone, making up the load I will bring back as justification for my trip

Night after night, I camp, and, eyes on the stars, brood. Men did these things to me, to my child, to Guapo, to many others. I would like to do things to them.

I have a spirit even if I do not have a name, and it would be honorable to die trying. Even nameless children can die honorable deaths. Nonetheless, I will not court death, like some. Being alive is more wonderful than it has ever been for me.

There is a cleanliness to the sea, earth, and sky absent from the places of men. If I sit and watch them long enough they may tell me how to understand what I know. Who I am. What is beyond the edges of this world. Who the presences that look through so many eyes are.

I must return. I set a stiff pace, pressing against my native reluctance. Even before I can see our settlement, I can smell the smoke and drying fish that tell me most things are well. For an instant, I am tempted to camp one final night, alone on the beach, to enjoy my solitude.

There will be decisions to be made as soon as I show myself. Sick to be tended, perhaps. On that thought, I lengthen my stride. They were kind to me, a stranger. I owe them my life.

When I start down the trail through the reeds, I hear someone running ahead of me. They have started keeping watch, then. My influence has held while I have been away. I drawn in a deep breath. Good.

Before I left, I suggested a watcher but the idea was rejected: there were so few adults that no one could be spared. In the daytime, though, a child, wise in the way of the marshes, will do. By the size of the footprints, it is one of Water Lily's twin boys.

Wondering if they guard our nights, I climb the palisade's entry ramp. Mist has my cup out, is making me tea already. She smiles welcome. Suddenly I long for night, my place by the fire, and sleep, deep and long. I have not slept like that since I walked south.

I put down my basket, and gesture to Mist, who will know what to do with its contents. She hands me the bitter tea and I squat by her as she sorts through my haul, exclaiming, questioning.

At my back a babble of voices tells me what has happened in my absence. All the problems I walked away to consider are that many days more urgent.

I set my empty cup down, make decisions simply for the sake of having them made and no longer bothering the headman and myself. Mist refills my cup without comment until I am done.

The villagers seem glad to yield up their anger. I would have wondered why there were so many matters left unresolved, if, my sight made clear by my journey, I could not see that Eye of the Sea is no longer what he was.

He sits, huddled on himself, eyes sunken, dozing.

The past winter strained the fiber of the headman's being, shortened the span of his useful days. Now he is an old man in truth and not just in weathered appearance.

He wants nothing more than a warm place when it is cold and a cool one when it is hot, and some small child to run here and there on little errands.

I look at him, hunched within his great cape of skins. I would feel sad if I were not so angry with him. He should have been good for another decade, long enough for one or another of the younger men to learn how to do a headman's job.

Village custom dictates a man hold the position, but no matter who holds the witches' eye of authority, the eye of the sea as they call it, the job will soon be mine by default if I do not find someone else to do it.

As for the thing itself, knowing what I do, I intend to take and burn it, if I can. Far away, on some beach where its white fire will flame unseen by any villager.

Eye of the Sea's death and the time for me to act might come suddenly. Meanwhile, I wear my obligations lightly, for when that time comes, I want to be gone. Not for me the comfort of this quiet village with its simple problems of survival. I am done brooding. I have larger concerns, larger obligations.

My hope lies in Mist, who may make a suitable marriage if her father holds on long enough. The villagers will accept the son-law as they would have the son, if he is a man for the job.

She stands little chance of attracting such a match as things stand. Our village is not yet rich enough, although the sea-going canoe we will soon have, the pilings that reinforce our islet, and the sturdy walls of our houses have brought us many more visitors than the place has seen in years.

But it will take metal tools and imported ornaments for us to be accounted truly prosperous. Although there is a good stock to trade, nothing has been heard of the traders while I was away.

The scant double handful of obsidian shards I gathered are welcome. We have two people with the skill to shape stone, and the brighter boys crouch watching, envying, and I hope learning.

By the hearth fire, everyone wonders, but they don't yet doubt that the traders' messengers will arrive and things be much as they were before. I say as little as possible and that cheerful.

North is where our best markets are. When we trade away south and west, the pelts and fish we have to offer are worth less, being luxuries, not necessities, in those warm, rich lands.

I have kept to myself how far south I went and that the way is closed, at least on foot. Good or bad, we will make no trades in that direction. Not this year. Maybe never.

Log by log we break up the last of the storm-built drift and put a low retaining wall about our reinforced islet. We lack only a secure water supply to be a self-contained fortress.

There is talk of driving a well down past the clay that underlies the marsh, although we are so close to the beach that there is doubt that the water would be fresh.

Remembering Orocan on its high cliffs, I suggest cisterns for rainwater, but the men began driving the well, intending to fill the islet to the top of the shaft's inner cladding if they hit freshwater. If not, they will close the bottom and make it a cistern.

It's an ambitious project: the villagers have grown used to massive undertakings, with only a few women doing the gathering and cooking, and the children supplying fresh fish.

While I was away the crude work on the dugout was finished, and day by day it is set floating and brought ashore again and again, as the workmen use sand and stone to smooth its surface and refine its balance. It is so good a boat that they cannot abide the slightest flaw in it.

The day when they will give it eyes and it will become live is not far off, and already people are leaving the project to gather clay, stone, food for next winter.

The smudge from the fires for smoking fish does very well to keep off the insects, and I roam far and wide for herbs to add to it.

Our smudge of smoke, hovering above the marsh, is a boast of how well things are going for us. I hope that distant young men and their fathers look at the horizon and think of the benefits of marrying Mist.

By late summer things are so well in hand that we and the next village, Small Cove, have time to talk together. We set a day, clean, paint, and replaster everything, build a firepit to sit around, bring in extra food.

I am pleased—and amused—when the entire unattached male population of Small Cove turns up with their faces patterned in festive white, waving wands of feathers and fur that boast their hunting skills.

While the young men parade for Mist and our two other nubile young women, their elders and Eye of the Sea decide to spare two of us and two of them for an expedition up the coast.

The traders' messengers may have come to some of the peoples scattered along the sand dunes and islands of the shore. If so, we can show them that we are still here, still worthwhile trading partners.

Small Cove has a heavy dugout big enough to take the four of us and seaworthy enough to coast up behind the off-shore islands.

We say New Place's canoe is unfinished, unsafe, and fill it full of trash and cold char. In truth it is worn glossy from hands smoothing it and floats like a seabird. We lie because we cannot afford to lose it.

We have not yet given it its eyes, although I have de-signed an exceptional pair and our finest stone worker has made them in secret. Usually eyes are merely painted; ours, of obsidian and shell pearl, will never fade.

It is decided the scouting party will take twelve days, no more: five to go, five to return, two for the possible trading or the unexpected.

We will fish and water on board to carry us throughout the trip, if necessary. It may happen that we cannot spare any time for fishing, gathering, or want to use a fire. No one mentions stealth; all understand. What has happened to the north is completely unknown to us.

Apparently what has happened to the south is known only to me, for I hear no mention of it, only puzzlement that this or that trader did not come up the coast with parrot feathers, monkeys, and dried fruit.

It is assumed that I will go, since Eye of the Sea clearly cannot. I delegate Mist to see to things for her father and in my absence, and hope she will handle things well.

The party sets off in high spirits, for the weather is fine and the coastal villages are more than hospitable when the food supply is good. We will trade stories for lodgings and gather news, and, if I am fortunate, I will find someone with a metal knife or two to spare.

Now that I live on the seacoast I understand why I saw no one on my long walk south: in summer everyone moves to the outer banks, fishes and gathers shellfish and sweet grass for baskets. No one with sense stays near the marshes when flies rise in black clouds and the scum of the stagnant inlets stinks.

Our first several stops are pleasant but the villagers tell us nothing significant that we do not already know. The traders have not been here either.

The fifth day of our voyage passes, and the four of us confer, awkwardly, for the paddling is such hard work that we have not become easy together, except in how to time our strokes.

That evening, anchored off shore, the four of us agree that it is not enough to return with so little information. We decide to press our luck a little. A favoring current further to sea will bring us back down the coast faster than we came. We can be home at the agreed-upon time, or close to it.

Something about the way the other three look at one another makes me sure they have in some way agreed before they consulted me. I wonder when and how, and most of all, why.

The coastline changes from the low dunes of sand broken only by the occasional rock, to the striated cliffs that will grow taller and more formidable until they become the towering heights of Orocan itself.

My journey down showed me this but I cannot tell the others without revealing myself. No one else has said they have made this journey before. I eye the wall of rock to our right with growing worry: I am nearer to the city than I want to be.

I forgot how quickly the canoe can move compared to my walking and wandering south. The trio I am traveling with seem too unsophisticated to cope with some of the people we are likely to meet this far north.

It has long been my habit to hide the necklace and the pouch with the turquoise bead, but still I tap my clothing to be sure they are concealed when we see the camp on the shore. Calling back and forth, we agree there is likely to be news here.

As we come close, I can see it is a regular summer port with substantial tents and a great central hearth. I cannot remember any sign of it on my trip south, although the beach is narrow and I must have passed this way.

We turn in-shore, the spume from the surf splatters across our faces. The dugout becomes difficult to handle as the water grows shallow, wallowing and threatening to swamp. It is not as well balanced as Seabird.

Bent to my padding like the rest, I can still see twin-tongued clan banners tasting the spirit winds, and hear the chink, chink of someone playing the bones for the weather. We ground our boat among a small fleet of craft, some with sails of one sort or another, and haul it far up the shore.

Even though we bear no arms, we are immediately sur-rounded by guards and summoned to the central fire. Red Snake of Small Cove steps forward to begin the parley and says, "Bring us the reward. We have brought the woman."

My mouth falls open with surprise. I turn to run, but strong men seize my arms and drag me backwards, off my feet. I am helpless as they bind and gag me.

A rough hand searches my breast and pulls the pouch with my jaguar bead out, then lets that go to take the golden jaguar mask from me. It crumples in his rough hands and he tries to reshape the metal.

There is a loud chorus of languages, many of which I don't understand, as I am led away. I do not bother to look back at those I thought were at least my allies, if not my friends.

If I could curse and bring death on them I would. As it is, I chew and mouth the knot of filthy rag that gags me,

and nourish myself with rage, a better meal than fear. I will
not let myself think of the long fall down the netless Well
or, more important, the waste of my knowledge of those
beyond the white fires.

The sun sinks and a chorus of web-footed hares from the
marshlands begins. No one bothers to come and feed me or
allow me to relieve myself. I lie, eye to eye with the
witches' eyes that foul the sand so close to the city, trying
my bonds one by one, as much to distract myself as from
any hope that they will yield. My guards have done a thorough job.

The alien pressure in my head is so intense that I am
only dimly aware of the sagging tent-cloth above me and
the gritty trampled rugs on the floor. The clinking of the
weather-bones throbs in my temples. The thing inside me is
desperate for me to escape. If there were aid it could give, it
would give it. I have become too interesting to be blithely
sacrificed.

Deep in my rage, it takes me a moment to realize someone has crawled under the edge of the tent. Red Snake
slashes the bonds on my wrists and hauls me out. Cursing
whatever has made me semiconscious, he slashes the rest of
the ropes, pulls the gag from my mouth. The Small Cove
man wads the scraps into some fold in his clothes and
creeps away on his belly, signing me to follow.

Joints aching, I do the best I can. Using my elbows to
drag myself is messy and slow, but I am moving. There is a
good stiff breeze that will erase most signs of our trail. I
think Red Snake will take me back to the others and we
will flee south together. But midway through the grass he
stops and says formally, "We part here," hand on the hilt of
his new steel knife.

I lie still while he wriggles away.

Evidently his conscience extends to not leaving me in
the hands of my enemies but not to being my friend. He

will crawl back, settle in, and wait for my absence to be discovered, just another one of those innocent of any wrongdoing.

Dangerous, if the leader of Orocan's delegation loses his temper, but guaranteeing that there will be no reprisals against the villages. The likeliest conclusion will be that, being a wise woman and possibly a witch, I have gotten away on my own, the only ones who might face blame being the wretched guards who bound me.

I wipe my grit-fouled mouth with the back of my wrist. I'm not sorry for them.

Crouching in the windy night, I feel the faint tracings of wind-blown salt and sand on my face, and think. I can't go south, I can't go north, I can't get one of these heavy boats to the sea, or paddle and steer one if I could, so I must go inland, and now.

Bending forward, almost running on all fours like an animal, I sprint into the darker darkness away from the camp and toward the beach. I have a long way to go, and maybe not even the presence in my head to help me. The first obstacle is the cliffs themselves, for there is no chance I can climb their unknown face in the dark.

Toes lapped by little waves, I look right and left and go to my left, north, on the chance that if they hunt for me they will be less likely to think of my heading in the direction of Orocan. If I am lucky there may be some path up the face I can take. Too afraid to creep and crawl, I run. With every stride I can feel the pouch with my jaguar bead at my throat bang against my sternum like a second heartbeat.

At least I have my bead.

Dawn is lightening the sky, creating a world of grays, blacks, silvers, but everything will be colored before long. I scan the cliffs as I pound past, see no way up. I smell the city's trash and garbage on the shifting breeze. There is no place that I can hide. Beggars and scavengers work and often camp at the cliff base.

They are dangerous to me. They may kill me for my clothes and glossy stone knife, for spite, or for no reason at all. They may capture and sell me, if they recognize me. I am a fortune running on two legs.

I run faster.

The sea and sky are ripening into blues when I submit to the inevitable and crawl into the portal in the base of the cliff. Following the sharp and feral scent of jaguar, I hope to hide myself in the shadows of the cave I once fled. I have come a wide and rugged circle, and for what?

For at least the time being, I am safe, for they will send no sacrilegious search parties here. Not unless the priests think to organize their own. If they know how I got out, they may think of where I am hidden.

With very little time left, I know I'd better conceal myself. Stepping carefully from stone to stone, trying to leave no sign, I go deeper into the cave.

There are three jaguars now, all white, but I know the one that was mine and she knows me, lapping my hands with a rough, warm tongue.

I go behind the stink and scuffle of their dens, and find a niche in the natural irregularities I can press my dark-robed body into. I am not really hidden, but staying still, I may avoid attention. It is too near full daylight to search for a better spot.

The presence in my mind has returned to signal warning, warning with painful insistence. I freeze in place, gut aching. I can hear them coming. Two men, muttering in the bored way of men who do the same thing day after day.

My back to them, although I must be in plain view if they look, I hear the yowl of an annoyed cat, smell the stink of oil-rag torches and the reek of overripe flesh, then some time later the sharp stink of fresh carnivores' dung.

Hood pulled forward, forehead pressed against stone, I am just another dark outcropping in the dark rock. I listen to the silence of the stone. I am deep in the earth and it may protect me.

Time passes and the warning pressure in my mind ceases: they must only come once a day to feed and care for the animals. The stone sings its silent song and I sing, silent, with it.

I wake from my trance, hearing the slow tock of water dropping into some hidden pool, and the whisper of wind moving out of the cave. The light changes, moves toward dusk, if I am to have any light at all, I must look about me.

Stiffly, limb by limb, I move, hoping they haven't left a guard. Tensed to run, I turn slowly to see the place is deserted, the animals replete and asleep.

For shelter, water, and food I must explore the deeper caverns. There are the troughs for the jaguars and I can drink from those, but it would be better to find a seep or trickle that does not bring me into the areas where the caretakers go. There will be days when they come for the animals for ritual purposes, and, underground, I have no sure way of knowing the day or time.

Licking a skinned palm from a failed climb, I feel the presence in my mind looking about. To aid it, I turn here and there that it may see better.

It, they, have left me alone for a long time, but now they are interested again. Having no plan of my own, I am willing to wait while it looks and thinks. For this moment, I think, our two interests may run together. I am, after all, amusing.

I pass a natural well, no wider than a chimney. I can hear the wind suck and moan in it. It may go to the very top of the cliff, although there is no way of telling if it is wide enough for me all the way up.

If that is my only choice, I will climb up into it, but fresh fallen stone is likely to give me away if anyone comes looking seriously. It is a choice of last resort. I keep on going.

Some distance along, there is what appears to be a narrow man-cut stair I had not noticed before, a smaller version of the one in jaguar house, although it runs through flawed rock, and the steps are covered with rubble.

This is in the lower cave through which the water that cut the Well must have left, and through which the tide must sometimes have risen before man built a sill across the exit.

There is no breath of air on my face when I stand in the black oblong of the stairway opening. Somewhere above the way is blocked, whether by a door or a fall of rock I cannot tell.

By the dusty, disused smell, it has been a long time since anyone climbed these steps. The stupor inducing air frightens me. I will see what I may do at ground level, before I try feeling my way blindly upward into that dead darkness.

I go toward the front again, where the aqueous light, reflected off the sea and the wet walls, illuminates the lower cave. It is possible to move around quickly once one's eyes are accustomed to the gloom. It is doubtful the caretakers ever come this way. It may all appear dark to them, for they carry torches of oil-soaked rags wrapped on stout sticks.

Tired, I stop and stand still.

My only real choice is to hide in the Well of Orocan itself, not a place I want to be, now that the season for storms is drawing near. I go as fast as I can without making noise, push my way through the overhang of foliage.

I fear seeing broken bodies, but the rock space is sun-baked and clean, overgrown with ferns and vines. I wonder if the jaguars are let in to feed on what falls here, for it is only after careful searching that I smell what might be old blood in a shadowed niche.

Understanding the truth, I snarl. The rank meat I smelled, that was fed the jaguars, comes from here. If the priest here is like those where I came from they are not likely to waste what could be used if it will leave more for them. They would see that there were religious reasons, too—

I have other concerns. There is too little cover to stay on the floor of the pit, even if nothing falls from above. Knotting my robe up, baring my legs, I climb the first shelving outcrop of the stone, levering myself over the sharp, crumbling edge. Toes pressing down and arms outstretched, I can drag my lower body onto the upper ledge. I look down.

Already I am higher than I would care to jump onto the rough, uncertain footing. My only escape is up. I look at small patch of blue sky, and start to clamber up the face of the rock, mouth gritty with loose dust, and hands and arms stained green by ferns and vines.

On the other side of the Well I see what might be Celia's apricot pit grown into a whip of a young tree, with no more leaves than you could count. It will be years before it bears fruit and yet it has begun its task. I must fulfill mine.

Higher, I find I am not the first to come this way. There is a small space that can only be entered by lying down and rolling cautiously sideways between two eroded layers of rock, but inside is a snug hollow and there is a hearth, no larger that my two outspread hands, backed into a crack in the cliff.

Judging by the thin and flaking layer of soot, it was seldom used. Perhaps it was a last resort when the cold grew too bitter to bear. I rub my fingers in the blacking and sniff them, but cannot tell what was burned. There is not much here. It would take work to gather a supply of fuel.

Hidden in the shadows is a jug with a wedge cracked from its lip, saved, perhaps, by a fall onto something soft and yielding, or salvaged from the city middens further along the cliff. I run a hand along its curve, wondering if there is a source of water in the Well, or if whoever-it-had-been made forays to the animal troughs.

Leaning out to judge the distance down, I bang my skull on the overhanging stone, and lie down, head spinning, to recover. Laughter bubbles out of me, and I jam my gritty fingers in my mouth to stifle the sound. I am probably safe. I may go thirsty, hunger, and cold, but I am, probably, safe.

My presence stirs uneasily. Mine, for now there is only one. In the past I could sometimes feel the surge of two or three in quick succession, now, sometimes, if I gaze at the same thing without moving, it goes away. Bored, perhaps, with an old toy.

I arrange my robe around me and sit, resting. This is as high as I can go and easily return to the floor of the pit. Until I find water, I am tied to the animal troughs.

The muscles of my arms twitch with the effort I have made. Licking dusty lips, I ponder whether it would be better to descend in the evening or at dawn. I fall asleep, sitting, where I am, staring at the blank and uninformative rock.

Some of my problems solve themselves. Not all the sacrifices they throw into the Well are living. There is a daily rain of bread and wine. I always have food and I drink very well whenever a stoppered metal jug falls onto a tussock padded with years of dead ferns.

In fact, apart from the days of horror when six or seven women at once splatter the Well-bottom with their life-blood, I live comfortably, keeping to my cave when they let the jaguars in to feed, or come to gather the meat themselves. I am inconvenienced only by the smell.

I spend much of my time thinking, staring at bare rock, being uninteresting to that inside my head. I am sure it cannot read my thoughts, although it may know me very well, but it certainly can look out of my eyes.

Often I think of my lady's books: *Navigation on Planetary Surfaces*, *Mining the Elements*, *A Guide to Determining Edibility*, and others less mysterious. I read all of them, although the words hanging in the cool morning air were sometimes just sounds to the person reading them, and probably to the listener too.

Now I spend my days remembering what I read by rote. I stare at a pebble, a stick, nothing, as if they all are of vast significance. Let me begin with the simple things and listen with my inner ear to the past.

Days pass and there is nothing to hear but the cries of the birds that roost up in the shaft and nothing to see but the shaft itself. I can tell the presence does not relish my occasional festive meal of wine, bread, and near-raw gull, singed of its feathers. I eat that as often as I can. I wonder what they feed on, and when, and why it cares what fills my stomach, but I know, if it is disgusted, it will leave me alone. I hope it has not figured out where I am.

I stare at one patch of stone wall, cracked here, marked by a fringe of grass there, flaking away in the sun and the dark, changing ever so subtly, until my head aches with the effort, pain so great my vision blurs. I knead my scalp with my fingertips, trying ease it.

Eluding one and another disaster, I came to this particular time and place. There must be a reason, a purpose, for that. Or maybe I am to decide what it is. I search within myself and find over and over what I want is something more than mere revenge.

As I press, trying to ease my agony, I feel it. A hard little strand that runs, ear to ear, across the back of my head, so thin that it takes extreme pressure and pain-induced sensitivity to be sure it is there. I am familiar with the hard knot at the base of my skull. I have never felt this before.

Hastily I pull my hands away, certain *this* must be the thing that lets them enter my mind. If they could put it in, then can I take it out? Trying could kill me; succeeding, I would be free.

Pushing aside my hair, I rub my head, probe my scalp. Now that I know it is there, I can feel the tug under the flesh. I shiver at the pain I imagine.

But.

Freedom.

When the slavers took me, I saw those who lived with their scalps cut off. I can survive pulling this free. So ill protected, the thing must fail naturally occasionally, and—I sway as I sit, leaping from conclusion to conclusion—then I might become one of the mass of people again: except I will have my knowledge of *them*.

I will do it.

It takes a number of forays before I get what I want, a knife so sharp that I can do what I must with a single, sure stroke.

The two men who bring supplies to the animals and re-leased them into the Well for cleanup do not leave their tools behind them. They do, from time to time, come to the man-built sill across the sea-opening, drink themselves into a stupor and then lie there in their pissed pants sleeping it off.

They would scarcely be allowed friends, wives, or con-fidants, and they have long since tired of one another. They cheat each other at dice, out of habit, for they gamble for nothing or that the loser take extra drink.

One of them chooses to get drunk alone. I pick his pocket while he snores. Booty: one small knife, with a sharp, narrow blade. I put it in my hideout and never look

at it while I wait for the next necessary opportunity, a sacrifice.

I keep close track of time to avoid being surprised by
any of the men or the animals. So the broken-lipped jug
brims with water and I have a packet of scavenged food
ready when I hear the meaty thud of one, then two, and finally a half dozen bodies on the stones at the foot of the
Well.

Tomorrow, then, is the day when I must act. Today the
jaguars will be let to feed, to save the trouble of moving
their food. By tomorrow there will only be vultures feeding
on the shreds and tags left by the cats. In a week the bones
will be overgrown.

I will be safe in my hideaway for a day or two. The two
men avoid the reek after a sacrifice once they have scavenged the valuables and hacked the carcasses into joints to
feed the animals.

Waking early, I check the pit is empty. In the silver light
of dawn, not even the carrion birds are there, only the buzz
and hum of insects that shroud the dead in a riot of color.
The jaguars, seeking water, have gone into their cages.

The stench is bearable so early in the day.

Reluctant to shave the hair from my head, for the knife I
stole will only do so much and, lacking a whetstone, I cannot give it a keener edge, I have devised another method.

I will cut a slit above one ear and pull the thing out as if
it were a parasite trapped beneath my skin. I had seen Mist
pull a worm from Reed's leg, rolling its length around a
stick so it wouldn't break and she could be sure of having
all of it. I think I have the willpower to do that.

Braiding my hair awkwardly to one side, I feel for the
end of the thing deep in my scalp, and make the cut. Blind
with tears, I sit for several minutes, blood streaming over
my shoulder, before I feel certain of the world and can cut

again, deeper, within the first slash, and claw with two fingertips to grip its end.

I pull.

And nearly faint.

But it is only the pain of my own body.

Again, and I feel it slide ever so slightly. Gritting my teeth I pull until a wave of darkness loosens my grip. Bit by bit I ease it out of me until I sit with its entire supple, segmented length in my hands, blood running down my shoulder, soaking my gown.

Reaching for a rock, I crush it, shuddering at white-hot pain as the thing at the base of my skull ceases to function. I lean back, too stunned to move, listening only as the thunder in my chest hammers at me.

I wake from soggy sleep a day later.

Now that I am dead, probably from a fall, I must get going before I am inconveniently seen to be alive.

The only safe way into the city is up and it is into the city I intend to go. I bind my head with fresh cloths, and climb, water and food strapped to my back. I take the snaky thing with me, crushed though it is.

This first day, I do not clamber very high. The animal caretakers do not seem aware that the inner wall can be climbed. I have another hideout, better hidden, better equipped. I will stay there while I heal.

It might be safe to stay where I stayed for so long, but I fear that the observer, believing me dead, might send someone into the Well to confirm the fact, collect the equipment in my body.

I can't take that chance.

Head throbbing with pain, I crawl from ledge to ledge, testing as I go. I've been this way before, made sure of my route. The water-rotted stone offers many handholds, but I do not want to knock much fresh debris down into the pit. Driven by a fierce desire to reach sanctuary, I press on until

I nearly slip from one ledge and know I must pause, gather my resources.

I lie, face down, staring at stone crusty with the droppings of nesting birds. They mortar together a slurry of broken eggshells and fluff. I cough and turn my face away.

Sweeping a clean place with my arm, I sit, wait for the wheeling flock to settle again. When the shaking in my arms eases, I shove a few lumps of rock between me and the outer edge, curl on my side and sleep. All night, the birds mutter to one another, annoyed but not alarmed.

My head, when I awake late in the morning, throbs so fiercely that I doubt my sense of balance. I know I must climb this section with deliberate care. Disturbed birds pouring from the top of the Well will draw attention as a bad omen.

I decide to stay where I am, hidden from both above and below. Since I carry water and food for several days, and the weather is dry and warm, I need not hurry to reach my hideout.

Instead I crush the segmented thing I brought with me, pounding until it is a coarse powder. I sweep the result into a crevice in the stone, and drop rocks in after. They, whoever they are, will have to break the cliff itself to recover the snake's remains.

The next day, slowly, carefully, I climb to the hideout I prepared, and there I stay, sleeping and drowsing while I heal. It is strange and pleasant to be so free of worry about when to go out, when to hide. I spend a lot of time, flat on my belly, chin on my folded arms, looking. Looking for myself, not to defeat some hidden observer.

This high, life swarms and flutters in the Well. There are all the flying things to which height makes no difference, the flies, and butterflies, and birds that roost on the uneven ledges in shoving, squawking pairs. The shared nests of the cave doves and whistle-fowl fill smaller niches.

There are others, too, lizards and skinks, perhaps escaped from being a meal, scampering through the swaths and fringes of ferns that hang from every support not fouled with guano. Cloven-toed rock rabbits, small as my fist, peek from the dark. Once I see a snake drive a blind frog from its cool crevice.

The sun's light reflects on the dropping-whitened rocks so that the whole middle shaft is filled with a kind of bright continuous gloom. At midday a long ray makes a half-ellipse down one side. There the flowering vines grow with special vigor, hanging in cascades of color that vibrate with their burden of vivid butterflies.

One afternoon a hawk, circling in the gulf of air, stoops into the Well, chasing a smaller bird that escapes by landing and scuttling into the cliff-face, sheltering in earth.

Although my head is still painful, I heed the sign, pack my remaining food and climb. A few dozen feet up I find a far more comfortable spot, sheltered by an overhang and carpeted with rough grass.

Back against rock, I sit listening to a distant trickle running deep within the cleft, where the split between the stones becomes too narrow for me to reach. It is a green and quiet place and several more days pass as my wound itches and heals.

I eat what I have, and find two scanty sources of water, one emptying into a basin so round and smooth that I would have taken it for man-made if it were not small as my fist.

Near evening on the sixth day, after I add a scratch to my calendar pebble and settle in my accustomed spot, something plummets past me.

It is a woman, and she sees me.

Battered by wind and the knowledge that death is instants away, I doubt that she understands what she sees, but her eyes widen and her head turns so she can look a little longer as she falls.

It is the wrong day or I have lost count.

Shaking all over, crying, I wedge myself into the crack in the darkness, afraid of heights as I have not been before.

I don't look, but I know when they pass, one by one, by the change in the light and the calls of the birds startled into flying. Six of them. There would, of course, have been seven actually flung over the lip of the Well. One had been caught in the net.

The one who might have been me.

It is full dark before I can make myself lie flat to sleep. I dream of falling, of the pain of lying crushed and broken and yet not dead.

Moons down, I wake with commonsense having taken hold. No one who falls from such a height would live to feel pain. I have seen the end many times by now.

Staring into the dark, I know that what I will do will be no private matter. The presences have placed one tool in my hands. Like the more fortunate of their sacrifices, I will return from the Well, just somewhat later than anyone might expect.

I sit down, facing the vast and shining gulf of air, water on my lips, earth in my hands. I call the spirits of my childhood. Singing and sighing through my skull, the spirits come, wrapping me in the protection of air, and water, and earth.

Fire is not for such as I.

When I stand again, hand knotted about my totem bag, I know my name. I am Turquoise Jaguar. I strip the bead of its concealment and rub it clean. Then, my hand closed around it, I sleep without dreams, resolute.

As long as I am willing to walk or crawl around and around, taking advantage of the cracks and splits in the rock itself, I can climb the upper half of the shaft with ease and in concealment, for the vegetation is heavy and the shadows and flights of birds confuse the light.

On the second day of my climb my questing fingers rub finished stone for a long moment before I understand that I have reached the top of the Well. The finished stonework is so old that water has eroded pockets beneath the lowest tier. I pull myself into one and lie, listening.

When I fell into the net, I saw that there was more beneath the floor around the plaza that surrounded the Well's top than one might guess. Now, in concealment, I can smell humanity: roast kid, peppers, charred and ready to be peeled, herbal soap, heated wine.

Those who serve the Well must sleep here. Possibly the jaguars' caretakers find beds among them, although I think the place where Tomás took me seems more likely for such rough types. By their voices, there may be as many as five here at one time.

Five who have no idea I exist.

I flex the muscles of my hands.

Five I may have to kill.

Climbing a little way down with caution, I catch my supper. As I sit gnawing the raw leg of a gull, its fishy flavor turns bad in my mouth. I have fallen and I can return and the words of one returned from death will be heeded.

But.

Things are more complicated than mere resolution and anger would make them. I must surprise the servitors and those who watch within them. To do that, I am going to need a length of rope to make the final few feet of the climb with speed and in safety.

In the Well vines grow everywhere there is sunlight for any part of the day, but after two or three attempts make rope of them, I give up. They cannot be braided together without splitting lengthwise.

I will have to rob corpses of their cloth robes before the men let the jaguars in, and to do that, I will have to descend the Well again. I touch my turquoise bead, but no reassurance comes.

I am on my own.

Knowing the routes up and therefore down, I descend, smooth and fast, and arrive while the shaft is still day lit. I doze, gathering my resources, in the stone shelter where I pulled the controlling device out.

When the hour comes, the women fall. It is hard to hear it happen; I do not watch. When the sixth body thuds and after a while there is no seventh, I go down, hand over foot with great care, to gather what I need.

I see an arm, with all its bracelets intact, resting many feet from any shoulder, and turn aside to vomit and then cover my mess. After that, I do not look around me, avoiding the torsos by the smell of burst intestines.

The women's outer mantles are what I want, for they are made of the same plain, tight-woven fabric I wear myself. Gingerly, I tug and pull at one, then notice another, unmarked, lying at a distance from the heap of corpses. Afraid that those who came to clear the bottom of the Well might notice if I take more than one, I take the unmarked one, carry it some distance up the Well.

None too soon.

As I finger its fine embroidered cloth, I hear the snarls of the jaguars below. I stay still lest I be seen by them or by their presences. I hope my own jaguar doesn't scent me and look up, searching.

I wait a long time after they go. It is full dark before I reach my newest hideaway, going slowly in the moonlit dark. It is g practice. I understand what the spirits want me to know: to succeed, I must go slowly.

Often I am lucky, a shoulder pin bursts as a woman flings her arms wide, and her mantle floats free to snag somewhere above the floor of the pit. Sometimes I have to go down and look, but not often.

I make it a rule never to take more than one, and to never go down into the pit twice in a row. Even with those restrictions, I soon make more rope than I can possibly need. The work keeps my fingers busy; my mind focused.

As I braid I run through every detail of what I will do. Other times, I go over the route—up, sideways, down—until I can do them with my eyes closed. Finally I am healed, strong, practiced, completely ready.

I find a knife, lost into the Well, and I claim it. Day after day, I caress it until it is part of me: black, obsidian, and sharper than any metal.

Like the madwoman I nearly am, I descend and walk to the beach, stand with the stars bright above me, dip myself naked in the sea, chant my mother's song very softly, re-membering. Coming back, I rinse the salt from myself in my jaguar's watering trough, almost courting her incurious gaze.

Ritually clean, dedicated, I climb back to my den. I dress in the clothes I will wear to climb, set my bundle ready, thank the space that has sheltered me. Then I sleep, hand closed around the turquoise bead reslung at my throat.

As the light of false dawn lights the walls of the Well, I start my last ascent. I take the easiest way, spiraling around and around, wanting there to be no bruise or scrape on my body to tell how I got where I am going or to suggest where I have been.

The clothes in my bundle are very like those I wore the last day I appeared before the people, in rich fabric in dark blues and greens. I have added what must be the newest fashion a spider web thin shawl, dyed with saffron.

Never before have I noticed the beauty of the Well as I do this day, knowing, whatever happens, I will not see it again. The flocks of butterflies, the stoop of the hawk into its shaft of air, the swags of leaves and flowers, all make me look, and look again, though I never pause, never fail to check where I put a hand or foot.

Several days before, I buried the sewing kit, sealed into a small unbroken jar with wax—both scavenged from the city's garbage—among the roots of the apricot tree I planted so long ago. A small loan, returned. There were bees, wasps, and butterflies everywhere feeding on the fallen fruit.

"Carry my prayers," I asked the short-lived insects. They will, I hope, reach the dead lands. My lady was kind and I, in her eyes, have cheated her.

Dead, we will not meet. I will go to my own kind, as she has gone to hers. But I can give my former owner her sewing kit—and, however qualified, my thanks.

Long before twilight I am where I planned to be, at the bottom of the section of the Well that has been lined. I am in position to climb the finished section of the wellhead before true dawn, when all should still be asleep.

No sacrifice fell past me yesterday so there will be one this evening. Tomorrow, the men will all sleep late. Sleep forever if I have my way. I know I am a little mad, but it is the madness the spirits send to those they favor.

I touch the ridged hilt of my obsidian knife, work my fingers into the cracks of the stone. The loop of rope, as fine and strong as I can make it, swings at my back. If I break off the wall, the rope will give me a second chance.

The sky overhead pales to pearl. Clinging to the rock like a lizard, I inch my way up unthinking, hand over hand, toes braced against the rock, gripping earth's maternal flesh.

When I reach the course of ornamental stonework that rings the Well, I force my way into the space between one huge stone leaf and its stem and rest. Only then do I see how strange the sky is, faintly green. There must be a mountain of clouds offshore that I cannot see.

Sheltered within the Well of Orocan, I did not think to worry about the weather. Now I do. Arms around my knees, I watch. Soon the patch of sky I can see is streaked with hurrying clouds, scudding before the oncoming gale. A low note sounds within the Well.

There is a jaguar wind coming.

If I make it up before the rain comes, the storm may strengthen my hand. Climbing the wet stone in a downpour I may not make it. I touch the bead at my throat. I am Jaguar Woman. Whatever happens will be the thing intended from the beginning.

I climb, living from grip to grip. Toes, knee, curled fingers, fist jam, fist jam. Finally my fingers brush the base of one of the narrow columns that ring the area where they rigged the net and caught me.

Swinging my weighted cord up and about, I get it around a pillar, use it to drawn my heavier rope into place, tie both off. I tug, gently, harder, then as hard as I can. It is secure.

Easing myself over the stonework rim, I undo the rope. After robing myself, I bundle everything I no longer need, and throw it down the Well. Seeking the earth, it flutters from my view.

At worst, no one will find it before I have won—or lost—my gamble. I touch my head, my heart, my groin, my feet, and silently ask the spirits to fill me with power. It pours into me like water filling a jug, cool and clear, shaped by what contains it, yet entirely apart from me.

Unsheathing my dark dagger, I pad down the halls, sniffing the residue of wine and food from the feasting of the day before. I smell human beings all around me, but no one is stirring.

The man in the first room I visit dies without a sound, throat cut. The second sleeps with his arms about his head. He moans as my dagger slides up under his ribs. Annoyed, I listen, but all is silent.

One by one I kill them with the throat-stroke as I come to them. There are five and one empty room. I prowl about the space to be certain that no one else is there, wash my bloody hands, go to the stair I ascended before with Tomás, when I was the reborn goddess.

If the old watchman were less punctual he might have lived, but the old rise early. He gives one shrill shout because I strike him in the gut before I dispatch him with a better stroke.

His messy death is a blemish on the occasion. Focus blurred by anger, I have to rededicate myself, touch myself with bloody hands. As my pulse slows, I know I have come to the time and place I first saw so long ago. The stairs. The door. The light.

Ascending, I pull aside the leather drape at the back of the altar, step through the fumes of burning grain and wine. I stand with the dagger in my hand, my clothes dark with man's blood.

Vacant-faced, the crowd of early worshipers stares at me. For a long cold moment, there is nothing but the sound of their clothing snapping and billowing in the fierce wind.

Then their faces change. Tall and grim, dressed as I was on the last day they saw me, they know me. I am no beauty, but people remember me.

In an instant, I am looking over a field of bowed heads and bent backs. The crowd says as one, "REBORN!"

I have no idea what that means.

They may not either.

"REBORN!"

I step forward, lift my arms to the stormy sky. I am bloody-handed, angry, and aware.

One fuego fantasma forms, and then another.

I point to them. "We are their prisoners."

The two fuego fantasmas swirl higher, and another forms above them.

"Yes!" shouts someone. "Yes!"

"Yes, yes, yes!" the crowd chants. "We are! Yes!"

"I have seen!" screams one woman. "I have seen!"

"The men in the flames!"

The crowd shouts, each one at his neighbor, telling what they know, what they've heard, what they guess. There is no need for my story of a threatening figure within a column of white fire. Many have their own stories. Many know.

Maybe we all know. It has been our mutual silence that enslaves us as much as any device. Someday I will hear their stories and tell them mine. I will not speak of the eyes watching from within their own, from within themselves. That will keep until later, calmer, times.

But now, as fuego fantasmas float above, I tell the city's people they must find every witches' eye and cast them into fires so hot they will melt iron.

Thunder rolling across the sea, lightning-dazzled, they surge from the plaza. Hammers beat on walls, smashing lenses free, a myriad sieves shake in unison, fingers grope in the dirt, every one dreaming of a time when no one and nothing will be watching us.

I hide my dagger in my belt.

Arms high, bloody hands open, I welcome the howling jaguar wind. It shreds the fuego fantasmas, blows them inland, reduces them to feathers of white flame against the slate-gray sky, sweeps them away.

They will be back, but not today. Today is ours. Mine.

The spirits' power drains from me like water through sand. I sink down where I am, alone on the steps of the temple of deceptions.

I have done the thing I was to do. Nothing that happens next matters. Not betrayal, not pain, not death. I touch my mother's bead, and am content.

Jaguar Child Marker

The Rosario Bay survivors are unique in that after losing contact with civilization at large they rapidly developed a culture both distinct and viable.

So distinct that it fell under the defense of indigenous cultures decrees. It was deemed illegal to recover and re-home the descendants of the original strandees.

The *Rosario* carried people who self-identified as Middle American Indo-Hispanic. Their homeland vanished in the first of Earth's great sea level rises.

During that rise, indigenous groups that did not wish to be assimilated were offered the option of forming an ex-portable colony. In the case of the Middle Americans the passengers themselves paid a substantial per head fee, augmenting mandated government funding.

In consequence, their colony ship, the *Rosario*, had ample resources, both material and informational, some of which survived its semi-controlled crash landing. Scattered escape pods released major live cargo spills, ecological disaster for indigene life.

The striving colony was not a just a fusion of Mexican, Guatemalan, and Nicaraguan—but also Oaxacan and Mayan elements entirely unexpected among people educated enough to give informed consent to cold sleep.

Observers, integrated into the population, were the first means of exploration. Later, argus and sight-distant technologies supplanted technicians on the ground.

It was only a matter of time before questions were raised about the ethics of the surveillance. Privacy concerns in particular attracted interest after some unfortunate recordings surfaced.

It always was difficult to insulate the observers from the observed. A pryros barrier was established, with mobile personnel enclosures. These upgrades did not go unnoticed by the study's subjects nor were they without consequences.

My own father was an integrated observer; my mother a runaway slave he took under his protection. Here I stand, a hybrid of two cultures. Let me speak to the specific question before us.

If it is decided to end this experiment based on an historical accident, then all implanted subjects will live out their natural span with their argus turned off. They will know some part of them has died.

There are only one hundred and three of them.

But their influence is far greater their numbers. We picked those in positions of power, those expected to rise, the skillful, the unusual. If these people lose part of themselves, the change will reverberate through their society.

Yet surely they have a right to be free.

As a plethora of documentaries and historical fictions attests, there is a power in these lives lived without personality backups, replacement medicine, even antivirals. It is a world painted with broad strokes in which small details matter, and willpower and courage can make major differences.

The stories we gather and curate affect our lives. We *must* be cautious. The most important may be missing. Delores-Luz, twenty years old, set motion a revolution that is still playing out, and then vanished from surveillance.

We cannot even guess what became of her.

I am her son. Frightened, alone, in the face of overwhelming odds, she came back for me. Persistence is in my very genes. I'll stay here, for her, for her people, for what have become—or always were—my people, no matter your decision.

www.ingramcontent.com/pod-product-compliance
Lightning Source LLC
Chambersburg PA
CBHW020826260626
47169CB00003B/851